BLUE PLANETS

BOOK I OF THE SOFAR TRILOGY

A Novel by

John R. Gentile

This book is a work of fiction. Places, events, and situations in this story are purely fictional. Any resemblance to actual persons, living or dead, is coincidental.

ISBN: 1-4140-3641-8 (e-book)
ISBN: 1-4140-3640-X (Paperback)
ISBN: 1-4140-3639-6 (Dust Jacket)

Library of Congress Control Number: 2003098621

This book is printed on acid free paper.

Printed in the United States of America
Bloomington, IN

1stBooks - rev. 12/30/03

ACKNOWLEDGEMENTS

I would like to express my sincere gratitude to the following individuals. Without their eager assistance and timely comments, the writing of this book would have been a much more daunting, if not impossible task. First and foremost, I wish to acknowledge my wife Katie Iverson, who not only acted as a source of daily inspiration, but provided editing and suggestions that saved me a lot of embarrassment. Among those who assisted with editorial suggestions and critique are Michael Barwick, Randall and Susie Claybourn, Chris and John Clifford, Lucinda Davis, Paul Maseman, Dr. Thomas Strong and Joia Wheeler.

Finally, a huge thanks to Meg Files, writing instructor at Pima Community College, Tucson, Arizona, who helped me develop the tools to get it down on paper.

For my father, Joseph A. Gentile, who introduced me to storytelling at the Roundup Drive-in on Friday nights.

Only those who will risk going too far can possibly find out how far one can go. - T.S. Eliot, Journeys

PROLOGUE

September 15, 2010

The third planet from the star glowed blue and white when viewed on the long-range visual scanners. The bizarre array of frequencies became more pronounced, luring the two travelers. At this distance, the ship's sensors revealed a planet with a sustainable atmosphere and vast bodies of water.

As the scanners separated the wave-forms, strange and wondrous voices began to fill the inside of the crippled vessel. It was as if a thousand beings were all speaking at once. The cryptic transmissions generated from the oceans on the strange world.

The travelers set a course for the water planet.

September 21, 2010 - The Seri village of Punta Chueca, on the northeastern shore of the Gulf of California, Sonora, Mexico

The triangular metal shard lay on the rough wooden table between them, the light from the kerosene lantern reflecting the strange inscriptions on its surface. Enrique Morales stood facing away from his young wife, Maria, and their five-year old son Jorgé.

Maria suddenly felt as if she and her family were being pulled into the center of the table by the cursed object like some ocean whirlpool yanking them into its vortex.

"You have frightened Jorgé," said Maria angrily, shifting her focus back to her husband. She placed her arm around the young boy.

"Instead of filling his head with useless tales of Sky People and fallen ships from the stars, you should be teaching him how to prepare to live among the whites and the *mexicanos*."

Enrique turned sharply, snatched up the shard and held the three-sided metal object in front of her. The light from the lantern exaggerated the deep creases in his weathered face.

"This should be proof enough to you, Maria. My father gave it to me, and he got it from his father, who gave it to him before that. The Sky People were here. This was part of their great flying ship."

"My grandfather told me the same stories," spoke Maria. "They were fine when I was a little girl. But that is all they are - stories. Ramblings of old men to frighten small children. Those fables do not put more fish on our table, nor blankets on our bed, nor clothes on the children's backs."

"You dishonor your grandfather's memory," said her husband disparagingly.

"I loved my grandfather, Enrique. I watched him waste his life looking toward the stars like all of the other elders. He waited for these Sky People to return. On his deathbed, he still believed they would come. They have not come. And do you know why? It is because they never existed."

Jorgé, deep brown eyes wide, looked to his father, then to his mother. His gaze returned to the metal piece. The circular symbols and lines appeared to dance off the burnt-orange surface. The piece appeared to grow before his eyes.

"What then of this piece of metal?" said Enrique, exasperation in his voice. "You cannot burn it, shape it with fire or scratch it. Even Martín's acetylene torch could not cut through it. It is not of earth."

"It could have washed up on the beach or been brought by the Spaniards," said his wife. "There are hundreds of explanations. But I will not allow more tales of visitors from the stars in this house."

"You cannot disregard the teachings of the elders, Maria. The Sky People will return. They will return at the end of time."

Maria shook her head in disgust. She stood and lifted the boy from the wooden bench. "Come, *mi hijo*, it is time for bed. Say goodnight to your father." She carried the boy around to the other side of the table. Enrique kissed his son's forehead.

"Tonight, you will dream of dolphins, my son."

Jorgé nodded. "Papa, will you tell me of the Sky People sometime?"

"Yes. Some other time. When you are older."

"*Buenas noches*, Papa."

"*Duerme con los angelitos, mi hijo.*"

The woman and the boy disappeared into the dimly lit house. Enrique cradled the strange metal shard in his palm, gazing at the series of lines and circles etched across its surface. He wondered again, as he had so many times throughout his life, what secrets these ancient hieroglyphics held. He placed the object in a small leather pouch that he wore on his belt, reached into his shirt pocket and produced a worn pipe. Lighting it, he stared skyward, contemplating the countless pinpoints of light. At that moment, a meteor's bright flare arced across the indigo sky and disappeared over the mountains of *Tiburón* Island.

CHAPTER ONE

September 24, 2010, Gulf of California, 29° 20′ W latitude, 112° 40′ N longitude

It was late in the afternoon when a lone kayaker rounded the point and faced into an expansive bay. The westerlies were whipping up a three-foot chop, leaving the ocean's surface a soupy mess. The sea kayak plowed through the waves without difficulty, the sharply defined bow piercing the breaking crests. Foamy water ran over the deck, splashing against Cooper Ridley's spray skirt and into his face.

Ridley squinted against the sinking sun. Even at this time of year, the late afternoon brightness off the water made his eyes red and weary. He didn't usually paddle at this time of day. In the northern Gulf of California, it was a pretty safe bet the winds would kick up in the afternoon, making paddling more arduous. Normally, he preferred to hole up under a tarp on shore during the time of the winds. A restless urge caused him to bypass the afternoon take-out point and put more miles of coastline behind him.

Through the glare and the salt caked on his sunglasses, Ridley saw a small boat taking the swells head on. The boat then reversed its position into a following sea, the backwash splashing over the transom. He recognized the craft as a Boston whaler. The captain was maneuvering the boat erratically, the bow pitching wildly in the white-capped swells. Something else caught Ridley's attention about thirty yards off the whaler's portside; a gigantic plume of spray erupted skyward from one of the waves. He glimpsed another smaller spout closer to the boat. It took him only a second to discern the geysers as being exhalations from large whales.

"Hey!" Ridley yelled above the wind and engine noise. "Don't get between the mother and her calf!"

There was no way the two occupants of the whaler could hear him. Ridley dug the paddle in and the kayak shot forward. He grew more furious with each paddle stroke. Drawing closer, he saw that the two occupants in the Boston whaler were women. Their frenzied gestures to each other indicated something was very wrong.

"Get that boat away from the baby!" Ridley yelled. "You're pissing off the mom!"

This time, the two women looked up to see where the voice was coming from. The woman at the helm angrily waved Ridley off. "Stay back!" she said. "You'll panic the whales!"

The other woman at the bow leaned down and lifted something out of the water and attempted to cut at it with a knife. Ridley realized the baby whale was trapped in a section of gill net.

He cautiously approached the boat. Timing the wave sequence, he paddled nearer, checking over his shoulder to keep an eye on the adult whale's position. She continued to circle the Boston whaler and her trapped calf.

"Get the hell away from the boat!" said the captain of the whaler, shifting her gaze constantly between the two whales and the kayak. She threw the throttle into reverse to avoid ramming the baby whale.

"Can you use some help?" said Ridley.

"Just stay back. I've got enough to worry about here," the captain said.

"I'm coming in," Ridley said. "I think I can help."

"You don't listen too well, do you asshole?" she said. "We have a baby whale that's about to drown and you're in the way. I'm not going to shut the engines down just to let you board."

The trapped whale thrashed in the water, churning it white. "It's getting more tangled!" said the Mexican woman, her voice frantic.

"Look," Ridley said. "I've worked with dolphins before. Something needs to be done soon. I think the winds are picking up."

The captain looked to the whale, then to the other woman. She nodded grimly. "Come up on the starboard side. Wait until I put the engine in neutral. Better tie up fast."

Ridley secured the kayak to the starboard cleats. He dragged his cramped body into the Boston whaler.

"What have you got?" Ridley asked the captain.

"Fin whale calf. Maybe six months old. We've been with it nearly two hours. The net is still wrapped around the flukes. We cut a big section away from the head. But the water's too rough now. Every time we get close, it just gets more tangled. It's getting weaker."

Ridley limped to the bow of the boat and peered into the deep green water. The young finback whale was as long as the boat. The slate-gray back tapered to a seven-foot wide set of flukes held in a downward position. Ridley saw why the boat was maneuvering so close to the infant. The women had rigged up two lines that were attached from the bow to four plastic fenders used in docking. The boat was part of a makeshift sling designed to buoy the whale's body up. The calf was nearing exhaustion as wave after wave crashed over its blowhole.

Ridley looked at the Mexican woman. "What's the mom been doing?"

"She charged the boat once. Mostly, she's been circling, calling to her calf."

"Have you been in the water with it?"

"We tried. Darcy cut away some net near its head. Then the baby started to panic. It just got more tangled. It's worse around the flukes."

"How long has it been like this?" said Ridley. The young fin whale opened its twin blowholes, expelling atomized droplets of water. The breath smelled fishy.

"Hours. Maybe all day." Tears of anger and frustration began to well in the Latina's eyes. "The damn gill nets are going to drown it!"

By the time the Mexican woman had turned around, Ridley was already at the stern, shirt peeled off and pulling on an old pair of jet fins retrieved from the kayak.

"What the hell do you think you're doing?" said the American woman.

"Keep the engine at the lowest idle you can, Captain," said Ridley, as he placed the mask and snorkel over his face. Lowering himself over the starboard side, he said, "I'm going to try to cut away the rest of the net."

"Be careful. There's fragments of gill net all over the place. The current is fierce," said the American. "I don't want to have to come down there and cut you loose, too. I almost got snagged in it a while ago."

Ridley nodded. He released his grip from the gunwale and immediately felt the strong pull of the current. He swam against it until he reached the bow of the boat. He guessed the visibility in the water was less than twenty feet.

A large shape loomed in front of him. As he finned closer, the shape of the baby finback whale materialized out of the frothy green. A length of netting was bound tightly around the whale's flukes. The other end had broken free from its floats and was ensnared somewhere below. Scattered throughout the net were the lifeless forms of fish and a large animal that could only be the corpse of a sea lion.

A deep rumbling sound enveloped him and penetrated down to his viscera. His entire body began to resonate with the pulsation. The adult finback was nearby, communicating with its infant.

It's okay, momma, I'm not going to hurt her, Ridley thought. He swam slowly along the infant whale's left side toward its head, keeping his arms folded close to his body and his movements as small as possible.

The finback infant still possessed strength enough to crush him under five or six tons of weight. Nearing the head, Ridley saw thin linear lacerations encircling the mouth and over the left eye, obvious cuts from the monofilament gill net. The young whale's large eye regarded Ridley with a mixture of fear and curiosity. Moving his hand out slowly, Ridley tentatively stroked the underside of the finback's jaw. The whale's rubbery skin recoiled from his touch. The second time he attempted, the whale closed its eye in acceptance.

Ridley's lungs were burning. He knew he was going to have to grab a breath soon. He was aware of something immense moving beneath him. Looking down, his heart pounded as seventy feet of finback whale glided just below his fins. Three large, black remoras moved back and forth across the behemoth's back as if it was an underwater soccer field. The great whale rolled onto its side as it passed underneath, regarding the small intruder. The finback swam seemingly without moving a muscle, a silent freight train gliding through liquid space.

Ridley was going to have to attempt to cut away the netting after he surfaced for a breath. He stroked the baby finback whale under the chin one more time and shot for the surface. He broke through near the bow of the boat and saw the Latina peering down at him, worry etched on her face.

"What were you doing down there?" said the Mexican woman. "I can't believe that whale let you touch it."

"Triage," said Ridley. "I needed to let it know that I wasn't going to harm it. I'm going down now to try and cut it loose."

"How's it doing?" she asked anxiously.

"It's getting tired." Trying to avoid inhaling a mouthful of seawater, he took three quick breaths.

"Good luck," said the Latina. "Be careful."

Ridley performed a surface dive. He swam dolphin-style to avoid thrashing his legs. The current was fierce. Ridley felt himself being pulled toward a tangle of netting just past where the young whale's tail was being pulled downward. Reaching for his knife, he swam below the whale and began slicing through the monofilament gill netting. Although the netting was incredibly strong for withstanding linear stresses, the razor sharp survival knife separated the strands easily. Ridley hoped the blade's edge would hold until the whale was released.

Reddish lacerations were evident where the netting was imbedded in the whale's flukes. Ridley continued slicing at the tangled netting. The skin flinched and shuddered as he moved the knife's serrations through the strands.

The right portion of the fluke was much more tangled than the left side, the net bunched up in thick balls around it. One strand was imbedded in the whale's flesh several inches. Ridley cut and pulled. The young whale bucked suddenly, knocking Ridley backward, the force sending the air from his lungs. He gasped, inhaling a mouthful of seawater. Panicked, Ridley kicked and pulled his way to the light.

Ridley broke the surface, gagging and choking. He vomited up seawater and nearly inhaled more before drawing a breath. With difficulty, he managed to get his snorkel back into his mouth. The two women in the boat were yelling at him, trying to tell him something. Ridley felt as if his head was caught in a wind tunnel.

Ridley struggled to catch his breath. Removing the snorkel from his mouth again, he called out, "Net binding to fluke… Won't pull loose…"

"I don't think it's got a lot left in it," said the American woman through cupped hands. "It's breathing faster now. Whatever you do, do it soon."

"Get ready to release those fenders," said Ridley, breathlessly. "Once it's free, things will happen fast." He placed the snorkel back in his mouth, hyperventilated three more times and dove down.

By now, the wave sets were cresting over the back of the fin whale. He swam directly toward the tail this time. Ridley swam below the level of the tail and ripped at the monofilament strands. It took more effort to slice through the netting; the knife blade was beginning to dull. The young whale's movements were less now, its tail barely flinching as Ridley cut the netting near the lacerated skin. Feverishly, he continued to tear through the strands.

Ridley was aware of a great life force very near. Turning his head, he was face to face with the female finback, just out of arm's reach. His entire body began to resonate with a deep bass humming. The female's huge eye regarded Ridley curiously. The parasites that clustered around the eye were as big as his thumbnail. He forced himself to turn his back on the enormous creature and continued cutting. *Hang on momma. We're almost there.*

Ridley sawed through a large section of net. He kicked continually with his legs to avoid being swept into the tangle of drifting gill net. Finally, the last strand of netting fell away from Ridley's knife. He touched the tail gently, urging the baby whale to move forward. At first, the finback did not respond. Ridley worried that it was too exhausted to swim. He reached down once more and attempted to move the fluke for the whale.

Suddenly, with renewed energy, the young finback moved its fluke in a wide arc, again knocking Ridley backward in its wash. He saw the fender lines go slack. The infant whale slipped over them. He sculled out of the way rapidly, fascinated, as the baby broke the surface and swam directly toward the mother. The female nuzzled her youngster and rolled slightly onto her side, allowing the baby to be supported by her great bulk.

Time's up. Ridley's oxygen-starved lungs screamed for air. He made for the surface, all the while facing the retreating female and her calf.

Surfacing, he spit the snorkel out of his mouth and yelled, "It's free!"

In the boat, the two women hugged each other and yelled something that Ridley could not hear. Then, the women stopped celebrating and pointed at the water beyond Ridley.

"Turn around! Look behind you!

Spinning in the water, he saw the whales returning.

Placing the snorkel in his mouth, Ridley dropped his head below the surface in time to see the female and the calf pass within ten feet of him. The whales stopped momentarily, suspended in the roiling water. Ridley felt electrified, his body attenuated to the energy field present between him and the cetaceans. For an instant, the gap was bridged between two alien species as each one regarded the other. Then, with powerful downward motions of their flukes, the huge female and her calf faded into the shimmering blue-green curtain.

Ridley swam back toward the boat. He wasn't sure if the salt that stung his eyes was from the seawater or from his own tears.

Draining the last of the Pacifico from the bottle, Ridley set it down between his feet and sat back. "As Doc Ricketts used to say - nothin' like that first sip of beer."

"Oh, so you read Steinbeck, too," said the American woman. "I think we may have one or two more cold ones in the ice chest, Mister..."

"Ridley. Cooper Ridley." He smiled a lopsided grin, made more comical by the layer of salt crusted around his eyebrows and several days beard growth.

Ridley guessed the American woman to be in her late twenties to early thirties. She was slender with light brown hair tied in a single long ponytail. He noticed how the reflected rays of light from the sunset shone on her, casting her in a golden glow. Even after being battered about in a strong sea for most of the afternoon, he noticed she had a beautiful calmness about her.

"Thank you very much, but that one will do me just fine," Ridley said. "Somehow, I don't think you're running a concession stand for stray kayakers out here. I know how researchers have to live close to the bone when they're out in the field."

"How did you know we're researchers?" said the American woman. "Oh, I'm sorry. I'm Darcy Billings and this is my colleague, Teresa Gamez." The Mexican woman smiled shyly, brushing her jet black, shoulder length hair out of her face. She was roughly the same age as the American woman, her features more gently rounded, but equally as beautiful.

"Nice to meet you both," he said. He wondered if the women were as attractive as he saw them at this moment, or if he'd been alone at sea too long. He indicated the large wooden plates and coiled black netting leaning against the stern.

"That otter trawl looks like it's seen some use."

"Yeah, it has," said Darcy. "How did you know it's an otter trawl? Are you a biologist?"

"No. Just crewed on a few research vessels from time to time. What are you studying out here?"

"We're conducting a census of the cetacean populations in the mid- to northern gulf," said Darcy.

"In the past two years, there have been inordinately high numbers of marine mammal die-offs and strandings," said Teresa. "Lots of bottlenose and common dolphins, sea lions, even the larger whales like the finbacks."

"We're trying to determine the cause of all the deaths and strandings," said Darcy. "In addition to performing necropsies, we've also been taking fish samples and water samples, and dredging the surface sediments."

We're working with IDO, the Institute for Deserts and Oceans. We're also funded by the *Insituto de Biologia* in Mexico City," Teresa said. She spoke clearly and slowly with only a hint of an accent. "A support team in Mexico City is helping us with the substrate analysis."

"So how are the whales doing?"

"Not so good," said Darcy. "Our examinations of tissues from stranded animals show excessively high levels of PCBs in their blubber. Most of the deaths seem to be the result of severe respiratory failure, like pneumonia."

"It's not unlike the AIDS virus," said Teresa.

"How are they getting sick?" asked Ridley.

"The oceans of the world have reached critical mass," Darcy said. "It's biomagnification, or the concentration of toxins as you move up the food chain. The animals at the top of the pyramid carry the toxins from all of the creatures below them."

"Any idea where the pollution is coming from in the gulf?"

"We have some pretty good clues," said Teresa. "But nothing definitive at this time."

"Fishing stocks are down, too," said Darcy, "so the fishermen are increasing their fishing intensity. They're struggling to feed their families. That's why you see more and more gill nets stretched out for miles. It's amazing anything slips around those damn things."

"We were lucky to find that baby when we did," said Teresa. "We were lucky you happened along when you did."

Ridley held up his hands. "All I did was finish what you both started. That buoy system you rigged up was brilliant."

"Just what kind of work do you do, Mr. Ridley?" Teresa asked. "That is, when you're not rescuing stranded whales?"

"Just Ridley. Right now, I'm in between jobs. I guess you could say I do a bit of everything. Some salvage diving here and there. Did a stint with the *Sea Shepherd* for a year. I taught SCUBA diving and kayaking in some of the resorts in the Caribbean and Canada. Crewed on a few research expeditions into the Silver Banks. I make enough to bankroll me through the lean times until another job comes along."

"Sounds like an exciting lifestyle," Teresa said.

"Or the wanderings of a lost soul," Darcy added, smiling.

"Ouch! The lady biologist hits a nerve. For what it's worth, it has its moments. But for right now, wandering along this coastline is just what the doctor ordered."

"You mentioned you worked with dolphins before," Darcy said. "In what capacity?"

"I used to train dolphins for special projects in the Navy."

"Oh. Did these special projects include death and mayhem?"

A shadow passed across Ridley's face. "Originally, no. In the last gulf war, the Navy brought back the program utilizing marine mammals for covert activities. They were to be used to help us patrol the harbors at night. Kind of an early warning system. Unfortunately, my former commanding officer had other ideas."

Several moments of uncomfortable silence ensued. Darcy broke the tension first. "Where are you headed from here?"

"Well, I guess I'm going to try to make Cabo San Lucas by New Year's Day." Ridley said. Darcy noticed his grin was boyish, with just enough mischief to make her wary.

Teresa whistled. "In that? Man, I think you are one crazy *gringo*."

"All the comforts of home."

"If you live in a sardine tin," the American biologist said. "That's a long way to travel by yourself. Do you have a support team along the way to re-supply you?"

"I was counting on my fishing prowess and the kindness of marine biologists for food and beer."

"How are your fishing skills?" Teresa said.

"Marginal, at best."

"*Buena suerte,*" said Teresa. "I think you will need it."

The sun dipped below the horizon, leaving the peaks on the Baja peninsula bathed in a vermilion hue. The winds had finally died down and the sea calmed into a silvery sheen. Ridley lowered himself into the cockpit of the kayak and cinched the spray skirt around his chest.

"Thanks again, Ridley," said Darcy as she handed him the bowline. "This day had the potential to wind up very badly. I think we scored a minor victory today." Suddenly, her tanned face took on a slight crimson color. "About that exchange earlier - I apologize about the … the asshole thing. Heat of the moment, you know."

Ridley laughed. "No worries. Trust me, if that's the worst thing I get called on this trip, then I'm not doing half bad," he said. "Good luck with your research. I think what you two are doing here is important."

"We certainly believe so," said Darcy

"Could we ask one more favor of you?" said Teresa after she untied the stern line.

"Name it."

"Could you write down the location of any strandings or dead animals you may encounter on your trip? Maybe include what species of animal if it's not too badly decomposed? You will be covering areas that we won't be able to get to." Teresa quickly produced a scrap of paper and jotted some information on it. "This is where Darcy and I can be reached in Kino Bay."

Ridley took the note and stashed it in the brim of his long-billed cap. "I'll be on the lookout," he said as he back paddled away from the whaler. Tipping his hat, he said, "Well, it's been fun. See ya around."

"Good luck and safe journey," said Darcy.

"*Vaya con Dios*," Teresa said. They both watched the kayak move westward until it was lost in the shadows of the point.

"Interesting man," said Darcy, straining to catch a last glimpse of the crimson kayak. "Do you think he'll make it?"

"He seems resourceful enough," said Teresa, as she pulled the cookware out to prepare the evening meal. "The Gulf of California is a strange place though. A lot can happen between here and Cabo San Lucas."

CHAPTER TWO

September 24, 2010, Kitt Peak Observatory, Arizona

Suresh Choudrury leaned against the cold, concrete wall outside of the observatory building. He took another pull off the almost spent cigarette, tilted his head upward and exhaled. He gazed at millions of points of light, quite a different perspective from what he had been seeing through the telescope for the past twelve hours.

There was the same static from the transceivers. Other than a small storm on Io, it was a night like most others on Kitt Peak. Dr. Choudrury shivered from the chill night air, and stepped away from the wall.

Gazing toward the northeast, the glow from the lights of Tucson stretched outward like a giant luminescent starfish, its rays extending to the foothills that bordered the desert valley. Those lights kept up their relentless push toward the western mountains as more and more people moved into the Sonoran Desert basin. Soon, the light contamination from so many cars and buildings would reduce the visibility for the scopes.

Highly recruited by the Phoenix Project, Suresh Choudrury had left a prominent teaching position at the University of Arizona Department of Planetary Sciences to oversee the installation of the new scope and assume the role of sector manager.

He had been the supervisor for the project for eighteen months. In that time, he still did not know who his direct superior was. All communications went through a secured phone system. The encrypted replies came by computer-generated voice response. Dr. Choudrury was never sure why the project resided in such a veil of secrecy. What was the final destination for the reams of readouts they produced every night from their celestial vigil?

He suspected that the pentagon was involved at some level, or else some obscure branch the average taxpayer knew nothing about. Stringent security checks were in place; he was to speak to no one outside the inner circle of scientists who worked on the project.

Dr. Choudrury believed the funding for this project must be clandestine. Only state-of-the-art technology and equipment were employed. Requisitions for capital equipment and supplies were filled within twenty-four hours. Even the reports from the eight other sectors located around the globe reflected a hugely coordinated effort. The entire operation proceeded like a finely tuned machine, run by some nameless faces linked to him only by the red phone.

Dr. Choudrury took one last pull from his cigarette, flicked it to the gravel, and crushed it beneath his foot. He was about to reach for the door when the cell phone in his coat pocket rang.

"Yes?"

"Suresh, I think you need to see this," said the woman's voice on the other end.

"What have you got, Gayle?"

"Just get up here fast. I think we have a live one."

Minutes later, a panting Dr. Choudrury climbed the last step to the platform to the scope and computer systems.

"This better be good, Gayle. I damn near had a coronary running up here."

Gayle Winters, the second of their team stood at a large monitor studying the readouts. She was in her mid-fifties, slender with gray-platinum hair that she kept in a tightly wrapped bun. A brilliant astrophysicist from Cornell, Dr. Winters had been assigned to the project three months after Suresh Choudrury. They worked well together and occasionally shared the same bed after a long shift.

"At approximately 10:26, we picked up an object from just beyond the moon's dark side. At first, I thought it was a meteor being pulled into the moon's grav field. Then, after I backtracked the trajectory, the object appeared to have positioned itself on purpose to take advantage of the moon's gravitational pull."

"What? Show me where this first registered."

"Here," said Dr. Winters, pointing to the coordinates on the screen. "Here is where it picks up the gravitational force from the moon and then slingshots around."

"Look at that. No meteor travels at that speed," said Dr. Choudrury. "Run the numbers again."

"I already have," said Dr. Winters. "Twice. I checked all systems. Diagnostics showed all systems functioning at optimum levels."

He looked up at Gayle. "This object is not ballistic. It's under power!"

She nodded. "That's not all." Dr. Winters forwarded the sequence. "Look here. See how the trajectory is shifted every few seconds. If I extrapolate the path, the object is moving in an erratic trajectory." She could not hide the excitement in her voice. "By the way it's moving, the flight path suggests a ship, not a meteor."

"Wait a minute. What do the French have up there right now?"

"I checked all scheduled shuttle flights. The French launch isn't until next Tuesday. Canaveral is coming up on the thirteenth. The Russians aren't planning another visit to the station until next month."

Dr. Choudrury whistled, more of a high pitched exhalation. "Where is it going down?"

Dr. Winters expanded the screen projection until a large relief of the southwestern United States and Mexico came into view. Across the screen, a flashing green dotted line indicated the trajectory of the object. "Looks like it's heading for us," Dr. Choudrury said, barely able to contain his own excitement. "How long before impact?"

"Three minutes, forty-two seconds until impact. And to think I almost missed it. I was about to take another series of shots on the Io storm."

"Can you get me the coordinates to touchdown?" said Dr. Choudrury, studying the object's elliptical path across the screen.

Dr. Winters moved to another terminal and keyed in commands. After a long moment, she looked up. "Got it! It's coming up on your screen right now."

"Well, it's not going to land in Arizona," said Dr. Choudrury.

The object moved rapidly across the screen as the two scientists madly tried to keep up with the data scrolling across the lower portion of the screen.

"It should have just entered the atmosphere," said Dr. Winters. "See the flare right about here?"

"It's moving a lot faster than we thought." Dr. Choudrury looked at the calculated speed of the object. "We don't have anything that moves that fast."

Suddenly, the object disappeared from the screen.

"It's gone below radar. "I'll see if I can extrapolate the flight path to impact point."

After several agonizingly long seconds, Dr. Winters looked up once more. "It's going to miss Arizona. It's headed for Mexico."

"Where in Mexico?"

"Hang on a second." Dr. Winter's eyes darted across the screen. She looked up at Dr. Choudrury. "It's going to splashdown in the Gulf of California!"

CHAPTER THREE

The greenish-white glow of bioluminescent fireworks briefly outlined the paddle as Ridley dipped it into the black sea and watched it trail away into the darkness. Occasionally, tiny sparks of light leapt from the wake as the streamlined bow of the sea kayak cut through the water.

The late September night was clear and cloudless. Away from the lights and pollution of the cities, the sky dome appeared three-dimensional. The sea was flat, the stars reflecting on the water like a mirror. For a moment, Ridley imagined himself hurtling through space, the nebulas sweeping by him.

Ridley loved to paddle at night. The sea was usually calmer and he tuned his other senses to the changes occurring on the water. His hearing became more acute, listening for the crash of surf on beachheads or projecting rocks. The breeze moving across his face kept him informed of wind changes.

His compact, five-foot-ten body propelled the kayak through the darkened sea. The sound of his paddle dipping gently into the water produced a trance-like effect on him. Sometimes he would hear the splash of something at the surface, probably the age-old reenactment of the bigger fish eating the little fish.

His back, stomach and shoulder muscles tensed and relaxed with each stroke of the paddle. In the past two weeks, his body had undergone a transformation. The regular paddling coupled with decreased food intake was now revealing muscles he had not seen in a while. Ridley stopped paddling and checked his dive watch. 9:30. If he paddled for a few more hours and then located a protected beach, he could catch five hours of sleep and be out again on the water with the sunrise.

He thought back on the afternoon rescue of the baby fin whale with the two marine biologists. Both of the women had that sharp intelligence that he admired in scientists. Both were exceptionally beautiful, Darcy in that freshly scrubbed southern California appearance contrasting with Teresa's more earthy features.

"Don't start thinking about the women," Ridley said aloud, as he executed a compensatory wide sweep stroke to alter his course a few degrees. The luminescent compass on the deck rotated until Ridley saw 55 degrees west-northwest. "You're just getting started on this little adventure."

His thoughts switched over to Liz. He couldn't blame her. The last two years of their marriage had been a circular hell for her. Shortly after returning from Venezuela, he heard that she was getting married again. That was when he began planning a kayak trip down the Baja peninsula.

A distinctive sound startled Ridley, breaking the night stillness. Dolphins. He broke into a smile and began tapping on the side of the boat. He heard the exhalations again, then several times all around him. Against the stars' reflection on the water, he could barely make out the silhouette of their triangular dorsal fins as they surfaced to breathe.

"Time for the evening show," Ridley said. "How's the fishing, guys?"

He reached into his deck bag and retrieved the mask and snorkel. Fitting it snugly to his face, he proceeded to tighten the spray skirt around his chest. After setting the stopwatch on his chronograph, Ridley hyperventilated three times and turned the kayak upside down.

The water was invigoratingly cool. Phosphorescence danced before his eyes. Ridley focused on slowing his heart rate while his eyes adjusted to the gloom. He was at home in the water. While in the Navy, he held the record for free diving in his SEAL unit.

A greenish-white fusiform shape bulleted past him. All around, the water was alive with the clicks and whistles of the dolphins. More dolphins shot out of the blackness, then disappeared in a flurry of bubbles. As they swam past, the dolphins left swirling bits of phytoplankton in their wakes.

The dolphins slowed their passings one by one until they were gliding by just out of arm's reach. Ridley dared not move. He did not want to spook them. A large dolphin cruised out of the primordial darkness and approached him. It stopped, close to him, suspended in the water column. Ridley wished he knew what the dolphin was thinking at that moment. The sight of this upside down half-creature had to be challenging a few neurons in the animal's cortex.

Ridley could feel the sonar pulses gently vibrating his sternum. The dolphin was reading him. Ridley's brain told him he needed air soon. He felt a pulsation at his temples that seemed to permeate deep into his skull. For a brief moment, he felt a heightened sense of awareness.

Ridley's lungs felt like they were going to implode. The dolphin seemed to sense this change and moved off into the black void with two powerful strokes of its flukes.

With a deft stroke, Ridley righted the kayak by performing an Eskimo roll technique. He gasped for air. Checking his watch, he noted that he had been down three minutes, fifteen seconds. Not bad.

The dolphins' exhalations faded off into the night. Ridley returned the mask back to the deck bag, checked all the riggings and felt under the spray skirt to see how much water he'd taken on while inverted.

He reached behind the map case on the underside of the cockpit. A small drybag was attached by velcro to the fiberglass body of the kayak. He pulled it free and unrolled the sealed flap. The Sig Sauer 0.40 semi-automatic pistol felt cool and dry.

He knew that it was bordering on lunacy to be carrying a weapon in Mexico. There were plenty of horror stories of stupid gringos languishing in Mexican jails for months after being arrested for having guns in their possession. Ridley had weighed the risks and decided that a lot could happen to a person on a twelve-hundred-mile kayak journey. He was prepared for inclement weather, lack of potable water, heat, and most of the creatures inhabiting the desert sea. He just wanted an ace in the hole in case any two-legged snakes showed up at his isolated campsite some dark night.

To smuggle the gun past the border guards, Ridley had welded a small metal box sealed with o-ring gaskets into the undercarriage of his old white Toyota pickup. Once he got to Cabo, a prearranged meeting with an old Navy acquaintance would rid him of the pistol and garner him a plane ticket back to the states. Ridley checked the magazine, placed the gun back in the drybag, and stored it.

Resuming his paddling, Ridley felt a heaviness cloud his spirits. An encounter with dolphins usually left him jubilant and energized. His mind drifted back to Charlie and Dali, the two dolphins that were his charges while he was assigned to the Cetacean Reconnaissance Project (CRP) during the last gulf war. No matter how many times he played it over in his mind, he held himself responsible for the dolphins' deaths. His mind played the final minutes over and over again. It was like a bad movie that got stuck in the worst part. He kept trying to think if there was something more he could have done.

Ridley shook his head. "Keep it up fool," he said. "You're going to be certifiable before Mulegé if you keep this up."

He felt very tired. Straining to see through the darkness, Ridley looked and listened for a break in the rugged coastline where there might be a sandy beach to take out. The unbroken line of rocky cliffs appeared to stretch northward forever. He remembered how this region of shoreline looked on the charts. Bad Points, or *Punta mal* as it was known to the local fisherman, had a reputation for unpredictable currents and submerged rocks, two obstacles Ridley did not want to reckon with tonight. He decided to skirt the shoreline well outside the surf zone and look for a shallow cove nestled among the craggy rock faces.

Suddenly Ridley sensed it was brighter. All around him, the water went from the color of midnight to pre-dawn slate gray. The tall cliffs became back-lit with a fierce illumination. He strained to look over his right shoulder. The light beyond the cliffs grew more intense. He heard a sound like a distant rushing noise that increased to a loud roar.

At that moment, Ridley saw the fireball come out of the sky.

CHAPTER FOUR

"I have a fix on it," said Dr. Winters. "Go ahead and bring it up on your screen."

Dr. Choudrury enlarged the image of the map on the computer screen. "Looks like it hit north of a place called Kino Bay. Sparsely populated area. Nothing much until you get further north. A few scattered fishing camps in between."

"We're receiving incoming messages from White Sands and Arecibo," she continued. "They want to know if we have a confirmation on the bogie. They lost the signal before impact, too."

"Tell them we're close and will run the numbers through as to where it hit as soon as we have a better idea."

He looked toward the red secured phone. "I think this warrants waking them up in Washington." He moved over to the phone, keyed in the complex identification sequence that he had memorized for just such an occasion and waited. A computer- activated voice came on the line. "Please provide voice imprint identification and numerical coding," it said in a monotone.

"Choudrury, Suresh. Tango-alpha-oscar. Six, three, two, two, seven, three, niner, niner, zulu."

Several seconds passed. All Dr. Choudrury could hear on the other end of the line was the click of connecting systems. Suddenly, a voice spoke.

"Go ahead, Kitt Peak." The voice was a soft southern drawl, almost lilting. It caught Suresh slightly off guard.

"Uh, yes, sir. At 10:26 P.M., mountain-standard time, my colleague Gayle Winters registered an object entering the atmosphere on an approach trajectory. It appears to have used the moon's G-force to slingshot into earth's orbit before it entered the atmosphere."

"You are sure it is not a meteor?" said the voice at the other end of the red phone.

"Positive, sir," said Dr. Choudrury. "Meteor signatures are fairly constant in velocity and trajectory. This entity was operating under power and traveling at speeds faster than any recorded meteor. We checked all NASA and foreign launch schedules as well. No one has anything up there at this time."

"Were you able to get a fix on its location?" said the voice. There was something vaguely familiar about the voice, but Choudrury could not place it. He nodded to Dr. Winters, who began downloading the information from the mainframe.

"Data should be coming through now, sir," said Dr. Choudrury. "From our projections, it appears the object crashed in the Gulf of California along a fairly deserted stretch of coastline."

"This information is incomplete," said the voice after a pause. "It gives an area of ten square miles where it could have possibly crashed. That is not good enough, Doctor Choudrury."

"Sir, once the object went below radar, the computer extrapolated the possibilities of potential impacts. What you have is its best estimate within one one-thousandth percent margin for error. I'll run the numbers again and try for a tighter location."

Dr. Choudrury keyed in figures into the computer while the phone lay cradled between his shoulder and his ear. After a moment's computations, he nodded and spoke into the phone again. "Sir, I narrowed the transects down to five square miles. You should be seeing the updated version coming through on your end now."

"Good. Very good, doctors. You are to be congratulated for your work. Have you reported your findings to the other stations?"

"Arecibo and White Sands both have confirmed the object's trajectory and destination. They also lost track of it shortly after it entered the atmosphere."

"I would like to take this opportunity to remind you both of your security channels. Any communication from this point on is to go through this secured line only. Do I make myself clear?"

Choudrury looked at his colleague, a puzzled look on his face. "Sir, you do not want us exchanging information with other members of the team?"

"The dissemination of all information from this point forward is not your responsibility. You have done your jobs well, and will be amply compensated for your efforts."

"Sir, please forgive me, but this could be the most significant discovery of the century. Dr. Winters and I would just like to follow up on our initial observations.

"Remember, Dr. Choudrury. Remember your obligation." The line went dead.

Dr. Choudrury muttered an epithet in Hindi, staring at the red phone still in his hand.

"What happened?" said Dr. Winters.

"I think we just were given the ... how do you say ... the bum's rush?"

Dr. Winters leaned against the console. "What about the next shift? What are we supposed to tell them?"

"Nothing. We are to tell them nothing of what occurred here this evening. Any and all debriefing will be handled by the directors, or whoever they are."

"Something's rotten in Denmark," said Dr. Winters. "Whoever heard of not disseminating information among the research team?"

Dr. Choudrury rested one hand on his chin, cradling his elbow with the other. "That voice on the phone. Where have I heard that voice before?"

"You knew that person?"

"No. But he had a voice and a manner of speaking that I know I have heard before - on a news program or something like that. Texas? I don't know."

"Well, that narrows it down to several hundred good old boys who haunt the hallowed halls of the capital," said Winters. "I sure would like to know just what the hell we saw go down tonight."

"Somehow, I don't think we're going to get the full picture," said Choudrury. He remained contemplative for a moment, then brightened suddenly. "I have an idea. Run a copy of all the data while I try to contact White Sands."

"What do you have in mind?"

"I'm going to arrange a little extra insurance for us, just in case they forget about their devoted and loyal employees."

Dr. Choudrury picked up the unsecured line and keyed in the number for the facility at White Sands. After several moments of waiting, he set the phone back in the cradle.

"The line is dead."

"What? We just spoke with them not ten minutes ago."

"There's something weird going on," said Choudrury. He picked up the phone and dialed the number for Arecibo.

"Arecibo's line is dead, too," he said.

"That's impossible," Dr. Winters said angrily. "They couldn't disengage both sets of phone connections that quickly. Could they?"

"I don't know. What I don't understand is why they forced us out of the loop. Can we still get hard copy on all the data from say ten o'clock through eleven-fifteen tonight?"

"Unless they locked us out from the mainframe, I think so," said Winters, inputting a series of commands into the computer. A moment later, the printer on the next table came alive and began spewing out the data accumulated over the last hour. She walked over to the table and retrieved the copies. Handing one to Choudrury, she said, "Are you sure we're doing the right thing?"

"I don't know. There was something sinister in that voice. It was cold, calculating. I would associate that voice with someone who could inflict great pain on a person and smile throughout the process."

"Now you're making me real nervous. C'mon, the voice on the other end of that phone is probably some pencil-necked bureaucrat who is following orders from someone else. Those types are as common as cockroaches in D.C."

"That may be," Dr. Choudrury said uneasily. "But do me a favor when you finish your shift this morning."

"What's that?"

Suresh looked at Gayle, his concern evident. "Please lock your door."

"There is a very competent security patrol on this mountain. They are always out there. Stop worrying, alright?

"Gayle, I -"

"Okay, okay. I'll lock my door if it will make you happy."

CHAPTER FIVE

The object appeared to skirt the top of the cliffs. It burned an arc across the sky, illuminating the walls of the cliffs like a spotlight. The roar of the meteor was deafening. Ridley detected something else; a strange odor was all around him. His brain took several seconds to process the information. He realized the smell was ozone.

The meteor had an odd shape. The pattern of the tail seemed more blunted than Ridley would have guessed. As the object roared overhead, Ridley thought he glimpsed black smoke against the starry canopy.

The thought came to Ridley suddenly. If that thing went down anywhere close, the wash from it would splatter him against the face of the cliffs. His imagination began to take over. Ridley thought of a meteor-induced giant tsunami rushing toward him. His thoughts flashed forward to years from now when some wanderer in the desert would gaze up into the skeleton of a once living cordon cactus and find the bleached out bones of a kayaker still sitting in the remains of a red kayak.

All he could do at the moment was watch, the flimsy kayak being the only barrier between him and the rapidly falling object. The meteor was now directly overhead. Ridley thought he saw bits of debris sparking off the object as it continued its fiery descent. From the angle of the trajectory, it looked like it was going to hit the water not far from where he was.

Panic gripped at Ridley's core. He realized he couldn't have picked a worse place to be at that moment. Using some wide sweep strokes, he aimed the kayak out to sea in the direction of the falling object.

Shards of debris began raining down all around him. The fragments hissed as the red-hot flakes met the cool seawater. A pea-size shard landed on the neoprene spray skirt and promptly burned through. Ridley felt a searing pain on his inner thigh and let out a yelp. He yanked back the spray skirt and flicked the ember off his thigh. It sizzled in the tiny puddle of water on the floor of the kayak. A smaller piece hit him on the shoulder, burning through his shirt. Ridley madly brushed it away. The heavy fallout of particles continued all around him. Another piece hit the foredeck and stuck in the fiberglass. Embedded, the triangular fragment glowed and sizzled. *A few more of those in the wrong place and I won't have to worry about riding the tsunami.*

Ridley pulled his life vest over his head and reattached the spray skirt. He entertained the idea of going inverted again, but did not want to risk getting holes in the keel.

Just as quickly as it started, the molten rain was over. The meteor was past him now and angling toward the water's surface. Ridley's nostrils were assaulted with the smell of burnt rubber, singed flesh and ozone. He saw from under the cover of his lifejacket that the object was going down.

The meteor hit the water with a resounding splash, followed by a huge hiss. The fire that had seconds before lit up the night sky was now extinguished, plunging him back into darkness. It was difficult to determine how far off the object crashed, but one thing Ridley knew for sure was that he needed to be a lot further away from the cliffs. He paddled harder than he had ever paddled in his life.

The explosion mushroomed on the dark horizon in front of him. Ridley was so surprised by the suddenness of the blast, that he almost capsized the kayak. Red flames shot skyward; arcing pieces of debris moved outward from the center. Then Ridley heard the detonation. *Do meteors explode when they hit the water?* His mind registered something odd about a time-delayed explosion from contacting the water. Perhaps there was a gas pocket in the rock that caused it to explode. Ridley did not know a lot about meteors, but this one was behaving strangely.

He heard the sound of pieces of debris hitting the water ahead of him. The object was close. Ridley heard another sound as the splashes subsided. It was subtle, like a gentle rustle on the wind. It grew progressively louder, the rustle turning into a rumble. He stopped paddling and listened. The rumbling sound became a roar.

Water! A lot of agitated water was bearing down on him. Ridley pulled the kayak toward the onrushing wave. He could hear the pounding of his heart in his ears. Straining his eyes, he peered into the darkness.

In the distance, where the night sky and the water fused, Ridley thought he saw a thin white line appear. He blinked and gazed intently at it again. The white line was thicker, more distinct now. The rushing sound of tons of seawater moving toward him was louder. Ridley made a last minute check of items lashed to the deck of the kayak. Uncleating the rudder line, he retracted the kayak's rudder. The less resistance when the wave hit, the better.

The line became a wall of white, foaming water. Ridley braced his knees under the gunwales and paddled ferociously toward the rogue wave.

Ridley felt a pressure wave of air. A roaring curtain of seawater grew before him, replacing the starlit sky. To his relief, the wave had not broken yet; the foamy crest was beginning its curl into the trough.

"Oh, shit!"

The kayak was carried up the immense wave face. He felt the kayak about to pitchpole over backward. Ridley's words were drowned out by the roaring sound all around him. Instinctively, he sucked in a big breath, ducked his head, and tried to lie as close to the foredeck as possible. Desperately, he held the paddle parallel to the boat's deck.

Suddenly, Ridley was immersed in water. The great wave tried to rip him from the cockpit. He dug his knees into the gunwales, the pain sharp as the kayak was lifted. In the next instant, Ridley felt air on his face. Squinting, he saw the night sky for a second. But something was wrong. The nose of the kayak began to dip downward and accelerate. Too late, Ridley realized he had punched through the wave and was now airborne on the backside. The kayak hit the water nose first, slamming Ridley into the deck and then trying to rip him from the cockpit. The buoyancy spit the kayak out of the water backward. Ridley braced himself to keep from tipping over.

Ridley yelled to the heavens in exultation and relief. Behind him, the sound of the rushing water slowly diminished. He performed a check of all systems. Head, torso and arms were intact. At that moment, he was aware of a deep aching in both of his knees. Next, he checked all the riggings on the deck. Compass and deckbag had withstood the wave's force.

Behind him, he heard the thunderous crash of the wave breaking against the face of the cliffs. Ridley breathed a sigh of relief, realizing how fatigued he was. It was time to find a beach.

Ridley resumed paddling toward the west. He noticed his shoulders were beginning to develop some stiffness.

The piece of debris from the meteor was still fused into the foredeck of the kayak. Reaching into the deckbag before him, he located his headlamp. He flicked on the switch. What he saw caused his heart to race in his chest.

Embedded in the fiberglass was a finely polished piece of metal. Upon closer inspection, he could see etchings on the face resembling some form of hieroglyphic writing, the likes of which he had never seen before.

"I'll be damned," he said softly. "That was no meteor."

CHAPTER SIX

Teresa Gamez stored the last of the dinner pots in a nylon pouch and placed them in the compartment at the bow of the Boston whaler. She returned to the stern and flopped into the cushioned seat across from Darcy Billings. The sun had set hours ago; their only illumination came from a butane lamp suspended over the transom. Schools of needlefish darted in and out of the light, taking advantage of the increased productivity.

Darcy poured more wine into her tin cup and then refreshed Teresa's. The night air was cool with only a slight breeze out of the west.

Teresa, took a sip from the cup. "I don't know about you, *mi amiga*, but I am exhausted."

"I think the wind and waves beat us up a bit today," said Darcy. "We were lucky that guy Ridley happened along."

"Yes. Thanks to him, there's a baby fin whale alive tonight."

"Hey, we didn't do half bad ourselves out there today." Darcy looked over the brim of her tin cup at her colleague and long-time friend. "What's your take on him, Teres? Do you think he is for real?"

"Do you mean, do I think he was telling the truth? I don't know. He seemed to be well informed. He is also quite at home in the water, if you hadn't noticed."

"Oh, I noticed," Darcy said with a smile. "I don't know how long he was down, but that guy has definitely got a set of lungs. I guess it's kind of strange to run into someone doing a twelve-hundred mile solo kayak trip."

"What's so strange about that?" said Teresa. "He said he was unemployed at the moment."

"I don't know. I kinda got the feeling he was - well, lost. Maybe he was searching for something."

"Perhaps he's coming off a broken relationship," Teresa said, staring out into the darkness. "A three- to four-month absence would not be tolerated by many women."

"He turned out to be a pretty nice guy," said Darcy. "That's more than we can say for a lot of our post-doc colleagues back at the university." She stood up and stretched her back muscles. "Man, I think I'm going to be sore."

"Where do you want to go tomorrow?" said Teresa.

"I was thinking sector twenty-four, near *Roca Blanca*. Let's see if any of the sea lions made it back there this year."

Darcy unrolled her sleeping bag and spread it out over the bench seat. She washed her face at the stern of the boat and turned to say something to Teresa. But her friend was already curled up in her own bag. Darcy extinguished the light, crawled into her bag and was asleep almost immediately.

Darcy was awakened by a strange roaring sound that was growing louder. She opened her eyes and thought that Teresa had lit the butane lamp again. It was light all around. She sat up and realized the light was not emanating from the lantern. Over the mountains, a fiery object was descending toward the ocean.

"Teresa, wake up!" She sat transfixed by the burning object as it arced across the sky.

"What is it?" Teresa sat up, eyes wide.

"My God, that's the biggest meteor I've ever seen," said Darcy.

"It's going to land close," said Teresa. "It looks like it's going to hit the water."

They watched in fascination as the meteor burned its path across the night sky, leaving a trail of fiery particles in its wake. It quickly dropped lower on the horizon and then disappeared into the blackness.

The sudden realization hit them both. "Oh, no," said Darcy. "What if it hits close by?"

"I think we'll be safe in this cove. It's protected from the open sea."

"Do you think we'd better pull anchor and head toward Kino?" said Darcy.

"I think we would be in more danger out there than if we stay here," said Teresa, in a voice that was far from convincing.

A brief flash of light appeared on the horizon followed by a muffled explosion several seconds later.

"Did you hear that?" said Teresa.

"Yeah, I did," said Darcy. "That must have been one hot meteor to explode like that."

They waited for what seemed to be an eternity, waiting for the giant tidal wave. Twenty minutes later, Darcy began to relax a little.

"What do you think, Teresa? Do you think we missed the wave?"

"Perhaps the impact was directed out to sea. It would have been here by now."

They settled in once more for the night. They had not been asleep long when the night stillness was broken by loud slapping sounds on the water. Darcy and Teresa scrambled out of their bags. Teresa lit the lantern by the time they made their way to the whaler's bow.

A great commotion was happening in the water. The sea was being churned to foam all around them. Dark forms moved quickly in and out of the light."

"Dolphins!" said Darcy. "Look at them all."

"They're agitated," said Teresa. "They're really close to the boat."

"I've never seen this kind of behavior before," said Darcy. "I wonder if that meteor has them flipped out."

The dolphin pod's actions became more frenzied, with several individuals performing arcuate leaps at once. All around them, Darcy and Teresa could hear urgent vocalizations. The group swam around the whaler in an ever decreasing circle, until Darcy could have reached over and touched their dorsal fins.

"I'm going to drop a hydrophone in," said Teresa. A moment later, she had rejoined Darcy at the bow. As she lowered the hydrophone into the water, the group of dolphins suddenly disappeared.

Teresa and Darcy stared into the darkness, then looked back at each other.

"That was too weird," said Darcy after a moment. "One minute they were here, the next they were gone."

"Was it me or did you get the strange feeling that they were trying to tell us something?" said Teresa.

"I had the same feeling," said Darcy. "But what?"

"I don't know. But I think it had something to do with that meteor."

CHAPTER SEVEN

Ridley paddled for another hour, searching for an opening in the rocky shoreline. Once, he encountered a small cove tucked in among the crags, but upon closer inspection, saw the small area of beach would soon be inundated by the flooding tide. He gave in to the rhythm of paddling, the movement of arms and torso becoming automatic, his mind attaining an altered state.

A burst of air off to his left yanked an exhausted Ridley from his mental meandering. A dolphin passed within two feet of the kayak. He heard a second exhalation behind him. And another. Suddenly, dolphins were everywhere. They seemed to materialize out of the depths. One of the things he loved about these cetaceans was their ability to appear and vanish easily.

"Hey, guys. Twice in the same night? Or are you another group?"

Strange, he thought. The dolphins were not moving in their normal traveling fashion. Instead of porpoising through the water, these dolphins were logging along the surface, hanging close to the kayak. Ridley gazed into the dark water below him. Elongate forms of dolphins undulated slowly, keeping pace with the kayak. Their bodies shimmered in the bioluminescent cast.

"What's the matter?" he said. "Are there sharks following you?"

Ridley thought about orcas, the dolphin's greatest enemy besides man. He had witnessed orcas relentless pursuit of dolphins and porpoises in Mexico and Canada before. Being the buffer between a bunch of panicked dolphins and hungry orcas was not a position Ridley desired this evening. Although there had never been a recorded attack on a human being by an orca, the frenzy of a feed could leave Ridley as one of the casualties.

The dolphin escort closed ranks on the kayak, the animals forming a tight living raft all around him. Ridley was afraid to paddle any more. Even if the dolphins were being pursued by orcas, the kayak offered little protection from an orchestrated attack. When the dolphins exhaled around him, tiny sparks of bioluminescence appeared briefly in the air. All around him was the permeating odor of fish.

The dolphins vocalized energetically. Their chatter even reverberated through the hull of the kayak. The pod appeared more anxious than agitated, Ridley thought. Not exactly the type of behavior one would expect from a group of dolphins under threat of attack.

Ridley decided to dip the paddle into the water, partly to see what the dolphins would do and to resume his search for a beach landing. Dolphins or no dolphins, he needed to sleep. Deftly, he brought the blade down to his left. As the paddle blade touched the water, the cetaceans moved out of the way enough to allow it to sweep by. Ridley was amazed. He dipped the paddle to the right with the same result from the animals on that side. Any one of these creatures could mete out serious damage to him and the kayak, yet they continued matching the kayak's direction and speed.

He heard the wash of surf on sand and peered toward the shoreline. Ahead, a faint glowing outline of white appeared out of the darkness. Behind the beach were a series of small, rolling hills leading up to a steep walled mesa.

"Well, boys and girls, it's been interesting, but this is where we part company," Ridley said.

Ridley attempted to turn the kayak toward the shoreline. To his astonishment, the bow of the kayak was brought around to its former westerly heading. The cacophony of sounds below him intensified.

"What the hell?" He attempted to turn in again toward the beach. This time, he felt a gentle push emanating from the kayak's stern. Once more, Ridley was headed in a westerly direction parallel to shore. With each course correction, the chatter from the dolphins increased.

"Don't tell me. I'm not supposed to go to that beach, right?"

An eerie feeling pervaded Ridley's brain. These dolphins appeared to want him to follow a particular tack. He had never witnessed this type of behavior in all his years spent in the company of marine mammals. Ridley attempted to turn the kayak out to sea. Again, the chorus of high-pitched vocalizations grew louder and more urgent. A dolphin gently pushed the stern and his course was corrected.

"Hmm. I guess we're going this way, then."

Normally, dolphins in Mexico are wary of humans. Most encounters spelled a nasty death for the dolphins in the gill nets or at least prop lacerations. Occasionally, an irate fisherman would shoot at them, believing that the dolphins were competing for the same dwindling fish stocks.

Ridley's thoughts turned back to the object that crashed. He wondered if there was a correlation between the dolphin's odd behavior and the fireball that went down nearby.

"Something out there got you spooked? Well, me too." Ridley shook his head. "I have to be crazy. Here I am, in the middle of nowhere in the middle of the night being shanghaied by a bunch of dolphins."

Ridley ceased paddling. Instantly, sounds of the dolphins grew louder and shriller. Some of the animals on the surface became agitated and pushed off one another. Flukes were slapped angrily against the surface. A dolphin pushed its rostrum against the bow, followed by several others. The water all around the kayak churned with the movements of the excited dolphins. At first, Ridley thought the pod was trying to capsize the kayak. Several times, he had to brace to avoid going over.

It took Ridley several anxious moments to realize a pattern was emerging in the cetacean's bizarre behavior. The dolphins were collectively attempting to move the kayak in the direction Ridley was paddling just minutes ago. At first, their efforts were clumsy and uncoordinated. The shape of the kayak made it difficult to push in a straight line. Soon a synchrony of movement unfolded as dolphins on each side alternated nudging the boat forward. Ridley was fascinated at how quickly the dolphins solved the hydrodynamics problem and the kayak continued along its original course.

"Okay, okay. I get it. You *really* want me to go this way."

Ridley began paddling again, slowly and tentatively. The pitch of the dolphin's vocalizations subsided. He still could not believe it. The dolphin entourage seemingly wanted him to continue in this direction and they were being insistent about it.

"This night will definitely go down as the weirdest night I've ever had."

It was about to get weirder still.

CHAPTER EIGHT

Ridley snapped awake, sweating profusely. Had it been the dream, or the continuous paddling? Overcome with fatigue, he had fallen asleep while continuing his trek along the desert coast.

The dolphins were still with him, moving slowly and purposefully beside the kayak. He wondered how much they had navigated for him or even if they realized he had nodded off.

Ridley was having trouble clearing the image from his mind. He could not remember the last time he experienced that dream. But there it was again, haunting his psyche and putting a lump in his throat.

The dream always began with Charlie and Dali leaping high into the air. Then it switched to Ridley's former superior officer, Richard Jenks. He gave the order to attach live limpet mines to one of the dolphins. Jenks ordered Ridley to deploy the dolphins to an abandoned ship sitting on a reef a mile offshore. In the dream, Ridley remembered protesting vociferously, feeling helpless and angry as the senior officer coldly relieved him of his duties and gave the signal to the dolphins to seek out the boat and place the mines.

An explosion occurred before the dolphins ever reached the target vessel. Ridley never found Charlie. Dali washed up near shore a half hour later, dying from the concussion of the blast. He remembered kneeling in the water cradling the dolphin's limp form, trying to keep it breathing. In the dream, he could not stop crying. Ridley remembered seeing Jenks standing over the dead dolphin and an uncontrollable rage overtook him.

He shook his head, trying to clear that image from his mind. That was seven years ago. Why couldn't he let it go?

Ridley could no longer feel his feet, the circulation being compressed from sitting far too long. A deep burning in his bladder told him that he had better relieve himself soon. Ridley stopped paddling and pulled back the spray skirt. Fumbling behind the seat, he located his bailing bucket. At sea, it also functioned as a urinal when the need arose.

"I'm sorry about this," Ridley said, as he poured the contents into the water. There was a change in the pitch of the dolphin's vocalizations briefly, then they resumed their normal chatter. He suspected that dolphins knew the health of other members of their pod because they were able to taste the waters around them. He wondered if right now they were saying, "Hey, lay off the *carne asada!"*

He shifted his weight side-to-side and lifted his butt off the seat by pressing down on the gunwales with his hands. The muscles in his back were a mass of knots.

He noticed the banter among his escorts had decreased, only becoming more active when the group passed along headlands or, Ridley guessed, underlying seamounts. He checked his watch. 1:43. He must have been asleep for how long? An hour? Two? The events of the night were running into each other.

He did not recognize this stretch of coastline in the dark. Perhaps if he were a little more alert, some of the contours might jog his memory. Ridley felt as if he were somewhere between fact and fantasy. He reckoned that he had traveled at least another four or five miles up the coastline.

Off in the distance, Ridley thought he heard the low drone of an airplane. He looked out to sea and near the place where the sky met the ocean. Then he caught a glimpse of a flash of light.

"I think we finally have some officious government types on the scene," said Ridley, trying in vain to alleviate the discomfort in his backside.

If it were the Feds in cooperation with the Mexican government, they had mobilized more quickly than Ridley had figured. He guessed that the initial search effort would be a spotter plane or a coast guard cutter sent to perform a preliminary survey of the area. He knew the place would soon be crawling with agents from both sides of the border and cringed at the thought.

The dolphins were traveling closer to the shoreline now. The rugged cliffs loomed overhead and the broken, eroded formations that crowned them appeared as eerie sentinels. Ridley could hear the sound of seawater being forced in and out of the crevices at the surface. In his fatigued state, the noise almost sounded like a distant conversation.

The dolphins stopped moving with the kayak. Suddenly, their vocalizations increased to a fever pitch. Ridley stared into the darkness, straining to see what lay before him.

"What is it, you guys?"

Reaching into the deck bag once again, he found the headlamp. He fit it to his head, and adjusted the lamp to emit a low narrow beam.

A cave materialized out of the darkness. It was not a large opening in the rock face; at high tide it would be completely submerged. Ridley did not remember seeing this formation on any of the charts he had studied. If a strong surge were present, this would not be a good place to be. He peered down into the water. Silvery shoals of small fish reflected in the light and then darted into the shadows.

Up ahead, the dolphins were milling about the entrance to the cave. Ridley saw them moving in and out in the low light. It appeared they were going back into the opening and remaining there for several minutes at a time. Ridley could see animals in groups of two and three jettison out of the cave, circle the kayak, and then swim back through the entrance.

"Is this where you've been leading me?" Ridley said. That bad feeling was back again. "I suppose you want me to go in there?"

Ridley thought the kayak would probably get stuck in the cave if he did manage to get past the entrance. He briefly entertained the notion of snorkeling in but decided that the strong surge coupled with the darkness could get him injured. Drowning was not at the top of his list of "Fun Things to Do Alone at Night on the Sea of Cortez."

Neither was getting stuck in the back of a cave in a seventeen-foot kayak. A voice in his head told Ridley to back the boat up and continue up the coast until he found the next available sand beach. The hell with the dolphins.

But the other voice was much stronger, that portion of his brain that talked louder and always seemed to get him in trouble. The dolphins had apparently brought him here for a reason. That much was clear. He needed to know what was inside.

Ridley pulled out a set of tide tables from the deckbag and studied them by the light from his headlamp. They revealed high tide to be around 3:30 in the morning, about an hour and a half from now.

"Oh, hell," he said as he rolled up the sheets. "If I go in there, will you guys leave me alone?"

He opted to stay in the kayak. Paddling slowly toward the entrance, he peered at the water's movement to gauge the strength of the currents. It was approaching flood tide stage; Ridley could see strings of algae being buffeted back and forth in the current.

The entrance of the cave was about eight to ten feet across. His head cleared the roof by about three feet. As soon as the kayak was in the cave, Ridley noticed a sudden drop in temperature. The air was damp in here. The walls were encrusted with barnacles. Something moved on his left, just out of his direct light. Ridley turned and caught a glimpse of several shore crabs scuttling away from the beam. Once at a safe distance, they would turn and watch, their claws held in a defensive position, their stalked eyes glowing. Large sun stars clung to the walls at the waterline.

Five or six dolphins had accompanied the kayak into the cave. Ridley watched them bullet ahead of him, while others swam in the other direction. The cave continued to snake back, growing narrower with each stroke of the paddle. He could almost touch either side of the cave wall with his paddle blade. Soon, he would no longer be able to paddle.

By his best reckoning, he had penetrated about fifty to sixty feet into the opening. All maneuverability with the paddle was lost except to push off the cave wall. When the walls narrowed to four feet, he thought about back-paddling out. A "sneaker" wave right now would smash him against the roof of the cave.

"Next time, bring your helmet, dipshit." He lashed the paddle to the deck with bungees and began pulling himself along by his hands contacting the wet walls. He swore as his hands were lacerated against the barnacles anchored in the wall.

A swell rose in the cramped space and the kayak was bounced against the wall. There was the sound of fiberglass grating on the sharp rock. Ridley tried to brace with his hands, but a projecting barnacle dug deeply into his palm.

"Dammit!" he said, pulling his hand back. The reverberation of his voice resounded off the walls. "I'm not having a good time here!"

As the wave receded, Ridley pushed ahead in the darkness. The ceiling was so low now that Ridley had to flex his torso forward over the deck. The best he could do was to inch along using his hands on the slippery walls. He was not going to be able to stay in here much longer. In ten minutes, he would have to push the kayak out of the cave.

Ridley lifted his head to see ahead of him but a jutting rock grazed his head and forced him to face-plant on the deck again. His back and neck muscles began to cramp from the contorted position. He decided to back out the way he came.

Suddenly, Ridley's hands were no longer touching the cave walls. He felt cool, damp circulating air brushing across his face. He adjusted the beam on his headlamp and looked up.

A large cavern loomed before him. The ceiling was at least twenty feet above him, laced with black fissures running in a lengthwise direction. Ridley focused the light ahead, hoping to see where the cavern ended.

Strange. He had been up and down this coastline a half a dozen times in as many years. He had never seen this before. He was sure it was not on any of the charts. Perhaps the ruggedness of the shoreline and currents had kept boaters away from this area. The entrance to the cave would be visible only at low tide. Surely the local fishermen must know about this place.

The dolphins were leaping in front of the kayak, spinning crazily about him. Ridley could see them in the headlamp, and then realized he could still see them when they surfaced out of the beam's arc. There appeared to be another light source in the cavern. Ridley shined his light on the nearest wall to see if there were phosphorescent properties in the rock. When he switched the lamp off, the cavern walls were black.

The light source was coming from the far end of the cavern. Once his eyes adjusted to the dim conditions, Ridley saw that the light was a soft, greenish-blue color, almost neon in quality. His nostrils picked up a smell, something that did not belong in a marine cave. His tired brain was slow in processing the information, but when the odor became stronger, he remembered.

Ozone. The same odor the fiery craft was trailing before it went down. Ridley was aware that the air around him had suddenly become charged, as if some low electrical current was moving about the great room. He felt the hairs on his arms and head become erect. The light source was brighter now, as he approached the far end of the cave. It seemed to be suspended about halfway up the wall. The light that emanated from the wall pulsated, the green-blue color swelling and shrinking slightly. A red corona outlined the light during its waxing phase.

With the rhythm of the light's brightness, Ridley could now hear a concurrent low-pitched humming in his ears.

"Hell of a place to put up a bug zapper," Ridley said, under his breath.

Drawing closer, he could detect a ledge just above the waterline. Below it, the dolphins were milling. Ridley thought it odd that they were floating like a logjam, bodies in close contact. They seemed to be looking at something.

Something stirred on the ledge. It was a subtle, almost imperceptible movement. Ridley's already frazzled autonomic nervous system got jump-started one more time. He switched his headlamp back on. Nothing. The batteries were spent and replacements were in one of the dry-bags stowed away in the front compartment. Where was that damn pink bunny when you needed him the most?

The creature on the ledge stirred again. The light intensity increased. So did the vibration in Ridley's ears. To his horrified amazement, he saw the orb was not hanging from the cave wall, but spinning, suspended over the now motionless form.

Ridley was within ten feet of the ledge. The raft of dolphins moved quietly out of the kayak's path as he landed against the rocks. The air was humming all around him. The vibrations pulsated within him down to his core. He felt as if he were inside a large turbine engine.

He reached under the deck, detached the Sig Sauer, and stuck it in the waistband of his shorts. The form on the ledge did not move.

Ridley transferred his feet from the kayak to the ledge, slowly placing one foot, then the other onto the rock. Pushing to stand up, he realized that he had no feeling in his legs. His legs crumpled beneath him and he fell hard onto the rocks. Panicked, he scrambled to his feet and drew the semi-automatic, engaging the slide mechanism.

The figure was lying in a semi-recumbent position, propped up against a small boulder. From this distance, it appeared to be human, but even in this diffuse light, something was wrong about the stranger's appearance. The proportions of the face were not right. The clothing was odd - something like a tunic that appeared to shimmer beneath the orb. Ridley saw that the right leg was bent at an odd angle. Something whitish was poking out of the clothing where the thigh would be, a large, dark stain surrounding it. The orb continued its revolutions, the spin and hum increasing as Ridley drew nearer.

Ridley took another step forward. In the next instant, he was thrown backward, the air driven from his lungs.

CHAPTER NINE

Ridley landed in the water and instinctively drew a breath. All he inhaled was seawater. Wracked in a spasm of coughing, more seawater flooded his windpipe. Fighting to reach the surface, Ridley became disoriented. Unconsciousness was starting to overcome him. He flailed wildly in the water in a desperate attempt to reach the surface.

Suddenly, something was pushing him upward. As he broke the surface, he found himself extended over the smooth, wet back of a dolphin. The next thing he knew, he was clinging to the rocks. Ridley vomited up seawater, his ribs aching from the coughing spasms.

Ridley lay face down, shaking, on the rocks for a long time. His legs and arms would not respond to the commands his brain issued. Finally, he managed to drag himself the rest of the way onto the ledge.

The injured humanoid was attempting to move now, trying to sit up. His eyes were focused on Ridley. Ridley looked back to grab the pistol. Gone! It must be at the bottom of the cave.

Perhaps it was a trick of the orb's light, but Ridley was drawn to the stranger's eyes. The eyes were of the most piercing blue that Ridley had ever seen. They were like the eyes of an animal caught in the headlights at night, burning with a light of their own. This color of cerulean blue reminded Ridley of some of the blue holes in the

Caribbean. The features of the head were human, but with some distinctive differences.

The nose was small, the nares possessing small flaps of skin that could cover the nostrils. The elfin ears, with less convolutions than human ears, were set back further on the skull. The skin was pale, with almost a bluish hue to it. Ridley was not sure if it was the man's natural coloration or the pallor of someone suffering from severe shock. In dimensions, the stranger was roughly the same height as Ridley, although more slight in build. *One thing was sure,* Ridley thought, *this guy was definitely not from around these parts.*

"Uh, howdy," Ridley said. *Nice going, stupid,* he thought. *This guy's lying here bleeding and all can come up with is "howdy"?*

The stranger coughed. A small glob of pinkish froth emerged from his lips. The orb sputtered and the light faded. Ridley realized that the orb was some type of barrier or force field. Contact with it had resulted in him being drop kicked halfway across the cave.

The stranger continued to look at him, but Ridley could see the eyes were unfocused. If he didn't intervene, the stranger would soon be dead.

The alien reached across his chest with his right arm and adjusted a small device with noticeable difficulty. Judging by the way he moved, Ridley guessed him to have internal injuries as well.

What do you say to an alien? The impact of that thought was mind numbing. Here he was, probably the first human to make contact with an alien race and he was at a loss for words.

"I, ah, …I think you're hurt pretty badly. Take down the barrier and let me help you." Ridley knew some basic first aid, but he doubted it covered triaging an extraterrestrial.

The stranger reached across his chest again, touching the shiny flat object on his chest. He cocked his head, as if he were listening to something.

"Was that your ship that went down out there?" Ridley said, gesturing with his hand moving downward. He wondered if the device on the alien's chest was some sort of amplifier.

"Can you understand what I am saying?" said Ridley in the slow, loud voice of someone hoping to be understood. He realized he was speaking like the *gringos* in Mexico who just talked louder when they weren't understood.

The stranger tapped his chest and tilted his head again, as if trying to clear some interference. Ridley was becoming frustrated. If they could not interface soon, the encounter would be over before it even started. Ridley tried another approach.

"Habla Espanol?"

The stranger fumbled at the device, shook his head. He weakly shrugged his shoulders and rolled his eyes in frustration.

"Where did you come from?" Ridley was hoping that his monologue would keep the alien awake. He was also hoping that the alien wouldn't vaporize him or whatever aliens do when they're pissed off.

"My name is Ridley," he said as he pointed to his own chest. "What is your name?" He thumped his chest once again. "Rid-ley."

The stranger did not move.

"Well, that's great. Just great," said Ridley, pulling himself up to a sitting position. "You're bleeding to death and there's not a damn thing I can do to help you. Hell, we can't even talk to each other. I think I'm the one who needs help. Coming in here's been a real bad idea so far."

Ridley looked over his shoulder. The realization hit him. The water level in the cave had risen another foot. It would be a long swim to the outside.

"Perfect. Now I can't even get out of here. I'm going to watch you die and then I'm probably going to get drowned for all my trouble." Ridley looked down at the dolphins that were still milling about the surface near the rocks. "Thanks a hell of a lot. This is all your faults. And I don't find anything funny about this at all."

Ridley stood up stiffly and turned toward the water. He thought about trying to snorkel out of the cave. If he could make it out now, he could always swim back in at low tide and salvage some of his gear.

"I understand your… language," came a hoarse voice from behind him. Ridley spun around, his jaw opening and closing in excitement.

"What did you say?"

The alien, his breath coming in gasps, was having difficulty talking. "You are ... speaking ... dialect... of... this planet. English. It took me ... time to ... encode."

"Look. If you don't let me try to help you, you're going to die very soon. I'm not sure if I can help, but drop the barrier and at least let me try."

The alien gazed at the human, looking as if he were trying to size him up with his last ounce of concentration. He shuddered from another wash of pain. Feebly, he reached up and touched the object on his chest. The orb began revolving even slower, the light fading to a soft blue in the cave.

Ridley advanced cautiously, fearful of another paralyzing jolt. "I'm not going to hurt you." He knelt down by the strange visitor. "What is that thing?" he said, looking overhead.

"It ... is ... personal particle ...force field," came the alien's stilted reply. "That is ... what ... dis- ... disabled you."

Ridley looked at the alien's ruined leg. He had to fight back the urge to vomit again. "That thing packs a hell of a punch. If you had the juice turned up anymore, I don't think we'd be having this conversation now."

"You had ... wea- ... weapon. Necessary to ... neutralize ..."

"Neutralize? That damn thing nearly killed me!" He saw the alien grimace in pain. "You better not talk for a while." Ridley began his examination. "Try to lay quietly while I check you over."

Ridley was close enough to the visitor now to see the details of his face and torso. The face was similar to his except the cheekbones were more prominent, similar to that of certain Native American tribes. The eyes were wide set and large for the rest of the face. The skin was delicate, almost translucent. The hands were slender, the four fingers longer and without nails. When the alien moved his hands, Ridley could see that the digits were connected by a thin membrane. The hair was shiny black and fine. This guy definitely wasn't a local.

Ridley steeled himself and began to examine the injured leg. He tried to peel back the tunic but found it adhered to the flesh. He reached for the Swiss army knife he kept in his pocket, opened the blade, and attempted to cut the material. When he touched the blade to the cloth, sparks flew off the blade. He tried cutting harder. The blade sparked again and broke in half, pinging against the rocks somewhere behind Ridley.

"Nice threads," said Ridley, staring at the broken knife blade.

"Wait," said the alien hoarsely, pointing a wavering arm toward the back wall of the cavern. "The cylinder. Bring it to me."

Ridley walked shakily over to the wall and looked down. A shiny metal cylinder that looked like a large thermos bottle was wedged between two rocks. He picked it up, examining it as he walked back to the alien's side.

"If there's an easy-off screw top lid to this thing, then it sure escapes me," Ridley said, handing the cylinder to the alien.

The alien moved his hands over the cylinder and one end slid open. He reached in and produced a small, metallic object that was shaped like a horseshoe. He activated it and a row of small colored lights flashed along the outside edge. He motioned for Ridley to take it.

Ridley held the metal half-ring in his hand. He could feel a vibration resonating from within the object. He moved it toward the alien's leg. When he was about eight to ten inches away from the leg, he felt the object grow warmer in his hand. An arc of light coalesced in the center of the ring and then projected outward. The beam touched the material of the tunic and the cloth parted with a sizzle.

There was an open wound about the size of Ridley's fist in the mid-portion of the alien's leg. The wound was oozing a fluid Ridley assumed to be blood. On closer examination, the blood consisted of two distinct colors; the main plasma appeared to be a deep fuschia, but there were striated blue streaks running through it. A pinkish-white nub of bone rose out of the laceration.

"You have a compound fracture of the upper leg bone," said Ridley. "You have lost a considerable amount of blood, but I don't think this is what your main problem is. Where else do you have pain?"

The stranger weakly indicated his right side. Ridley moved his hands over the area, probing as gently as he could. The alien stifled a cry of pain and writhed on the ground.

"Sorry! I think you've got some internal injuries as well. I can set the leg, but there's nothing I can do about this. You need a doctor."

Through clenched jaws, the alien spoke. "Hold han- … hold hand like this," indicating a pinch grip of the thumb and first two fingers. "Cover red … yellow … and bl-blue lights."

Ridley did as he was told. He held it over the injured alien's right side. A broad beam of light sprang from the metallic horseshoe. The heat from within kept building in Ridley's hands. Suddenly, Ridley felt like the ring was an extension of his own hands. It was as if he could visualize the torn and bleeding internal tissue repairing itself as he moved the device. Ridley's fear that he might be doing more damage to the stranger gave way to fascination of the images projected into his brain.

The alien's eyes were closed now. The last wave of pain had taken him under. Ridley wondered if he was dead, but then realized that a throbbing at his temples was not his heartbeat, but that of the stranger. As Ridley finished the final pass over the torso, the alien's eyes fluttered open. Ridley noted that there were actually two sets of eyelids, the inner one being almost transparent, like a shark's nictitating membrane.

"I'm not sure if I'm doing this right," he said. "But I swear I could see your organs repair themselves. If you live through this, I want to know how this thing works."

The alien looked down at his leg. "Will not … Re-repair." Then, indicating with his long fingers, he signed "break." Ridley nodded in understanding.

"I get it. The device can heal the tissue after the fracture is reduced. Well, I hope this contraption has a pain killer in it, because you're going to need it."

Behind him, Ridley heard the exhalations of the dolphins. He glanced over his shoulder. Dorsal fins still cut through the water near the rocks. The entrance was now completely submerged. The water lapped at the rocks almost level with him and the alien.

"We may have to look for higher ground soon." Looking around, he added, "If there is higher ground."

The alien spoke, his speech barely a whisper. "Hold on inner circle … like this." He again gestured with his hands. "Pass over … like this …" His hands moved over the top of his head. Again, Ridley moved the device over the alien's head, holding it in the position he was instructed. A small multi-colored beam arced across the alien's skull. Ridley made one pass over the area and the beam disintegrated.

"Proceed," said the alien.

Ridley rose stiffly, went over to the kayak that was moored to the rocks, reached inside the rear hatch, and produced a first aid kit. On the way back, he grabbed the two halves of the spare paddle.

"This is going to hurt you a lot more than it'll hurt me." He straddled the alien, facing away from him. "Hang on."

Ridley began to traction the leg. He could feel the alien tense up beneath him. "Breathe and try to relax." The break was not yet aligned. Ridley leaned into the leg with all his strength. The alien groaned and made a feeble attempt at throwing Ridley off. Even in the coolness of the cave, sweat dripped off Ridley's face from the exertion.

Slowly, the bone began to disappear back inside the wound. More blood oozed forth. The stranger passed out again. When Ridley was reasonably sure the fracture had been reduced, he held the leg in position with one hand and placed the halved paddles on either side of the leg with the other. From the first aid kit, Ridley found a roll of duct tape. He strapped one paddle on the inside and one on the outside of the leg, then bound the makeshift splint together snugly with the duct tape. Satisfied the leg was immobilized, he found the metallic ring.

Ridley fumbled with the device, trying to remember the sequence he used before. His fingers located the inverted and opposed placement on the ring over the red, yellow, and blue lights. Passing the device over the leg, Ridley saw the now familiar beam projected.

As he watched, the oozing from the wound slowed, then stopped completely. The angry ragged edges of the wound began to turn lighter, shrinking as the beam moved over the injured area. The beams healing effect continued to cauterize the wound until only a small opening was visible. A moment later, the wound was completely closed; the area of the break was now only pink and slightly raised above the rest of the leg. He finished the leg by wrapping a sterile dressing over the newly closed wound.

Sitting back, Ridley felt a wave of exhaustion wash over him. He looked at his watch. Twelve minutes past 3:00. Was it morning or afternoon? Delirious from sleep deprivation and too much adrenaline, he lay down on his side a few feet from the motionless alien. He needed to check the time of the high tide, but he could not get up. Whether the stranger lived or died was out of his hands now. The last thing Ridley remembered was how cold and damp the rock floor felt on his face.

CHAPTER TEN

At four forty-five the following morning, Dr. Choudrury and Dr. Winters stepped out of the Phoenix Project observatory and into the chill morning air. They walked down the gravel path toward the bungalows that housed the scientists working on Kitt Peak. The Phoenix Project had arranged for the more spacious quarters to be given to the two astronomers.

"That's not like Donaldson and Petty to be late for their shift," said Dr. Choudrury, shivering from the cold.

"Yes, I know," Dr. Winters said, walking close to her colleague. "This is all so surreal. How can Donaldson and Petty accomplish anything with the mainframe down?"

"I think that someone wants this information kept hidden. Don't let that data get out of your sight."

"What's our next move?" she asked.

"It's probably a good idea to lay low for a while," Dr. Choudrury replied. "At least through the next shift. Let's get this data off the mountain. I knew I should have asked for the car in the divorce settlement."

Somewhere off in the trees, a great horned owl called. It startled the two scientists and Dr. Winters found herself leaning against the shoulder of her colleague. "Damn you, Suresh, "she said. "Now you've got me jumpy. What with all this conspiracy nonsense. There has to a legitimate explanation for all of this. We're just too tired to figure it out."

Dr. Choudrury cast quick glances into the darkness all around. "You didn't hear that voice on the phone!" he snapped. "I'm sorry about being so paranoid, but I don't have a good feeling about our esteemed employers."

"Why would they be a threat to us?" Dr. Winters spoke, her voice slightly higher than usual.

"I wish I knew. Suddenly, all this secrecy. The loss of communication with the other facilities. I'm really nervous."

"Suresh, I'm scared too. Maybe we shouldn't have downloaded the data."

"No. We may need it as insurance later."

They arrived at the Dr. Winter's quarters. All of the apartments were dark. The only other resident was away. Dr. Choudrury's apartment was another hundred yards up the hill.

"What do we do now?" said Gayle.

"Try to get some rest. I'll arrange transportation. I'll ring up Petty or Donaldson. See if I can borrow one of their vehicles. Maybe I can requisition one of the maintenance trucks. I'll call you soon."

"Oh, Suresh. I'm not so sure I want to be left alone right now."

"Get some things together quickly. Once we get the data to Tucson, we can be back for next shift, no problem. Oh, and another thing. Conspiracy or no conspiracy, lock your door."

"No problem," Gayle said. "Please hurry." She gave him a quick hug, turned, and disappeared behind the door. Choudrury heard the clink of the deadbolt.

Suresh Choudrury hurried up the path, which was barely discernable in the pre-dawn light. With each step, he imagined hands reaching out of the darkness for him, just beyond the limits of his vision. He quickened his pace. The blood rushed in his ears.

The owl called out again, this time much closer. Choudrury broke into a run, scrambling up the winding gravel path. The small pebbles acted like ball bearings. He pitched forward, landing hard, scraping his hands and knees, temporarily knocking the wind from his lungs. The pain was muted by the irrational terror he was feeling. Picking himself up, he retrieved the folder with the data, now scattered before him on the path. He sprinted the rest of the way until he saw the outline of the residence building ahead. He thought he heard footsteps but was not about to slow down to find out who they belonged to.

Dr. Choudrury arrived at the door, fumbled for his keys, and when the right match was made, flung himself inside. He dead-bolted the door and then leaned against it, breathing laboriously, his body drenched in sweat.

He closed his eyes and breathed deeply, trying to calm himself. Opening his eyes, Dr. Choudrury started to reach for the nearest light switch when he froze. Across the room, the red glow of a cigarette flared.

"You really should consider a regular exercise regimen, Dr. Choudrury," the voice said cheerily. "I could hear you huffing and puffing all the way up the hill."

"Who…who are you?" Choudrury stammered.

"Just another stargazer out on a chilly evening, that's all. Leave the light off, please. Hurts my eyes, you know."

"My money and credit cards are in the top drawer of my dresser in my bedroom. Take them. Take them all."

"Well, that's mighty generous of you, Suresh. But I'm more interested in what you have in the folder under your arm."

"It's nothing. Some scientific papers from a colleague. Black holes. The papers concern the formation of black holes. How do you know my name?"

The cigarette flared again. Suresh heard a long exhalation of air. "The one thing that really irritates me," the stranger said, "Is a bad liar."

"What do you mean? I'm not lying. I swear." Choudrury discerned the man's silhouette in the darkened room. When the cigarette glowed, he caught a glimpse of close-cropped blonde hair and sunglasses.

"I'll take that folder now," said the intruder. Set it down on the davenport in front of you and then step back."

"Please don't hurt me. I just…"

"Put the folder down now."

Choudrury set the folder on the back of the davenport. Then he backed toward the door.

Another red light appeared. This one hurt Choudrury's eyes as he gazed into it. He realized too late he was looking directly at an infrared targeting laser.

In the next instant the astronomer's head was jerked backward by the impact of the silenced nine millimeter slug. His head hit against the door once and he crumbled to the floor.

The intruder stood up and spoke into a handheld radio. "Conference complete. Commencing cleanup."

From the other end, he heard a voice say, "Meeting adjourned here. The reception is waiting for us in Mexico."

The intruder walked over and retrieved the folder, then nudged the corpse with a black sneaker. "A very poor performance review, Dr. Choudrury. I'm afraid your services here are no longer required."

The great horned owl sat perched in the pine tree, its two yellow eyes tracking the movement below. It watched while two inert bundles were loaded into a nondescript white van located behind the grouping of buildings. The four figures dressed in black moved quietly and efficiently.

A subtle breeze came out of the west, ruffling the owl's feathers. The night hunter stared indifferently as the assassins got into the van and disappeared down the gravel road.

CHAPTER ELEVEN

Ridley awoke not knowing where he was. Turning his head, a sharp pain shot down between his shoulder blades. Sleeping on the cold rocks must have kinked his neck. He had been dreaming - something about images of dolphins flying through space. He remembered being underwater with them, too. He could not define any order to the dream sequences; random disjointed images were all that he remembered now.

Groggy, he sat up and looked at the motionless form nearby. From here it was difficult to tell if the alien was asleep or dead. After a moment, Ridley saw the slow rise and fall of the stranger's chest.

He looked at his watch. Nearly 7:00 a.m. The sun would be up and the tide would be out. Ridley looked toward the other end of the cavern; in the entrance there was plenty of room for passage. He entertained the thought of quietly getting in his kayak and slipping away before the stranger awakened. He still did not know what the alien's intentions were.

But he could not leave. There were too many things he wanted to ask the traveler. It was worth the risk to find out. Besides, there might be a reward if he were the one to bring the alien to the authorities. And what of those wonderful gadgets!

Ridley stood up slowly and stretched. Every joint in his body protested as he hobbled over to the ledge and looked for the kayak. It was still moored to the rocks, eight feet below where it was last night.

Ridley's stomach rumbled. He realized he had not eaten since midday yesterday.

Climbing down the ledge, he opened the forward hatch and retrieved the lightweight butane stove and old aluminum cook pot. From the rear hatch, he removed one of the five-gallon plastic water cubes. The bulk of the kayak's payload was in water. Between here and Cabo San Lucas, water was a precious commodity. Ridley continued rummaging through the compartments until he found the dry bag marked "breakfast." He tossed the bag onto the ledge.

Within five minutes, he had water boiling and was straining coffee through a filter. He felt like fifty miles of bad Mexican road. His joints creaked, his back was sore, his head hurt where he'd slammed into the cave ceiling, and his hands were raw from the barnacled walls. The coffee would taste especially good this morning.

While preparing breakfast, Ridley cast an occasional glance toward the inert alien. Ridley never did buy into UFOs and from what he had read, an alien life form, if it did exist, wouldn't resemble humans at all. Perhaps it was disguised, so as not to draw too much attention to itself. If that was the case, the stranger had done a poor job of blending in. Ridley was still tormented by the images of the alien's internal anatomy.

Ridley noticed the stranger not only had webbed hands, but when removing the footwear, membranes were present between the toes. The skin had a cool, almost damp feel to it. The alien resembled a human more than not, but alien he was.

He glanced back out at the cave entrance. Somewhere outside, he thought he heard the drone of an outboard engine. Figures, he thought. They're probably combing the area right now looking for the downed spacecraft and its occupant. He wondered what would happen to the stranger if the American or Mexican authorities picked him up. Then, another thought occurred to Ridley. What would they do to him? He hoped the cave was cryptic enough to hide them from the outside, even if just for a little while. Would the feds treat the alien like a visiting dignitary or whisk him off to some secret government laboratory to access his technology? Ridley did not envy the stranger's predicament. He shook off the thought as he poured a steaming cup of coffee.

He had not seen the dolphins when he awoke. It all still seemed like a dream. Had the dolphins really brought him here? What was the connection between them and the strange visitor?

"What is that liquid you drink?" a voice disturbed Ridley's thoughts. He turned back toward the stranger to see him propped up on his elbows looking at him with deep blue penetrating eyes.

"This is coffee," said Ridley. "Would you like some?"

The alien looked at the human suspiciously. "Cah-fee."

Pouring another cup, Ridley approached the alien cautiously. In his other hand, he held a Nalgene water bottle.

"It is a popular beverage on this planet." Stopping just before he reached the alien, Ridley said, "You're not going to zap me again, are you?"

"The personal force generator is deactivated. There is no danger."

"Here. Drink this first," Ridley said, handing the alien the water bottle. The stranger sipped cautiously at first, then tipped the bottle back until the bottle was drained. "Well, at least we have one thing in common. We both need water. Careful, the next one is hot."

The stranger took the tin cup from Ridley and took a small taste. He quickly pulled the cup away from his mouth and regarded it for a moment.

"Cof-fee," he repeated. The alien took a long and purposeful draught. Ridley saw him wince as the last of the liquid was drained and he set the cup down. "Bitter…taste."

"Well, that's just great. I'm sitting here drinking coffee with the extraterrestrial version of Juan Valdez." Ridley half-smiled. "Yeah, maybe it's not so good after all."

He fired up the stove again and then reached into the dry-bag. He produced several packets of freeze-dried meals and when the water was once again boiling, dropped them into the cook-pot.

"I figure if you can drink, then you also can eat," Ridley said. "Hungry?"

The stranger said nothing.

"My name is Ridley." He pointed to his chest.

The alien stared at him.

"R-i-d-l-e-y. Ridley. This place is called earth."

The alien continued to study him.

Ridley spooned the contents of the cook pot into a shallow aluminum bowl. He stirred it and handed the steaming gruel to the alien along with a spoon.

"It's okay. It's breakfast. Chicken-a-la king. Here, watch me." Ridley spooned a portion into his mouth. "It's not four star, but it will help get your strength back." Ridley took another few bites, and noticed the alien was still staring at him, the bowl of chicken-a-la-king cooling on the rocks beside him.

"This stuff isn't that great when it's hot. It's nasty when it's cold." He scraped out the last few bites, set the dish down, and poured another cup of coffee. He was still quite stiff and sore, but the coffee was beginning to loosen him up.

Ridley gathered up the used cookware and started for the water's edge. He didn't know what social taboo he had broken with the stranger. All of a sudden, the alien had gone mute. Perhaps he thought Ridley was trying to poison him with the nasty tasting beverage and foul-looking food.

While rinsing off the cookware, Ridley glanced up to see the alien tentatively placing a spoonful of the freeze-dried meal into his mouth. He chewed pensively, then scooped up more into his mouth. The alien's face twisted into a pucker.

"Well, that's two things we have in common," Ridley said. "We both don't like chicken-a-la king."

When he got back up to the campsite, Ridley saw that the stranger had finished the contents of his bowl.

"Still hungry?" Ridley motioned toward the empty bowl. The stranger gave a brief nod. Ridley went down to the boat and retrieved the lunch dry-bag. Within minutes, he fashioned a peanut butter and jelly sandwich on a *bolillo*, a small Mexican bread loaf he had picked up in Kino Bay a few days earlier.

The visitor bit into the sandwich after turning it over and over in his webbed hands. He bit down on it and began chewing furiously. The more he chewed, the wider his eyes became. Ridley stifled a laugh. The alien reminded him of his old dog masticating peanut butter.

The alien held out the tin cup and said, "Munffh."

Ridley quickly poured another cup of the rapidly cooling coffee. The stranger drained the rest of the cup. Ridley hoped he wasn't killing the visitor with all this new cuisine.

After a few moments, the alien figured out how to take a bite of the food, then wash it down with a swallow of water. *He's a quick learn,* Ridley thought. He was about to put the last dry-bag away when the alien spoke to him.

"How did you find me, human-of-earth?"

"The name's Ridley. Cooper Ridley. But Ridley works just fine. And since you're so interested, they brought me to you." Ridley indicated the water, where the dolphins had been. "They didn't leave me a lot of choice in the matter."

"Rid-ley," the stranger practiced. He then spoke in a dialect that Ridley could only describe as high-pitched clicking and chirping.

"I hope that's not your name, because I'm never going to be able to say it, much less introduce you at cocktail parties."

"I am called Azrnoth-zin," the alien said slowly and deliberately.

"Where are you from, Mr. Az-r-noth-zin?"

"The seventh world of the Yllantros system," the alien said. "The name of my homeworld is Delphinus."

"Delphinus? Like in dolphins?"

"I do not understand," said Azrnoth- zin. "Explain dolphins."

"Those are the creatures that led me to you. They live in the sea. They are mammals, like me."

"Delfids. They are not like you, Rid-ley. They are…" Azrnoth-zin struggled with the words. "…They are connected."

Connected, Ridley thought. *What does he mean by that?*

"I'm amazed at how quickly you are picking up the language," said Ridley. "Not bad for being on earth less than 24 hours."

"I have this," Azrnoth-zin said, pointing to the small device on his chest. "It is a translator. It assimilates your language and relays it to an area in my brain. I can then process your words into understandable dialogue."

"That thing works that fast?"

"Yes. The images of the translation take only as long as formation of thought."

"Incredible," said Ridley. "Can you understand other earth dialects as well?"

"It has more than 20,000 languages stored in its processors."

Ridley looked at the stranger in amazement. "20,000? Are there that many intelligent life forms out there?"

"The galaxy is vast and boundless," said Azrnoth-zin. The alien looked at Ridley. "Your planet earth is the only planet that supports life in this system?"

"That's right. As far as I know, we are the only inhabited planet in this solar system. About a decade ago, scientists here were real excited about Mars, our neighboring planet."

"You have not explored the proximate worlds that are close to your home-world?"

"Well, if you can count the moon, that's about the limit of our manned space exploration. We have sent probes to Mars and Jupiter to gather scientific data, but we're still a ways off from getting a man to touch down there." Ridley eyed the alien suspiciously. "You know, I'm not sure I should be telling you all this. For all I know, you could be a preliminary scouting party for a strike force that's getting ready to invade earth."

Azrnoth-zin looked at the ground. Ridley wasn't sure, but it appeared that a great sadness had come over the stranger. *That's good*, Ridley thought. At least he appears to have some demonstrable emotions.

"I saw your ship go down last night. It seemed to explode after it hit the water. Did you detonate it once you were free?"

The alien nodded. "Yes. After I ejected the command module from the ship, it was set for automatic destruct. I was lifted to the surface by the … dol-phins. They brought me here."

"Is there anyone else with you?"

Azrnoth-zin looked away. "My sub-commander, Porin-fah. He was…he ceased to exist."

"He died?"

"Yes. He died."

"I'm sorry to hear that," said Ridley. "What went wrong with your ship?"

Azrnoth-zin's face flushed a bluish color. "I made an error in my navigational computations. The ship emerged out of subspace into an ion storm. It damaged the drive system before we could react. I was forced to land here."

"What interest do you and your people have in this planet?" said Ridley.

The alien stared beyond Ridley for what seemed like a long pause. After a while, he took a deep breath and began to speak.

"Among my people, there are stories - mostly for the children - of another planet, a planet that is inhabited by beings similar to us. Until recently, no proof of this world existed. Then, I began receiving a very unusual transmission as I moved through your system."

"Radio waves?" said Ridley.

"Initially that is what brought me closer to... investigate," said Azrnoth-zin. "But that was not the transmission of which I speak."

"What was it then?"

The stranger pointed to the water. "It was the voices of the delfids I heard."

Ridley looked incredulous. "The dolphins? You mean to tell me you picked up their vocalizations hundreds of thousands of miles out in space?"

"It was not a signal in the manner you are thinking. I do not...have words to describe now."

"That's a hell of a note," said Ridley. "But then again, I am not really surprised. Maybe humanity has been ignored by extraterrestrial visitors. We're not exactly the most stable of species. Maybe the whales and dolphins have been the chosen contacts all along."

"You do not communicate with them?"

"Only on the most basic levels. If trained, they understand our language a whole lot better than we understand theirs."

Azrnoth-zin was reflective. "They are wary of humans. They told me they are at conflict with most of your race."

"Well, there are members of my people that think of these creatures only as food, or, at best, competition for their food."

The alien gave Ridley a hard stare. "To destroy such an intelligence is...unthinkable."

"You've been here less than 24 hours and already you're condemning the entire human race," Ridley said testily. "Why don't you hang around for a while before you pop off about the locals."

The alien's hard stare continued. Ridley's gaze matched the intense blue eyes. After an uncomfortable moment, the alien looked away. "I spoke with anger. I do not mean to offend."

"If it's any consolation, there's a hell of a lot of us living here who don't like what's happening to the whales and dolphins any more than you do. We do what we can, when we can. What else did they tell you?"

"They say that many of their numbers develop the sickness. It begins with a bad taste in the water. Many are unable to reproduce. More die shortly after birth."

Ridley shifted his weight on the rocks. "Sickness? I wonder if those biologists were really onto something. A lot of really putrid stuff is getting dumped into the waters all over the planet."

The alien pondered this statement for several minutes.

"The delphids that brought you to this place," said Azrnoth-zin."They knew you would not cause me harm."

"How did they know that?"

"They scanned you when you entered the water with them."

Now, Ridley's eyes grew wide. "You mean the dolphins who approached me last night? The ones that echolocated on me when I rolled the kayak?"

"They told me that you were inverted in the water at first. They had never seen a human in this position before. At first, they thought you were sick or dying."

"Yeah, right," said Ridley, shaking his head. "They told you all that?"

The alien nodded. "There is much humans have to learn about communication with these aquatic species."

"Hell, most of us can't even communicate with our own kind without starting a war over economics, politics or religion."

"You are at war?" Azrnoth-zin said.

"There are factions on this planet that are in perpetual states of conflict," said Ridley. "I can not recall a time when there wasn't a coup or a revolution igniting somewhere around the planet. The last great war was seven earth years ago."

"Then the people of earth are not united?"

Ridley considered this. "No. We are not united in that sense. We are divided into sections called nations. The nation you crash-landed in is called Mexico. The nation I come from is called the United States of America. It is due north of Mexico."

Azrnoth-zin was struggling with this idea. "You mean there is no ruling body? No central form of government?"

"Nope. Each nation has leaders it elects or appoints. Every nation has its own set of rules to live by."

Azrnoth-zin was quiet for a moment, appearing to be deep in thought. "Chaos," he said finally.

Ridley laughed. "Yeah. I guess you could say that."

Azrnoth-zin picked up the empty cup and appeared to be examining it. "So many governments. I think earth would not survive an attack from outside."

A chill went through Ridley. "Just what do you mean by that?"

"I request some more of the bitter beverage," the alien said, holding the cup toward Ridley. "What is it called?"

Ridley knew this part of the conversation was over. "Coffee. It's called coffee."

CHAPTER TWELVE

The Blackhawk helicopter set down before sunrise in a secluded section of the Guaymas naval station. The tires barely touched down when the door was flung open and three figures emerged. They walked briskly toward several men gathered near the dock.

In the lead, Richard Jenks, special agent in charge of field operations for the Phoenix Project, walked purposefully toward a group of military personnel. Over six feet tall and heavily muscled he wore his gray-blonde hair in a close-cropped buzz cut. Jenks was dressed in a field jacket with fatigue pants.

A former Naval Commander with ties to intelligence, Jenks had been called upon to supervise the field operations of the Phoenix Project when his naval career stalled. After twenty-two years of service to his country, Jenks knew he would not make Captain's grade. Calling up some favors to a former Admiral to whom he was attached as an aide led to his present lucrative position in the private sector.

Even in the cool morning air, beads of sweat were forming on his forehead. As he drew closer, he noticed there were officers and enlisted men from the Mexican navy standing with his men.

"Shit," he said softly.

A man dressed in khakis and a baseball hat moved to intercept him.

"Sir," the man said, grasping his hand. "I hope you had an uneventful flight."

"Roberson, what the hell is the Mexican Navy doing here? This is supposed to be a covert recovery mission."

"There's been a communication problem, if you catch my meaning, sir," said Roberson, matching the larger man's stride. "Apparently, Number One has not been able to convince the commandant of this God-forsaken facility to requisition a boat to us without an escort. Captain Garcia wants this to be a joint effort - all in the name of good neighbor relations between countries."

"What is the status for the search and recovery?" Jenks asked impatiently.

"All transports, air and water, ready and awaiting your orders, sir."

"What about the equipment for our group?"

"The recovery equipment, tanks and salvage gear are already stowed below. A trawler has been retrofitted for deep water recovery operations and will join us at the target zone," Roberson said. "It should arrive within an hour of when we do."

"Where's our boat?

Roberson pointed to a mid-size gunboat moored at the end of the pier. "That's her. Fastest boat in the Guaymas naval yard."

Jenks shot Roberson a look. "I assume we are to take extra personnel on all of the vessels?"

"That's about it, sir. We can have anything we want as long as there is a complement of Mexican personnel along for the ride."

Jenks and Roberson strode up to the Mexican officer and his men. After introductions, the commandant began a long and flowery speech in Spanish.

"We don't have time for this," said Jenks, under his breath.

"I think he's planning on doing this in English when he's done in Spanish," said Roberson.

A cellular phone's muted ring caught Jenks's attention. One of the agents handed him the phone and said, "It's for you, sir."

Jenks turned away from the commandant who was in the process of acknowledging the various government agencies participating in the joint project.

"Jenks here."

"Ah, Number Two, you have arrived. I trust the clean-up at section forty-six went as scheduled." The voice had a distinctive southern drawl.

"It went without incident, Number One. On my way here I received confirmation from Team Beta. Sections forty and nine are secured. They should be arriving here in Guaymas within the hour."

"Well done, Number Two. Thank you for personally overseeing the operation at Kitt Peak. There was potential for loss of very valuable data."

"All part of the job, Sir. Number One, we have another problem here. It seems the local brass insists that we take along half the Mexican navy for this recovery mission."

The voice on the phone was unwavering in its chilling calmness.

"Unfortunately, I was unable to convince the president of Mexico to supply us with all of the ships without the accompanying personnel. He was most insistent that this was to be a joint effort. It seems they are suddenly quite interested in our visitor. I'm afraid you'll have to make do."

"Yes, sir," said Jenks. "Once we secure the area, we'll see about arrangements for the crew during the recovery stage."

"I know you will be resourceful," said the phone voice.

"I will contact you when we reach the target zone," said Jenks.

"I'll be waiting, Number Two." The line went dead.

Moments later, Jenks and the other agents boarded the gunboat. On deck were three Mexican seamen and a captain. A fifty-caliber machine gun sat pointed at the sky on the foredeck. Jenks smiled as he lovingly stroked the barrel of the deck gun.

Introductions were made. The gunboat cast off while Jenks and the captain went below to pour over the charts. It was going to take nearly four hours to reach the target zone. Jenks was anxious to get there. Eight hours had passed since the object crashed into the gulf.

The sea was calm and the first rays of light were appearing over the mountains in the east. One of the Mexican crew members had laid out a breakfast buffet for Jenks and his men. After Jenks and the captain ascertained the heading and position, they grabbed a plateful of food and went to the wheelhouse to familiarize the American with its workings.

Jenks moved about the wheelhouse easily, asking questions of the crewman at the helm. Although his Spanish was not polished, he could make out the gist of what the Mexican crewman and the captain told him regarding the workings of the ship. Jenks continued to act the part of the maritime enthusiast, smiling and nodding whenever the captain pointed out something of interest.

The first two hours were uneventful. Everyone went about their tasks with business-like efficiency.

Shortly before eight o'clock in the morning, one of the Mexican crewmen came below where Jenks was sitting at a small table in the galley, going over the charts of the area.

"*Señor, por favor. Vengas con migo. Hay una launcha,*" said the seaman, indicating there was another boat nearby.

Jenks stood and followed the crewman up the narrow steps, making his way to the wheelhouse. The captain handed Jenks a pair of high-powered military binoculars. He pointed to an area of ocean about a mile and a-half to two miles in the distance off the starboard bow. Once Jenks located the object, he adjusted the focus. A small boat, possibly a Boston whaler was sitting alone in the water. Two figures were in the stern, hauling a large object into the boat.

"What do you have, boss?" Roberson said, entering the wheelhouse. "I thought we had another two hours to the target zone."

"We do," said Jenks. "But I think we need to check this out, none the less." He indicated to the captain to make the necessary corrections to bring them alongside the smaller boat.

Within ten minutes, they were pulling alongside the whaler.

Jenks was surprised to see that the occupants of the whaler were women. As the realization of this reached the crew of the gunboat, lascivious remarks were exchanged. Jenks and Roberson went forward to the bow. Jenks ordered one of Mexican crewmembers to stand ready at the fifty-caliber deck gun. By now, the two women had stopped what they were doing and were staring at the much larger ship looming over them.

"You are in restricted waters," Jenks said matter-of-factly. "What are you doing here?" With his aviator sunglasses and Aryan appearance, Jenks was a formidable sight on the flybridge.

"Since when is this area restricted?" said Darcy Billings. "We have no knowledge of any restrictions."

"What are you doing out here?"

"We have been doing research in this area for the past two months. Our permits were issued through the Department of Ecology in Mexico City."

"The Mexican government rescinded all permits for this area until further notice," Jenks said. "What is that equipment used for?"

"This is an otter trawl. We're taking fish samples," said Teresa. "I think I would like to see your papers. I don't think the Mexican government has anything to do with this."

"I'm sorry, but this is not a matter open for discussion. Please do not try my patience any longer. Prepare to be boarded," Jenks said, his face expressionless.

"What?" said Darcy furiously. "You can't just board us without some kind of warrant."

The gunboat pulled alongside the whaler, its momentum causing a jarring collision, which almost rocked Darcy and Teresa off their feet. Two of the agents jumped down onto the whaler. The Mexican crewman threw down two lines to secure the whaler to the larger vessel.

One of the agents passed by the two women, leering as he went to the stern. Another went toward the storage bins forward of the cockpit. The agent at the stern inspected the pile of netting with the large pallet-like structures.

"Hey!" Darcy was visibly shaking. "A lot of that stuff is our personal belongings. Just what do you expect to find anyway?"

"So what else are you hauling up with that net?" Jenks said.

"We told you, mister. We're taking fish samples. We are research biologists. What's your problem?" Teresa's eyes blazed in fury.

"I don't have a problem, missy, but you're about to."

By now the whaler looked like a small tornado had touched down inside it. Papers were strewn about the floor. Equipment lay scattered. The scientist's clothes and camping gear lay exposed. Suddenly one of the agents produced a thirty-five millimeter camera from under the dash area of the whaler. He held it up and Jenks nodded. The agent opened the back and ripped the film out of the back of the camera. He then proceeded to throw the exposed film overboard.

"You son of a bitch!" Darcy said. "That's two weeks of research you just ruined."

"Nothing here, boss," said the agent at the stern.

"All clear up front," said the other from the bow section. "Should we search these two?"

Jenks considered this for a moment. "No. I believe they're telling the truth."

Although Darcy could not see past the mirrored lenses of the blonde man's sunglasses, she could tell that he was enjoying himself.

"Please do not make me come back here and confiscate your boat. It is a very long walk back to civilization from these beaches."

Before the agents re-boarded the gunboat, they untied the lines from the whaler. Darcy stared at Jenks as the naval boat pulled away. Teresa muttered a string of epithets in Spanish. Darcy could not stop shaking. As the boat motored out of sight, Darcy defiantly held up a middle finger.

Teresa went about gathering up the papers that were being picked up by the morning breeze. Although her face was hidden from Darcy's, the occasional sniffle told Darcy that Teresa was crying.

"Why do I feel like I have just been violated?" Darcy said as she sat next to Teresa. "Government restrictions, my ass."

"Those are *hombres muy malo,*" Teresa said. "Are all government agents from the United States that rude?"

"I'd bet you good money those guys aren't affiliated with any regular agency," Darcy said, shifting a pile of data sheets back together. "No badges, no ID, just a lot of bluster. You know, ever since we saw that meteor last night, things have been getting more and more bizarre."

Teresa looked up. "What do you mean?"

Darcy stood up, stretching her back. "Do we have any beers left?"

"I think there's two more in the ice chest. Unless the *gringos pendejos* took them. What's weird?"

Darcy popped the tops off the bottles, handing one to Teresa. “Here. This will calm your nerves.” She took a gulp from the bottle and made a face. Warm beer in the morning left something to be desired.

“After that thing went down, we saw the dolphins around the boat. We’ve never seen wild dolphins behave like that before. And then this morning, we’re over run by the testosterone fraternity. I can’t remember the last time I ran into that many assholes at one time. They were looking for evidence - but evidence of what?”

“I still don’t see what the connection is between the meteor, the dolphins and those men,” said Teresa.

“I’m not sure either, but those clowns aren’t out here to film a documentary about the wonders of the Sea of Cortez.”

“I do not feel good about staying out here longer, Darcy. If they were to come back - well, I just don’t want to be around if and when they do.”

“I agree, we should go back. There’s some people in Guaymas and Mexico City we need to talk to,” Darcy said, her voice even. “And by God, we’re going to get some answers.”

Teresa stood up and they both inspected the wreckage left by Jenks and his men.

“Damn,” said Darcy. “I haven’t seen anything like this since my first dorm room at the university.” They both broke into laughter. “Let’s get this mess cleaned up and head back into town. I don’t know about you, but I could use a shower.”

CHAPTER THIRTEEN

Ridley finished putting away the camp stove and the last of the cookware. He still felt bone weary, though nothing 12 hours of undisturbed sleep wouldn't fix. His mind wrestled with what to do about the alien. He thought of the potential threat this stranger could be. Ridley had no way of knowing whether the alien was telling the truth.

Then there was the money. Ridley could be set for life if he could acquire some of this technology and sell it to the highest bidder. Let's face it, he thought. He wasn't exactly on the road to financial security. Before the trip began, Ridley had cleaned out his meager bank account.

On the other hand, there were a lot of other people that had their own motives for capturing the traveler. It wouldn't be difficult to imagine an international power play to procure the alien and his technology. Ridley truly despised bureaucrats.

He approached Azrnoth-zin, this time with his field medical kit. "Let's have a look at that leg and your abdominal area," he said, kneeling beside the alien. "This is pretty Neanderthal compared to your device, but at least I know how this one works."

Ridley unwound the gauze from around the leg wound just enough to see the injury without disturbing the splint.

"How does it feel?" Ridley said. The skin was still reddened and swollen but the wound was completely closed.

"There is deep soreness. And itching," said Azrnoth-zin. "There is tightness in my chest and some discomfort when I inhale deeply."

"And I thought I was a fast healer," Ridley said, shaking his head. "I'd really like to know how that little gadget works."

"It focuses the body's energies, speeds the healing process. Both the personal force field and the surgical disc have small, rechargeable cells."

Ridley was looking at his future right now. This technology would revolutionize medicine. Yep. Things were looking brighter all the time.

He began his examination of the alien's torso. He palpated along the ribcage. Several times, the alien winced as Ridley encountered tender structures.

"I haven't a clue about your internal organs, so I'm not sure what I should be feeling for."

"Use the disc and place the first two digits on the white lights. That is the scan function."

Ridley did as he was told. The disc then registered a series of flashing lights in rapid sequence.

"The bleeding inside has stopped," said Azrnoth-zin. "Your energy was adequate to begin the healing process."

"My energy? That disc used my energy to heal your injuries?"

"If it had been administered by another Delphinian, I would be now walking about and without discomfort."

"Oh, I get it. Not bad for a hu-man," Ridley said sarcastically. "You know, I could have worked on you with this." He held up the small surgical scalpel he had retrieved from his own medical kit.

"I do not think I would welcome such intervention," said the alien. "Your surgical field skills are competent."

"I'll send you my bill." Ridley thought he heard the drone of a distant motor. "Did you hear that?"

"I did not register any auditory signal other than the sound of the immediate environment," said Azrnoth-zin. "What do you hear?"

"Well, it isn't every day that we get an honest-to-God extra-terrestrial crashing into our planet. My guess is that I'm not the only one who saw you enter our atmosphere. There are people out there constantly monitoring the skies looking for fellows like you. They have very sophisticated tracking equipment, at least for earth standards, and I wouldn't be surprised if they are converging on where your ship went down."

"I cannot allow myself to be taken into custody by the powers that govern your planet. We are forbidden to make contact with non-technological civilizations. Your people cannot assimilate this technology presently."

"I have some breaking news for you," Ridley said. "Contact has been made. Come on. What are you? Are you the first wave of some pre-emptive invasion force? Because, if you are, I'm going to be real pissed off that I helped patch you back together."

Azrnoth-zin's gaze was intense. "I assure you, Rid-ley, that I am nothing more than an explorer and observer." He looked down and flexed his webbed hands. "It is not from my people that the threat to earth arises."

"That's the second time you have alluded to some ominous event," Ridley stated. "Why don't you stop beating around the bush and tell me what's going down."

Azrnoth-zin looked at Ridley, puzzled. "I do not understand the context of your speech. I did not strike at a small low-growing plant."

"That's an earth saying which means just tell me the facts. Don't talk in circles."

"I do not think you can understand the magnitude of the destructive force that is present in the galaxy," Azrnoth-zin said, his voice distant.

"Try me. I'm a good listener."

Azrnoth-zin shifted his weight against the boulder and began to speak. He was not looking at Ridley now. His eyes seemed to be focused beyond Ridley, beyond the confines of the marine cavern.

"There is another war," he began. "A war that has been fought longer and has been more devastating than all the conflicts in your earth's history combined. There exists another race, a society of soldiers whose sole purpose is to consume. They invade each system they encounter and all habitable planets that lay before them fall to their countless numbers."

"What do you mean consume?" Ridley was skeptical. "What would they want from us?"

"Everything," was the alien's reply. "These invaders consume biomass. They feed on all life forms, plant or animal. When they have exhausted the carbon-based life form supply on each planet, they turn to the mineral elements, leaching all of the organic compounds from the planet's surface. What they leave behind is an uninhabitable sphere of ash."

"How did your people escape them?" Ridley said, caught up in the alien's story.

"We did not escape. We have been at war with them for..." Azrnoth-zin hesitated, "...more than 900 of your earth years."

Ridley was skeptical. "My God. The resources that a war of that magnitude would require is mind-boggling. How can your population survive in a war that is endless?"

"We are not fighting well any longer. Their numbers keep increasing. Ours are diminishing. The birth rates of my people cannot keep up with the deaths as the battles continue to rage across the systems."

"Why don't you just cut your losses and stop fighting?"

The alien gave Ridley a hard stare. "You do not understand. There is no place to go. There is no escape. They moved out from the center of their system and they are like a living pestilence that consumes everything in their path."

A chill ran up Ridley's spine. "Are they headed in this direction?"

Azrnoth-zin looked at the water. "I do not know. If not now, then sometime in the not distant future."

Ridley said, "Maybe they'll miss earth completely. Hell, they may miss our entire solar system. The universe is a big place. You said it yourself."

"Your planet has already sealed its own fate. Your communications networks are sending signals into the far reaches of space as we speak. I was picking up weak transmissions outside of your system, which led me here. It is only a matter of time before they intercept one of those transmissions, and direct their forces toward your planet."

Ridley realized his rear end had fallen asleep from sitting on the hard stone. He stood up slowly. "So what can we - I mean the people of earth - do about it?"

Once again, the cold blue eyes of the alien stared at Ridley. "Nothing. There is nothing you can do."

CHAPTER FOURTEEN

For several moments, the only sound that could be heard in the cavern was the gentle lapping of waves on the rocks and the steady drip-drip of water from the fissures overhead. Ridley stared at his feet. Suddenly, he laughed out loud.

"What is that sound you make, Rid-ley?" Azrnoth-zin said, tilting his head to listen.

"That is called laughter. We humans do that when we find something to be humorous."

"What is humorous?

"I'll tell you what's humorous. What's funny is that human beings are no longer on the top of the food chain. History's quintessential consumers are about to become intergalactic lunch. We call that irony."

The alien looked puzzled. "The translator does not have a word equivalent for humor or funny. Was something said that was humor?"

"You mean you don't laugh where you come from? No jokes?"

Azrnoth-zin looked puzzled. "What is a joke?"

"It is a short story or set of words arranged in such a way to make you laugh. Humor comes in many forms. For instance, if I was walking in front of you and I fell flat on my face, you might think that was funny."

The alien's expression was blank. "Do you laugh when others of your race fall down or injure themselves?"

"Okay. Bad example." Ridley pondered momentarily. "I'll have to get back to you on this."

After an extended silence, the stranger spoke again. "You are considering whether to turn me over to your authorities," Azrnoth-zin said.

Ridley's face blushed crimson. "What makes you think that?"

"You do not deceive well, Rid-ley. You have thoughts of reward from your government to turn me over and to sell the technology."

"Well," Ridley said, "I'd be lying if I said it hadn't crossed my mind. Give me one good reason why I should help you. You have been nothing but bad news since the damn dolphins brought me here."

As if on cue, several sharp exhalations broke the stillness of the cavern. Ridley could see at least half a dozen shiny backs and dorsal fins cut through the waters in the cave.

Azrnoth-zin pointed to the group of loudly blowing cetaceans. "They chose you to help me. You are not like the others."

"Don't be so sure. I just might surprise you."

"Just as they can read your intentions, so can I," said Azrnoth-zin. "I have been listening to your thought patterns since you first arrived."

"Hey! Don't you know that's an invasion of privacy? It's impolite to read peoples' minds here." Ridley wondered if the alien had picked up all of his thoughts for the past twelve hours.

"I must send a signal to my people," Azrnoth-zin said. "If I can reach our forces, perhaps we can draw the Trochinids away from your system. Perhaps we can give you some time."

"Time for what?" said Ridley. "Time to bend over and kiss our asses goodbye?"

"To prepare your defense systems should such an attack become imminent."

"Oh yeah? And who is going to be telling them all this? Me? I don't think so. I don't carry a lot of credibility in official circles. In fact, I'm considered what you would call a *persona non gratis* with my government."

"I can think of no one better," Azrnoth-zin said. "The people will listen to you."

"The people will lock me away. I can just see it now. Me on a street corner with a big sign, the one saying, "Repent! The End is Near!"

Azrnoth-zin looked at Ridley. "Was that humor?"

"What did you call them? Troco-?"

"Trochinids. We know them to be a nomadic race. They colonize worlds only as long as there are resources to consume. Once they have depleted a planet of its organic compounds, they begin searching for other worlds to process."

"Are they intelligent?"

"They have a colonial intelligence. We have never been able to search out the primary leaders because they behave collectively."

"Like insects?"

Azrnoth-zin considered this while the translator fed his brain the information on the word "insect." He raised his chin in acknowledgement. "Most interesting. You have many species on this planet that have some similarities to the Trochinids. Only they are quite small in size. And your insect species lacks the knowledge to use technology and fire weapons."

Ridley was incredulous. "You mean you're fighting big insects that can shoot back?"

Azrnoth-zin nodded solemnly. "They have the ability to absorb technology as well as the other resources."

Ridley had a sick feeling in the pit of his stomach. "I think we're in a lot of trouble here."

The stranger looked at Ridley directly now. "You are faced with a most difficult decision. Choose well, Rid-ley. The future of your world may depend on it."

Ridley walked over to the alien, knelt, and began redressing the leg. If Azrnoth-zin was fabricating all of this information, Ridley was going to go down in history as one of the greatest suckers since P.T. Barnum coined the phrase. But then, what if he was telling the truth? It sounded like his home world was about to be listed as the late great planet earth.

As Ridley finished re-splinting the leg, Azrnoth-zin noticed a change in the human's facial features. The earthman's mouth was pulled back, revealing his evenly spaced teeth. Ridley shifted his attention to Azrnoth-zin's torso and began to tape the damaged ribs.

"Oh hell," said Ridley, grinning. "I really didn't want to paddle all the way to Cabo anyway."

CHAPTER FIFTEEN

Ridley tossed the last of the dry bags onto the ledge from the boat. The alien could not see what Ridley was doing, but loud exclamations coming from the water's edge told Azrnoth-zin that whatever the human was doing was not going well. Other sounds came from below the ledge. A rasping noise followed by a clatter on the rocks.

Finally, Ridley's sweaty head popped above the ledge. He clambered over the top and approached Azrnoth-zin, two lengths of metal in his hand.

"Rid-ley, what were you doing?"

"Preparing your vessel of deliverance," Ridley said flopping down next to the alien.

"Do you mean we are to both leave in that?

"What? So it's not the Enterprise and I'm not Captain Kirk, but it's the only chance you have to get out of here."

"How will we both fit in that…?"

"Kayak. It's called a kayak. I emptied out all the gear, removed the rudder brackets and then cut away the bulkheads. If you only knew how much it hurts me to trash my boat."

"Where will I sit?"

"You won't. You'll be lying on your back on the floor. There should be enough room for you to stretch out with those bulkheads removed. I'll be doing all the paddling."

"This is no way for a warrior to travel," the alien said, obvious disgust in his voice.

"Sorry. Maybe you'd prefer to wait around 'til the Millennium Falcon shows up. Hey! I just carved up my ride to give you a place to hunker down in so we can make an attempt to get out of here. Since when did you get to be so special?"

The alien was quiet for a moment, casting his eyes downward. "I spoke in haste. I am in your debt."

"Bet that damn near killed you to say that, too. Look, Az-er-noth-zin or whatever your name is, the chances of us getting out of here without getting shot or caught are remote at best." Ridley let out a long breath. "Here, let me have a look at that leg again."

Ridley unstrapped the paddle shafts from Azrnoth-zin's injured leg. He aligned the smaller brackets along the break and taped them into place.

"That'll do," Ridley said, admiring his handiwork. "Now, you can fit inside the boat."

Ridley looked ruefully at the pile of dry bags on the ledge.

"Looks like we're going to have to leave the majority of this stuff behind. Damn. It took me three years to accumulate all of this junk."

He pondered the situation for several moments. "Ah, what the hell. I always preferred to travel light anyway. Guess I'll sink this stuff on the bottom of the cave - weight it down with rocks. The less evidence for the feds to find, the better our chances of escape. We'll only carry enough water and food to get us back to Kino Bay."

"How far is that place from here?" asked Azrnoth-zin.

"About a day and a half to two days paddle," said Ridley. "If the conditions are right."

"Is it safe there?"

"There is no safe place for you," Ridley said sharply. "Right now, you're front page news - any earth government would do just about whatever it takes to get a hold of you and these great little gizmos of yours. I don't make a lot of wagers, but I'd bet my mother's teeth that the ocean and beaches are crawling with unpleasant government types as we speak."

"When do we leave?" said Azrnoth-zin.

"Sundown," said Ridley. "We no longer have a rudder and we're going to be heavier than usual. I want to go for the calmest seas possible."

Ridley went over to the piles and began sorting gear. Throwing several gas canisters on the pile, he said, "Once we get to Kino, I have a friend who I think will help us. Lives just outside of town. He has a truck and might be able to get us back to my vehicle. I'm going to call up a couple of owed favors."

By midday, Ridley had separated out the water, foodstuffs and essentials that were to go back in the boat. All but five gallons of water were emptied out.

Sitting down to lunch, Ridley asked, "Where are your people going to pick you up?"

"That will be determined after I transmit my coordinates," said Azrnoth-zin. "Unfortunately, it is impossible to transmit from the confines of this cave. I must have a clear night sky."

The alien seemed to enjoy the spaghetti and marinara sauce Ridley cooked up. He even asked for seconds. *Nothing wrong with his appetite.* Ridley popped open two packets of juice.

"Eat and drink hearty, because after sundown, we're on light rations," he said, handing one of the juice packets to Azrnoth-zin.

The tide was high again. Ridley spent the rest of the afternoon loading the meager rations into the kayak. He moved his seat as far back as possible and placed the water containers behind him. Basic cookware was stored at the stern. The dolphins and Azrnoth-zin watched the entire proceedings intently.

Ridley did not have a great deal of confidence in their escape plan. Traveling at night may give them an edge, but he had never paddled a kayak with a living being lying inside. He was unsure of the kayak's tracking and how it would ride in the water with this odd weight distribution.

Ridley swore from the contorted position he put his back in to push the last of the water containers into place. He sat by the kayak, rivulets of sweat running down his face. "I gotta be out of my mind. This isn't going to work. We'll probably both drown the first wave that broaches us."

Azrnoth-zin saw the agitation in the earthman and spoke. "As warriors, we know the necessity for proper preparation. There comes a time when you can prepare no longer. You must face your task."

"I can't help but feel that I'm leaving something out here. But I don't know what it is. This little voice in the back of my head is banging loudly on the inside of my cranium. I usually hear that voice right before the feces hits the fan."

Ridley stood up, peeled off his shirt and kicked off his old canvas tennis shoes. He retrieved the mask and snorkel from the deck bag.

"May as well get to it," he said picking up two of the dry bags. "I guess we're going to see just how waterproof these things are." He eased down to the water's edge. The dolphins, seeing Ridley entering the water, were energized into playful leaps and rolls.

Ridley methodically squeezed as much air out of each of the bags as he could. Diving down, he kicked hard to the bottom of the cave floor. Even in the dim light, he could see schools of scissortail damselfish and sergeant major fish darting about. Ridley located several good size rocks and set them on the dry bag.

He couldn't decide which he felt worse about. Littering the ocean floor with his personal flotsam or losing all of his hard earned gear. Right now, he was not practicing low impact kayaking. But then again, there was nothing in the guidebooks regarding smuggling an alien in a kayak. Groups of two and three dolphins came down to inspect Ridley while he worked at concealing the gear. He marveled at how close the dolphins came to him. He held out his hand. A large dolphin glided by allowing Ridley to touch its soft underside. A visible shudder passed along the dolphin's flank as it pushed against his palm.

After two minutes, Ridley's lungs ached. He surfaced, grabbed another dry bag, inhaled deeply and went for the bottom once more. Wedging the bags in between the numerous crevices took a bit of eyeballing to match the crack with the dry bag. Ridley was careful not to disturb the rocks. Creatures lived on, above, around and in every available space down here.

On the next dive, Ridley located a large crevice that would hold the bulky bag containing the extra cooking equipment. Nearing the crack he attempted to wedge the bag when he caught sight of a large green form snaking out toward him. He back-pedaled in time to see a flash of pointy teeth going toward the dry bag in his hands.

Ridley had never seen a bigger moray eel. Judging by the size of its head, this one must be close to eight feet. Once Ridley's heart stopped pounding, he watched the enormous creature. The moray's mouth opened and closed rhythmically with its breathing. The green sentinel slowly receded back into the rocky lair until only its head was visible. Nearby, Ridley found a more suitable crack to stash the last dry bag.

"Wow!" said Ridley as he clambered up the rocks to the stony platform. "That was the mother of all morays. Had to be close to eight feet."

"Are you damaged?" said Azrnoth-zin.

"No. Just a little surprised. I think that eel has lived here a long time. It was kinda particular where I stashed my gear."

"Is the creature dangerous?" Azrnoth-zin said, sitting up.

"That depends," said Ridley, toweling himself off. "They can be if you go sticking your hands in their hidey-hole or if you're carrying a stringer of bleeding fish with you. I think this old gal didn't want me blocking her driveway. Now that I think of it, I can't think of a better security guard to watch over my gear until I can get back and retrieve it."

"You do well around the water, Rid-ley. Are all humans as adapted?"

"No. Not all of us. Some of us have a downright aversion to water. It depends on who you talk to."

"On my homeworld, all are adapted to a water existence."

Ridley stopped toweling his head and looked at the stranger. "Why is that?"

Azrnoth-zin stared across the cave. "Delfinus is covered by one great ocean. The land masses are much smaller than here. Most of our cities lie on the ocean floor or suspended at specific depths."

"Then that would explain the membranes between your toes and fingers," Ridley said. "Pretty neat adaptation."

The alien nodded. "We can exist entirely out of the water throughout our lives. There are some, how do you say - ceremonies, that are still conducted in the places of our origins."

"Have your people been coming here for a long time?"

"I do not think so," said Azrnoth-zin. "I believe I may be the first. There is nothing in our data logs that speak of another water planet. There are tales spread by off-world traders that speak of another planet similar to Delfinus. Until now, these stories were thought to be a diversion for the traders during transactions."

Ridley pointed toward the dolphin entourage milling about the surface. "Got anything like them back home?"

"Not in the time of my existence. The last delfid was seen ..." Azrnoth-zin's brow furrowed deeply, "...more than three thousand of your earth years past."

"What happened to them?"

The alien's body appeared to slump. "I do not know for certain. I was told as a child that they left to colonize another world because they were unhappy with the people." Azrnoth-zin shifted his position and moved to face Ridley. "As a warrior, I believe they were casualties of the Great War."

"So, there are none left?"

Azrnoth-zin shook his head. "Regrettably, no. All of my life I wanted to interface with the ancient ones. I may not be able to make it back to my homeworld, but I have finally contacted the delphids, or beings similar to them."

"Have you contacted the others yet?" said Ridley.

"The others?" Azrnoth-zin's eyebrows raised. "Of what others do you speak?"

Ridley smiled. "Oh, you've met just one species of delfids. Here we call them cetaceans or whales. These guys are known as bottlenose dolphins. They're probably the most widespread dolphin on the planet. Dolphins are small whales. Some, like the blue whale can reach one hundred feet in length and weigh one hundred tons."

Azrnoth-zin regarded Ridley suspiciously. "You speak like an offworld trader."

Ridley laughed. "I guess if someone sprung something like that on me, I'd be hard pressed to swallow it too. There are something like eighty-four species of whales that live in all parts of the oceans."

The stranger digested this information. "That explains the range of sounds we monitored from outside your atmosphere." A concerned look came over the alien's face. "Do the other ce-ta-ceans face the same sickness as these delphids?"

"Probably so," said Ridley sadly. "Some people think the oceans are a personal dumping ground. Everything from raw sewage to toxic chemicals to nuclear waste gets thrown in. For many years, most of the great whales were almost hunted to extinction for the products that humans desired - oils for machinery, pet foods, fertilizer, makeup."

"The Water Council must be apprised of these delfids," said Azrnoth-zin. "We Delfinians are forbidden to intervene in primitive cultures, but the Water Council will make an exception if they learn of the Delfids' existence. I am sure of this." The alien's eyes burned with a renewed intensity. "Rid-ley. I must be able to contact my people. The delfids must be preserved and protected from the Trochinids."

"While you're at it, how about a little protection for all of us humans as well?" Ridley said.

"I can only present the data to the council. They will make the final decision."

"Well, that's a start anyway. I guess we need to begin thinking about getting you to a safer place."

Blasts from the water signaled that the dolphins were becoming active again.

"The delfids request your presence," said Azrnoth-zin, gesturing toward the leaping dolphins.

Ridley's face grew into a great grin. "Well then, who am I to keep them waiting?" Springing up, he headed toward the water.

CHAPTER SIXTEEN

By sunset, all the remaining gear was crammed into the furthest reaches of the kayak. All but the drinking water, which Ridley kept behind the seat. The jettisoned gear now rested at the bottom of the cavern. Once they emerged from the cave, Ridley would take a GPS reading on their location to return for all of his belongings at a later date.

Azrnoth-zin hobbled about the cave using one of the paddle shafts as a makeshift crutch. Ridley cleaned up the last of the afternoon meal. He was sated, almost uncomfortable. In a silent celebration of departure, Ridley had cooked up most of the dinner items that could not be taken along. It turned out to be a tasting lesson for the alien. Azrnoth-zin sampled each of the dishes Ridley prepared. Ridley watched for expressions of interest or disapproval as the stranger put different foods in his mouth.

"I have discovered two desirable aspects of your world," said Azrnoth-zin, testing the weight on his leg. "There are the delfids and your food has many interesting flavors."

"Hmm. Only two, eh?" Ridley said, not looking up from the last pot he was scrubbing. "I take it Delfinian food is bland."

"We do not have time to focus our energies on elaborate rituals of food preparation."

Ridley laughed. "If you think this was elaborate food preparation, you would go nuts in a restaurant. Too bad we won't have time to introduce you to the finer aspects of gourmet dining."

The alien snorted in disapproval. "Too much time is spent by your people in wasteful activities. It is no wonder you are a backward race."

"I didn't see you push any of the food away," Ridley said. "Are all Delfinians this anal retentive?"

"Please explain anal retentive."

Ridley thought about it for a moment. "Forget it," he said. "We don't have the time for a lengthy discourse now."

Azrnoth-zin placed more weight on his leg and his gait improved while Ridley watched.

"One thing I've got to say is that you are one fast healer," said Ridley, marveling at the alien's determination. "Yesterday, you were circling the drain and today you're feeling good enough to rail about the human condition."

"We are able to focus our energies on the healing process. Almost all Delfinians have been seriously injured in the wars. Unless it is a mortal wound, we heal ourselves to fight again. If it were not for your healing energy, Rid-ley, I would have ceased to exist."

"You're welcome. Az-r-noth-zin, this is going to be a long, uncomfortable trip. I'll keep the spray skirt pulled back as much as possible. But any time we're approached by another boat, the cockpit gets buttoned up. It may get unpleasant in there."

"I understand," said the alien.

"Oh, and another thing. As much as I like their company, you had better tell the dolphins not to hang too close to us. We don't need any extra attention drawn to the kayak."

"The delfids will know long before we do when someone approaches us by water," said Azrnoth-zin. "They will serve as an effective early warning system."

"I never considered that. Maybe we might make it out of here after all." Ridley stared at the water.

"What is it? Did you forget some detail in your preparation?"

"Yeah. I scoured every crack and crevice down there for my semi-auto. I couldn't find it anywhere."

"Even if you did, the weapon would be beyond repair," said Azrnoth-zin. "The personal force field neutralized it."

Ridley turned back toward the alien. "If we get out of here, you owe me for a new forty caliber." He looked around the cavern ledge one last time. "Well, I think that's about everything. It's time to put some daylight behind us."

Ridley and Azrnoth-zin negotiated the slippery rocks to the water's edge. The kayak bobbed gently in the darkening waters. After several failed attempts, Ridley finally got Azrnoth-zin lowered into the unstable kayak by hoisting him up from behind. This was a cause for great discomfort to the passenger due to his freshly healing leg and ribs.

Finally, Azrnoth-zin lay supine in the length of the kayak, only his head and shoulders were visible, framed by the oval of the cockpit.

"How's it feel?" Ridley said.

"You are correct, Rid-ley. It is going to be a long journey."

Realizing the absurdity of their situation, Ridley laughed out loud.

"That's one hell of an image, your face looking up at me from the floor of my boat."

"Perhaps we could trade positions at one time," Azrnoth-zin said disgustedly. "This is no way for a warrior to travel."

"I don't think so, *amigo*. I'm not the one they're after." After a moments pause he concluded with, "Yet."

Ridley kicked off his shoes and dropped them behind the seat. He untied the bow line from the rocks. Gingerly stepping onto the seat of the kayak, he lowered his weight, with one leg on either side of the reclining Azrnoth-zin. Gripping the paddle, he pushed away from the rocks and began slow, steady strokes across the cavern. The kayak felt wobbly to Ridley. The weighting was not right. All he could do was to hope for calm seas.

"No kidding, this is going to be a long paddle. I've done some pretty insane things in this kayak before, but this is the first time it's been used to smuggle an illegal alien."

Ridley reached the opening at the far end of the cavern. Ahead he saw light filtering in. The tide was at its lowest ebb, exposed rocks protruding in several places.

"That's a good sign. I don't think there's a boat other than a kayak that can get in here."

The kayak scraped against the rock outcroppings on its winding path to the outside. Even though the sun was behind the cliffs now, Ridley's eyes were not accustomed to the light after the dark confines of the cave. From a world of perpetual dusk, they were borne into a dazzling panorama of brilliant colors washing across the Mexican sky. Gazing across the water to the south, Ridley saw a silvery sheen on the water with a sky that was painted in hues of peach and rose. Low-lying clouds scudded across the horizon, the first sign of approaching winter storms.

Ridley inhaled deeply. The fresh saline air felt exhilarating. He kept the sprayskirt peeled back for now so Azrnoth-zin could partake of the sea air. The boat still felt awkward and Ridley adjusted his paddle strokes often.

"You okay?" said Ridley.

The alien nodded. "I am happy no other Delfinian can see my position of travel," he said. After a few moments, Azrnoth-zin broke the silence. "Ridley, how does one eliminate bodily wastes in this vessel?"

"Glad you asked," Ridley said, reaching behind the seat and producing an old plastic water pitcher. Then, raising his eyebrows, he said, "that is if ..."

"It will be adequate."

"I'll try to stop whenever it looks safe so we can stretch our legs and eat. We lucked out. The sea is pretty flat. There's only a light breeze out of the west. And that's good, because this kayak isn't responding like she usually does."

After Ridley took a reading from his GPS, they traveled in a southeasterly direction for the next hour. He followed the contours of the coastline, except when they encountered a bay or cove. By now, night had fallen, and once again Ridley found himself staring at the stars. Several times, Azrnoth-zin queried Ridley about the particular constellations that he was able to view from his limited portal. Ridley did his best to name the common ones.

Looking around, Ridley noticed the dolphins, constant companions for the last few days, were now strangely absent. "Where did the dolphins go?"

"They are close by. By your request, they are traveling parallel with us, spread out across some distance. They are monitoring the other vessels that are in the area."

Ridley smiled. "That's some more good luck. They can be our eyes and ears out here. Are you in contact with them now?"

"Yes."

"Anything to report?"

Even in the dark, Ridley could see the blazing cerulean eyes of the alien, until he closed them.

"There are eleven vessels in the area. Three have converged on the location where my ship went down," Azrnoth-zin said.

"Is there any evidence of your arrival that was left behind?"

"There will be small fragments of my ship and the command module I was strapped into. I believe it is still lying on the bottom along with my environmental suit."

"Well, I hope it's in deep water. Deep enough to give us a good head start," Ridley said.

Conversation between the earthman and the alien lulled. Ridley could no longer see Azrnoth-zin's eyes. For a while, Ridley assumed the stranger was asleep or in a deep trance. It was not until he heard some faint whistles and a string of bizarre clicking noises that Ridley realized what was transpiring. Azrnoth-zin was communicating with the dolphin pod. Ridley felt a pang of jealousy; all of his adult life he had desired a link between himself and the cetaceans he spent so much time around. Ridley wondered if Azrnoth-zin's universal translator accomplished this feat or if it was accomplished telepathically.

A vaguely familiar sound brought Ridley out of his reverie. It took him a moment to process; the noise was muted, sounding far away. Then, a shot of adrenalin pumped through his arteries when he realized where the sound was coming from.

From beyond the cliffs to the east, Ridley heard the distinctive "whump-whump" of helicopter rotors growing louder. Suddenly, a light appeared in the sky beyond the tops of the cliffs. Remembering at the last moment, he pulled the sprayskirt over the cowling, completely covering the face of the alien.

"Sorry about this," Ridley said. "I'm not sure how close they're going to get."

Bright lights appeared over the cliffs; then three transports flew by a short distance away. Ridley judged them to be Blackhawks, recognizing the pitch of the rotors and their outline in the night sky. The three choppers were flying below five hundred feet. The lights from one helicopter briefly illuminated the kayak and for a second, Ridley was thrown into daylight.

The helicopters passed quickly, moving in the direction of the open sea. Ridley followed their blinking lights until they disappeared into the night sky.

"That was a bit on the close side," Ridley said. "Are you all right in there, Azrnoth-zin?"

"Yes," came the muffled reply. "What was that disturbance?"

"It seems you are commanding a lot of attention. They're pulling out all the stops to locate your ship. I don't think we were spotted. Otherwise, they would have come back for a second look."

"The delfids tell me that two of the vessels have located the crash site," said Azrnoth-zin. "Can you take the cover off now?"

"Not yet," said Ridley, continuing his paddling. "Let's see what else is around before we let our guard down again."

During the ensuing hour, Ridley began to notice an increase in boat traffic as well as air support flying to and from the area where he reckoned the ship had splashed down. Another formation of Blackhawks flew down range of them. Ridley noticed there were cargo crates suspended by cables as the choppers angled toward the crash site. Ridley doggedly paddled on. Out to sea, lights played off the water intermittently, flashing in their direction, then moving away.

"They're setting up search grids out there," Ridley commented. "Looks like they're closing in on each other."

They were going to have to run a gauntlet of boats and planes. Most of the traffic appeared to be further out, at least two miles. It would not be long before they expanded the search toward the shoreline.

"I'm going to try to stay close to shore," Ridley said. "It seems those boys are preoccupied, at least for the moment."

By the third hour, the dolphins had returned in all their exuberance, leaping around the kayak and splashing head-first into the water. Ridley could hear the calls through the hull of the kayak. Then, he heard a sound that emanated from within the cockpit. Ridley felt a slight vibration in his legs and gut. It was Azrnoth-zin. Ridley slipped the sprayskirt back and gazed upon the alien.

Azrnoth-zin, in the low light appeared to be asleep. The only clue that he was not was in the sounds that emanated from his head. Bursts of high frequency energy caused the alien's head to reverberate slightly. The exchange lasted several seconds between the alien and the dolphins. A lull followed, then a glissando of whistles, groans, and clicks filled the air. Ridley listened intently, fascinated by the excited level of discourse. It was an alien conversation, carried on by two sentient species and Ridley was probably the only human ever to witness it. He longed to be part of this conversation, to be able to understand the dolphin's cryptic code.

Suddenly, the dolphins ceased vocalizing and disappeared into the night. It was several moments before Azrnoth-zin came out of his trance-like state. He opened his eyes, once again revealing their brilliant blue reflective glow in the darkened cockpit.

"The delfids have returned to the crash site," Azrnoth-zin said. "Presently, there are six vessels converged on the location. The vessels are well equipped. They are using sonar to locate metal objects on the seabed. Two of the larger vessels are equipped with devices to retrieve objects from the bottom. These ships are large, four or five times the size of your boat."

"They told you all of that?" Ridley said incredulously.

"It is difficult to explain. They projected…sound images to me. It was similar to a holo-image. It was not like the words that you and I speak."

"Did you use the translator for that?" Ridley said.

"The translator does not work for this type of communication. It is…within us."

"What else did they tell you?"

Azrnoth-zin drew in a long breath. "Two of the ships are carrying armaments."

"The dolphins know what guns are?"

"It seems they have numerous encounters with your race that do not end pleasantly for them," said Azrnoth-zin.

Ridley felt the hot lash of remorse once more. The image of Charlie and Dali flashed before his mind's eye. He saw the dolphin with the live limpet mine attached to it, followed by the explosion.

"You were not to blame," said Azrnoth-zin.

"What?"

"The death of the two delfids in your charge. The ones who commanded you are to blame."

"How in the hell did you know about them?" Ridley said angrily.

"It is a recurrent image in your cortex," said the alien. "Easily retrievable through a mind link."

"Do me a favor, Azrnoth-zin. Stay out of my head, and we'll get along just fine. Next time you do that, I'm dumping you at the first beach I see."

"I meant no harm, Ridley." After a moment of concerted thought, Azrnoth-zin said, "I a - pol - o - gize for the intrusion."

Ridley sighed. "Forget it. Let's keep focused on trying to get by all these boats."

The next two hours passed with agonizing slowness. With every point they rounded, Ridley expected to see the relentless government search teams. His back and legs were beginning to cramp. Ridley cast regular glances toward the shoreline, hoping to find a sheltered beach where they could rest. He was concerned about the alien. Water orientation or no, lying in the damp bottom of the kayak could not be good for Azrnoth-zin's injuries.

Most of the air and boat traffic was behind them now. Occasionally, Ridley could hear the sound of a distant helicopter. He was tired. The stress of flight and anxiety of being discovered had depleted his adrenaline stores.

Ridley heard the gentle splash of sea meeting sand ahead. Peering through the darkness, he saw a break in the contour of the cliffs. A small reflection, a tiny apron of sand, appeared on a steeply pitched beach.

He looked down at the stranger. For the past hour, Azrnoth-zin was quiet. Ridley observed the regular rise and fall of his chest.

"Azrnoth-zin, wake up," said Ridley. The alien's eyes came open instantly. It was still a little disturbing to see the double lids fold back.

"I was not sleeping, Ridley."

"We're going in for a rest. My legs are asleep and my spine feels like it fell through my pelvis," Ridley said, maneuvering the kayak for a beach landing. "Sorry, but I have to cover you up again. This could be a wet exit." Ridley pulled the sprayskirt over the cockpit.

He stopped paddling long enough to listen to the way the surf was breaking on the beach. From the rolling of the kayak in the gentle swells, Ridley could tell the surf was breaking at about a thirty-degree angle to the beach. He focused on the shoreline, listening for any telltale signs in the night.

All seemed clear. Ridley pointed the kayak toward the beach and paddled several hard strokes until he felt the grip of sand on the hull. He yanked the sprayskirt back and lifted his butt onto the rear deck. He stood, rushed to the bow, then hauled the kayak further up on the sloping beach. Azrnoth-zin was already squirming to free himself from the cockpit, like some larval stage of moth, emerging from its chrysalis. Ridley helped him out of the boat. With support, Azrnoth-zin was able to hobble about. The alien massaged the life back into his cramped legs.

Ridley walked to the back of the beach where the sand met the cliff face. He relieved himself there and noticed a deep depression in the sand near the wall. It would provide them adequate cover from any boats approaching from the sea.

"This is a good a place as any to rest for an hour. I need to grab a nap before we push on," Ridley said, stretching his back and legs. Walking back to where Azrnoth-zin was pacing to and fro, he said, "Let's have a look at that leg and your ribs."

After examining Azrnoth-zin's fracture site, Ridley decided it no longer required a dressing. The last one was soaked through with water from the bottom of the boat. It must have been an uncomfortable ride, yet the alien had not complained. The injury was healing at a surprising rate. Only a raised pink area remained where yesterday a splinter of bone was showing.

"I am not tired, Ridley," said Azrnoth-zin. "I will watch while you sleep."

"This is no time to be stoic. I'll let you. Thanks."

Once the kayak was hauled further up the beach, Ridley hollowed out a small depression on the backside of the dune and promptly fell asleep.

Ridley awoke to being shaken. He opened his eyes and seeing Azrnoth-zin's face close to his, jumped slightly.

"Wh-what's up?" he said groggily.

"We are being approached," said the alien, pointing a webbed finger toward the water.

"Shit! The boat! They'll see the kayak," Ridley said, spinning onto his stomach.

The boat was not on the beach. "Where is it?" he said turning to Azrnoth-zin.

"After you went to sleep, I dragged it over there." He indicated the sand depression at the base of the rocks. "I think it is well hidden."

"I'm glad one of us is thinking," said Ridley. From his vantage point, he could see a light approaching from around the point to the west. A halogen searchlight was panning across the cliff face, moving toward them.

"Looks like they're expanding the search pattern." Ridley kept his head down so as not to be spotted, but still able to see the approaching boat. "That means they've probably found your ejection seat."

Azrnoth-zin and Ridley hunkered down behind the shallow dune and waited. Suddenly, Ridley felt trapped and silently cursed himself for allowing the two of them to be cornered like this. The search beam illuminated the rocks above them. Ridley and Azrnoth-zin quickly ducked their heads. They heard voices talking softly. Straining his ears, Ridley picked up snippets of conversation coming from the boat.

English. They were speaking English on the boat. From his last glance, Ridley thought the boat was good size, certainly not a *panga*.

The boat's engines went silent. Oh no, thought Ridley. They're mooring here for the night. The searchlight moved across the beach and out into the water away from them. Ridley took this opportunity to peer over the dune once more.

The boat was thirty to forty yards off the beach. It still had its running lights on and Ridley could see that it was a military ship, probably something the Mexican navy used. There were three figures moving about on the bow. One man passed in front of a forward light. He was carrying an automatic rifle.

Ridley knew the large boat would not approach any closer without running the risk of grounding itself. Waiting to see if a landing party was to be assembled, Ridley dared not move or take a deep breath. The searchlight came around for another pass. Ridley was barely able to pull his head below the dune in time. Just as quickly, the light was extinguished. The voices continued in that low level just out of Ridley's full comprehension range. He thought he heard someone say they were going to anchor here for the night.

Ridley checked his watch. What had appeared to be an eternity was only twenty minutes since the boat had entered the cove. His mind racing, Ridley tried to think of a diversion to draw them away from this spot. He doubted Azrnoth-zin and he could slip by the boat undetected; they were just too close.

The boat's diesels coughed and then roared back to life. Ridley took a chance and peered over the top once more. The ship backed out of the cove and into the deeper channel. Turning around, it steamed toward the south. The fugitives stayed behind the dune until the sound of the diesels was gone.

"Well, that was a little closer than I'd like," Ridley said, dusting the sand off of his legs and arms. Then, turning to Azrnoth-zin he said, "How did you get the kayak up here and manage to cover your tracks from the waterline as well?"

"With great difficulty," said the alien. "Covering the track was simple." He produced the orb from under his tunic. "I buried it in the sand near the water. The oscillations caused the sand tracks to dissipate."

"I think you just saved our collective asses," Ridley said. "That's a handy thing to have around."

Azrnoth-zin helped Ridley haul the boat down to the water's edge. Ridley then assisted the alien back into the supine position in the cockpit. Climbing back into the cramped kayak, Ridley pushed off the beach with the paddle and headed in a southerly direction, paddling easily. Again cloaked by the blackness of night, Ridley felt some of the tension lift.

"I'd sure like to know what branch of the government is down here using Mexican naval ships and personnel. Whoever they are, they're packing like they were getting ready for a major insurrection."

"I do not understand, Ridley. The men on the boat...were they warriors?"

"No. They were just armed like warriors. Not your run of the mill government agents. What I meant to say was that someone is very intent on finding you. They have money and manpower behind them to mobilize very fast."

Several times that night, Ridley dozed while paddling. The long-shore current pushed them gently in the direction of Kino Bay. Ridley awoke from one of these naps to find the water like glass. The stars reflected off the inky surface, and he felt the sensation of being suspended in the void of space. Azrnoth-zin's head lay outlined in the darkness; he appeared to be in a state of sleep. Ridley wondered if the Delfinians actually did sleep or did they achieve some meditative state?

Ridley dug the paddle in and pulled the kayak forward. So far, so good.

CHAPTER SEVENTEEN

Dawn on the Sea of Cortez was spectacular that cool September morning. The rising sun outlined the mountains to the east with orange to golden rays arcing across the sky. Ridley had been paddling solidly for five hours. He could no longer feel his legs. Ahead, a long stretch of empty beach curved around the larger bay they had entered.

"There's a beach about a mile and a half from here," Ridley said. "I think we're going to chance it."

"That is acceptable," said Azrnoth-zin. "I am not sure which is worse: the injuries I sustained from the crash or the travel accommodations that I must endure."

"Whine, whine, whine," Ridley said tiredly. "For a warrior race, you sure are vocal about your discomforts. Besides, where's your sense of humor? I want you to know that I'm having the time of my life."

"The Delfinians have endured more in the thousand-year war than any human could possibly imagine," the alien said defensively.

"Right. Hang on. We're going in."

Landing on the beach, Ridley was acutely aware of anything that looked out of place. He could see no roads that led from the beach, but still wanted to be sure. He and Azrnoth-zin moved quickly and quietly up the beach and into the dunes beyond. The dunes gave way to a small arroyo. The landscape changed to scrub and cactus almost immediately. Small lizards darted in front of them, disturbed from their early morning sunning sessions.

Rounding a curve in the wash, Ridley's nostrils were assaulted with the stench of flesh rotting in the sun. Ahead of them, Ridley and Azrnoth-zin saw a pile of material that had a green chiffon-like appearance. Drawing nearer, Ridley realized what they were looking at was a huge section of monofilament gill net. Inert forms were outlined in the thin veil of netting. Ridley realized what the source of the noxious smell was.

Encased in the net were the putrid corpses of dolphins, their smiles turned into a grimace of death. Ridley recognized the two species that were common to this area. The crumpled mesh outlined a large green sea turtle lying on its back. A young, male sea lion stared back at them, its teeth pulled back in a final snarl. It had become so entangled in the netting that the monofilament had cut through its hide and flippers. Scattered about were the rotting remains of fish, sea birds, and a small manta ray, all hung in grotesque postures of death.

"Maybe we're not worth saving," Ridley said. He turned from the carnage and headed back for the beach.

Azrnoth-zin heard Ridley say something as he was walking away, followed by a brief outburst of kicking at a dead cactus. The alien took another look at the repugnant scene and went to find Ridley on the beach.

He found Ridley sitting next to the kayak, his knees drawn up to his chest, staring out to sea. The alien sat next to him. Neither spoke for a time.

"Can your people save them?" Ridley said, breaking the silence.

"I do not understand," said Azrnoth-zin. "Save them?"

"The delfids. Can you transport them off the planet? I don't think we're capable of ensuring their survival."

The alien thought about this statement. "I think the delfids are ingrained in your culture as much as they were in ours. There would be much psychological damage were they not present."

"You saw that scene back in the arroyo. At the rate we're going there's not going to be any of them left for you to tell your Water Council about."

"I do not know what can be done, Ridley. We are at war with the Trochinids. To transport their numbers off this planet would require almost all of the fleet."

"Maybe you could arrange to take enough of each of the animals to ensure the genetic diversity of each of the species. A modern day's Noah's ark, so to speak."

The alien looked puzzled. "Please explain."

Ridley shrugged. "It's a story from the Old Testament. That's a book certain members of humanity base their rules on for living and conduct. Anyway, it was probably a myth concocted a long time ago. This guy named Noah received word from God that humanity was a mess and that he was going to teach them a lesson. He ordered Noah to gather a male and a female pair of every representative animal and put them in a great wooden boat. Then God flooded the planet for forty days and drowned everyone and everything else."

Azrnoth-zin considered this for a moment. "Your people believe this?"

"I guess some do," said Ridley.

"That would be an impressive undertaking," said Azrnoth-zin. "But logistically impossible. Even with the best of collection methods, such an undertaking would take a fleet to accomplish."

Ridley turned his head, squinting at Azrnoth-zin. "Right." Standing up, Ridley brushed the sand off. "Let's get out of here."

Ridley took another reading from the GPS. It was mid-afternoon and the instrument indicated they had covered more than thirty miles since they had paddled out of the cave. The Sea of Cortez continued to bestow its good graces on Ridley and Azrnoth-zin: the water remained flat with only a hint of breeze out of the west. However this created another problem as the sun climbed to its apex in the fall sky. It was uncomfortably warm paddling and even warmer in the cockpit. Ridley had removed his shirt, dipped it in the water periodically and draped it over the opening, creating a crude evaporative cooling system for the alien.

His limits already tested, all Ridley wanted to do was find a beach and crawl under his tarp and sleep for twenty-four hours. The severe sleep deprivation was causing his eyes to play tricks on him.

He and Azrnoth-zin kept the conversation to a minimum to conserve energy. The heat made it too much of an effort to talk. Ridley kept hanging on to the thought of reaching the village at Punta Chueca, just outside of Kino Bay. Once there, his old friend Enrique could hide them, and Ridley could take the siesta of the century. With Enrique's help, he could get back to his truck and hopefully spirit Azrnoth-zin across the border before their pursuers realized they were gone.

Ridley never saw the spotter plane until it was too late. It shot out from between some low-lying hills and headed straight for them. He did not even have time to cover the cockpit with the sprayskirt. The plane passed overhead not one hundred feet off the water. The twin engine Cessna buzzed past and then began to bank for a return run.

"I think we've been made," Ridley said. "Let's hope they think I'm some *gringo muy loco* out here kayaking the coastline, frying his brains."

The plane passed overhead once more. Ridley could see one of the doors had been removed. A figure was hanging in the open doorway, holding in his hand what appeared to be a camera.

Ridley waved his hand and smiled at the cameraman. "You can kiss my ass, you sorry sons of bitches."

The plane did not make a third pass. It veered off and headed in a northwesterly direction. Soon, the engine noise faded and all Ridley could hear was the gentle lapping of water against the hull of the kayak. He pulled his shirt off the cockpit and revealed the face of Azrnoth-zin staring up at him.

"Ridley, you often use words that I cannot translate. It is most frustrating," said the alien.

"Sorry. When I get nervous, I tend to swear a bit. You probably shouldn't translate everything that comes out of my mouth. It may ruin your translator."

"Is there danger from that flying craft?" said the alien.

"Don't know. They seemed to be checking us out. There was some guy shooting pictures of the kayak. I hope he doesn't have an infrared camera or we're screwed before we get to the big dance."

Ridley kept on paddling, a new reserve driving him toward Kino. Beginning to think they had pulled a fast one, Ridley started to relax, when all of a sudden, several dolphins appeared out of nowhere, vocalizing frantically.

Azrnoth-zin's brow furrowed. He began producing those strange emanations again, reverberating the inside of the kayak. The dolphins arched their dark gray backs and just as quickly were gone.

"It seems a vessel is approaching. There are eight humans on it. They all appear to be armed," said the alien.

"The plane must have called us in. How soon?"

"They are on the other side of the projecting landmass in front of us."

Ridley looked ahead to the jutting point, which formed a low-lying peninsula. The sand dunes and rocky outcroppings hid any trace of an approaching vessel.

"Got to cover you up again. Sorry," said Ridley, cinching the sprayskirt over the face of Azrnoth-zin. Ridley took a deep breath and resumed paddling steadily toward the point.

It was not long before a sleek, gray boat came steaming around the point. There was no mistake. The vessel was headed for the kayak. Ridley's stomach did some flip-flops. He recognized the boat as one of the Mexican naval boats. Utilized primarily to fight drug traffickers, it was designed as a pursuit boat and carried enough firepower to sink boats much larger than Ridley's kayak.

"This isn't good," Ridley said. "If they pull alongside us and decide to search the kayak, I'm going to dump the boat. Once I clear the cockpit, get yourself out fast while I flounder about to distract them. Get as deep as you can and call your pals."

Ridley suddenly realized the metal shard that was still fused into the foredeck of the kayak. Working quickly, he adjusted the deckbag so that it lay over the piece of Azrnoth-zin's ship.

Ahead, the boat came off plane, the big diesels idling as it drew nearer. Ridley could see four men on the bow. Two were standing behind an ominous looking fifty-caliber machine gun that was pointed at the kayak. The two behind the gun looked like regular Mexican Navy. Judging by their clothing, the other two were Americans, who also wore aviator sunglasses and baseball caps.

"*A donde vas, señor?*" one of the Mexicans called out.

Ridley put on his best dumb tourist face. *"Yo - voy - a - Guaymas,"* he replied deliberately.

Another man dressed in fatigue pants and a field shirt came forward from the wheelhouse. His close-cropped gray-blonde hair and dark sunglasses were a dead giveaway. These guys weren't from Mexico. The big man came to the bow rail and studied the kayaker. He removed his sunglasses, blinking in the harsh afternoon light.

Ridley's butterflies turned to stomach-churning rage as he realized who was standing on the bow leering down at him.

"Well, I'll be damned. If it isn't Cooper Ridley. Of all the places. What's it been? Six, no, seven years."

"Hello, Jenks," Ridley said. Then, nodding toward the machine gun he said, "Doing some fishing?"

"You know this guy?" said the American standing next to Jenks.

"Yeah," said Jenks tersely. "I know him. This loser served under me in special projects during my last years in the Navy." Jenks fingered the uneven line of the bridge of his nose. Jenk's nose had never quite healed right. It had taken several surgeries to repair the crushed septum from Ridley's crashing fist.

"Ridley received a dishonorable discharge. Washed out of SEAL training and then washed out of special projects under me." He glared at Ridley. "I still owe you one for the cheap shot when I wasn't looking."

Ridley felt the old hatred boiling to the surface.

"What are you doing out here?" Jenks demanded.

"Not much," said Ridley, trying to maintain his composure. "Just a little coastal exploration. You know, Jenks, you look kinda hot out here. Next time you guys ought to try one of those great cabin cruisers they charter out of San Carlos if you want to go fishing."

"Save it for someone who cares, Ridley. Where are you coming from?"

"*San Felipe*," Ridley lied.

"How long you been out here?"

"About a week, maybe nine or ten days. I lose track. What's it to you?"

"Have you seen anything strange or unusual in your travels?" Jenks said.

Ridley laughed. "Does meeting up with you bozos count? I'd say running into a Mexican gunboat manned by a bunch of rednecks falls under the category of strange and unusual occurrences."

Behind him, the two Mexican seamen snickered. Jenks looked past Ridley for a moment. Then in a lightening fast movement, he produced a semi-automatic pistol from inside the waistband of his trousers. He aimed the gun directly at Ridley's head.

"You're a long way from home, asshole. People just up and disappear down here all the time. I doubt anyone would miss you."

Ridley stared at Jenks. The muzzle of the pistol looked ominous from this angle. Both men could feel the corridor of hateful energy between them.

Another American emerged from the wheelhouse. "Sir, we have confirmation from the recovery boat."

Jenks blinked, then lowered the gun. Ridley inhaled deeply.

"Another time, Ridley," he said with a slight smile. "You are in a restricted area. By authority of the Mexican Navy, you can be arrested or shot if you are found anywhere in this area again." Turning to the others on the deck, he said, "Prepare to come about."

The diesels roared to life and the gunboat powered up, creating a wash that nearly swamped the kayak and sucked Ridley into the prop wash. Ridley braced and paddled backward frantically to avoid the larger boat.

The gunboat moved out toward the center of the gulf and then veered to the north. Ridley leaned forward in the seat and let out another long breath.

"Son of a bitch," he said. "Jenks. I don't believe it. Azrnoth-zin, there are some very bad people after you."

From underneath the sprayskirt, Azrnoth-zin's voice was muffled. "Is that why you taunted them?"

"Jenks and I go back a long way. He used to be my superior officer for Special Projects when I was in the Navy. He was the one who gave the order that got some friends of mine killed. If I had acted passively, he would have searched us or maybe worse."

Ridley could still not believe his bad luck. Of all the people to run into in one of the most desolate places on the planet, he had to run into Jenks. Just behind his eyes, he could still picture that last day.

His last thoughts were of being pulled off Jenks and his right hand throbbing.

"It is quite warm in here, Ridley," Azrnoth-zin said. "Would it be possible to get some fresh air?"

"Oh, sorry." Peeling the sprayskirt back, Ridley felt a rush of warm, moist air escape. From all of the tension, his increased metabolism had turned the inside of the cockpit into a sauna.

"That was the commanding officer responsible for the death of the delfids?"

"One and the same," Ridley said coldly. "What I can't figure out is what in hell Jenks is doing out here looking for you. You can bet he's no scientist."

"I was unable to read those men well from my position," said Azrnoth-zin. "One thing I was able to ascertain was that they have all killed others of your race. All except the ones who spoke in the other language."

"How did you know that?"

"It is -" Azrnoth-zin struggled with the idea for a moment. "It is like a mental signature, an imprint. Once you kill for pleasure, you wear it like a scent."

"I didn't think Jenks had it in him to kill…a couple of dolphins, maybe, but a man…"

"I do not know if this is a good time to tell you this, but the killing scent was very strong with that one. He was about to kill you."

"You're right," said Ridley. "Not a good time to tell me." A smile passed over Ridley's face. "His nose is still bent out of shape," he said, resuming his paddling toward Kino. "My only regret is that I didn't hit him a little harder."

"You were close to these delfids, the ones that died?"

"About as close as a human can get to another species, I guess," Ridley said. "I started training them for the Cetacean Reconnaissance Project during the last war in the Middle East. Initially, I was told my assignment was to prepare them for routine patrols of the harbors where our ships were anchored. In fairly short order I found out my superiors, Jenks included, had other plans for them. What they wanted was an elite killing machine. These dolphins were to be trained to neutralize anyone foreign in the bay after dark. My job was to teach them the difference between our people and the enemy. Later, they had me begin instruction to the dolphins on the deployment of limpet mines onto the hulls of ships. I was working on the placement of the charges, using dummy mines, having the dolphins target the propeller shafts of the ships."

Ridley drew in a long breath. "They were both quick studies. Only problem was neither Charlie nor Dali had been exposed to live mines. I came on duty one morning to find Jenks and some muckey-mucks gathered at the pens. They informed me there was to be a live demonstration of the dolphin's skills. The target was to be an old rusted out hull in the harbor. For authenticity, they wanted live mines to be set on the hull. I argued that they weren't ready, that the risk was too great. I got into a shouting contest with Jenks and was relieved of command. The lieutenant junior grade who worked with me on the project was ordered to continue. Something went wrong with the detonator. It exploded on contact with the hull. We never found Charlie. Dali washed up on shore a short time later - dying from massive internal injuries as a result of the concussion. I don't remember much after that."

The alien was contemplative for several moments. "They did not die by your design, Ridley. You did what you could.

"Somehow, I just can't convince myself of that. I should have figured out a way to keep them out of harm's way."

Azrnoth-zin weighed each one of Ridley's statements carefully, as if he were savoring each word. After another pause, he spoke again. "You were right about one thing."

"What was that?"

"You did not hit the human Jenks hard enough."

Ridley smiled thinly. "Yeah, I guess so. His due is coming sometime. Maybe not from me, but I still believe the universe provides."

They rounded the point and Ridley adjusted the course to hug the shoreline as closely as possible.

"Hey, let's get to Kino Bay, eh?" Ridley said. "You have a ship to catch."

CHAPTER EIGHTEEN

After rounding the northern end of Tiburón Island, they landed in Punta Chueca after dark, tired, dirty, and dehydrated. Ridley beached the kayak on a sand spit and was immediately surrounded by a throng of Seri children. Recognizing the intruder, they crowded around him, talking excitedly and looking for sweets. Ridley fished into his deck bag and passed out what was left of his trail mix and energy bars.

Seri was a very difficult language to master. Ridley was still struggling with his Spanish. Fortunately, most of the Seris spoke Spanish as well as their native tongue. Ridley asked the children to go find Enrique in the best Seri he could muster. The children laughed at him, but were able to get the gist of his request. Several of them disappeared among the small concrete and ramshackle wooden homes.

Ridley had used this tiny village as a place of embarkation and take out for more than ten years. Over that time, a relationship was forged with the people of Punta Chueca. Ridley developed a unique friendship with Enrique, one of the village elders. Initially, Ridley rented a space from Enrique to store his truck while off on kayak trips. Enrique would keep an eye on Ridley's truck and personal belongings while he was kayaking.

A deep bond formed with Enrique, his family, and others in the village. He soon became an advocate for these proud people on both sides of the border. Whenever Ridley came to Mexico, he piled his truck to bursting, bringing in much needed food, medical supplies and equipment, most of which he smuggled across to avoid the miles of red tape at the border.

Punta Chueca was one of three main Seri villages in this part of northern Sonora. The livelihood for thousands of years was fishing until the northern gulf was decimated by the shrimp fisheries and foreign fishing interests. The Seris had felt the brunt of this decline.

From out of the shadows a lanky figure approached the kayak. Ridley recognized the gait as Enrique's. Even at fifty-one years of age, he still possessed a spring to his step.

"*Buenas noches,* Enrique. *Como estas?"*

"Ah, *buenas noches, mi amigo,* Ridley. *Bien, bien."*

Continuing in Spanish, Ridley asked after Enrique's family and how life was going in the village. Ridley remained seated in the kayak. If he thought it strange, Enrique did not let it show. He squatted beside Ridley while they conversed. Enrique's dark eyes reflected light from the lanterns placed near the shore.

"Enrique, I need your help, but I am afraid to place you and the rest of the village in danger."

"There are many men in Kino these days. *Federales* and men from *Los Estados Unidos.* They come and ask many questions, search our homes. Are these men after you?"

"Not yet," Ridley replied. "This has something to do with that fire in the sky the other night. Did you see it?"

"Yes. It was like no falling star I have seen before."

"It was no falling star, old friend."

"Perhaps this is not a good place to talk of these matters. Let us go to my home. Maria will fix you something hot to eat."

"That sounds wonderful, but before we do that can you get everyone to step back for a few moments. I have to show you something."

Enrique's weather-lined face showed concern. He spoke rapidly in Seri and the small crowd laughed and dispersed to other parts of the village.

"What did you tell them?"

Enrique smiled. "I told them the crazy gringo had lost his *pantolones* at sea and he was modest."

Ridley almost laughed at this. Then, peeling back the sprayskirt, Ridley said, "Enrique, I'd like you to meet Azrnoth-zin, from the planet Delfinus."

The Seri's eyes widened and he spoke softly in his native language.

"That fireball was his ship," Ridley went on. "And those men are looking for him. Somehow, I do not think their intentions are friendly. He needs to get to a place where he can be picked up by his people. I intend to see that he does."

The alien began speaking in Seri. Enrique, startled by this, lost his balance almost falling over backward. Azrnoth-zin assimilated the dialogue quickly, yet his cadence was erratic. Enrique began speaking to the alien. The exchange lasted for several moments when, finally, Enrique turned back to Ridley and said, "I will help, but I must bring this matter before the village elders."

"I understand," said Ridley. "I don't want to endanger your village in any way."

"There is much for us to discuss," Enrique replied. "But for now, we must get you hidden, fed, and rested."

After the crowd dispersed, Enrique found an old woven blanket for Ridley to wrap himself in. Together, both men lifted the kayak containing the alien and struggled up the sloping beach until they reached Enrique's house. It was a small, squat, two room concrete building with a corrugated tin roof. They set the kayak down in front of the house.

Turning to Ridley, Enrique said, "Wait here for a moment while I prepare Maria for our guest."

Two small children shot out the front door. Enrique's children, Jorgé and Anita, leapt into Ridley's arms and hugged him tightly around the neck.

"You were gone for a long time, *Tio* Ridley," said Jorgé.

"Yes, *sobrino,* far too long. It is good to see you both."

"*Tio* Ridley," said Anita, age four. "Did you bring us *los dulces?"*

The American usually had something sweet in his pockets for the children. Ridley did not disappoint them this evening. He set the children down and from under the makeshift serape, he produced what was left of his deck bag stash. Anita and Jorgé grabbed it and studied their treats for a moment. Ridley was rewarded with two beautiful smiles.

Enrique appeared at the door and summoned the children inside. He motioned for Ridley to bring Azrnoth-zin into the house. The alien had to be assisted through the doorway. The prolonged cramped position at the bottom of the kayak had stiffened Azrnoth-zin's muscles.

It was an austere dwelling, yet considered upscale because it had a concrete floor. The front room was for dining and gathering; the back room had woven floor mats arranged along the walls for sleeping. Maria sat on the floor before a cookstove in the front room. On the stove, an old blackened pot simmered on the low flame. The aroma of frijoles and tortillas filled Ridley's nostrils.

Maria stood up and warmly greeted Ridley. She was at least twenty years younger than Enrique. Her large dark eyes held wisdom far beyond her chronological age. Her shiny black hair was braided into two distinct coils on either side of her head. Her gaze shifted to the stranger. The smile disappeared and was replaced by a look of incredulity. She quickly realized she was staring and refocused her gaze to the cookpot. The children huddled behind their mother's flowing skirts and peered at the stranger.

Enrique spoke softly, but intently, to Maria and the children. Maria nodded solemnly, avoiding the burning blue eyes of the alien. Ridley was able to pick up only a word or two that he recognized. What he understood was that Enrique was telling Maria and the children that they had nothing to fear from the stranger.

Azrnoth-zin spoke in Seri. Maria's eyes grew wider and she stepped back as if she had just landed on a snake. As the alien continued speaking, Maria's shoulders relaxed and she began to converse with him. Ridley noticed that Azrnoth-zin's command of Seri was improving rapidly. Maria excused herself and went about preparing the meal for the visitors.

"I'm sorry," said Ridley. "But you three left me in the dust back there. What did she say to you?"

Azrnoth-zin's eyebrows raised. "Strange," he said. "She spoke of hearing stories of off-world visitors with eyes that burn blue from her grandfather. She tells me that I speak in the dialect of the old ones. It is not spoken very much now."

"That's no surprise. Hundreds of years ago, the Spaniards landed here and were deified for a while until the locals started becoming indentured or murdered."

"That is not of what she speaks. She informed me that these visitors arrived here a long time before that. And that they appeared from the sky."

"So, does that mean that your people have been here before?" said Ridley.

"Among my people there is no record that we have encountered your planet before."

"Funny that she would mention blue-eyed visitors. If that's the case, where did your translator pick up the language? Someone had to encode it."

The alien looked pensive. "I do not know. When I - if I return to my people I have many questions that must be answered."

The meal consisted of pinto beans, rice and a few pieces of fish, served in chipped ceramic bowls. From under a small folded cloth, Maria produced steaming corn tortillas. Ridley inhaled the food. Glancing over at Azrnoth-zin, he could see the alien was enjoying his meal. Enrique and the alien continued their conversation in Spanish for Ridley's benefit.

Ridley set his plate down, complimenting Maria on the meal. She smiled and asked if he wanted more. Ridley patted his stomach and graciously declined, but the alien took another helping of the beans and rice mixture.

"I have determined that Maria's food preparation is superior to yours, Ridley," Azrnoth-zin said in Spanish.

"What?" Ridley said, making a wry face.

Enrique explained the comment to Maria and the children. Laughter erupted in the small house.

"Great. Just great. Everyone's a critic," Ridley said. Enrique slapped him on the back and Ridley joined in the mirth.

After the meal, Ridley went outside and removed the rest of the food and supplies from the kayak. He presented them to Maria, which she accepted graciously. Enrique and Azrnoth-zin were speaking in low tones while they sipped coffee.

Azrnoth-zin stood and approached the mat where Ridley lay. In his hand, he held a triangular metal object that caught the reflection from the fire.

"I see you finally pulled that out of my boat," Ridley said.

"This is not from your boat," said Azrnoth-zin, a troubled look on his face. "Enrique presented this to me. He said it has been kept by their people for hundreds of years."

Ridley sat up. "What?" He took the object from Azrnoth-zin and examined it. "Looks similar to the piece that's fused into my kayak." Standing quickly, Ridley left the house and stepped out into the night. Several moments later, he returned, the metallic shard from Azrnoth-zin's ship in one hand, the one from Enrique in the other.

"This thing didn't pry out of the deck easily," Ridley said, handing both of the metallic objects to Azrnoth-zin. He followed the alien back to the fire.

By the light of the small fire, Azrnoth-zin examined the two shards. When he looked up, his face registered confusion. Enrique sat back, watching the alien's expressions.

"This is strange," said Azrnoth-zin. "Many of the runes are similar on the two pieces. On this one, the encryptions appear to be an old dialect of Delfinus. Some of the characters I recognize from the ancient scrolls. Then, why is it I have no recollection of this water planet being in our data systems?"

"Maybe like you, they got lost a long time ago," Ridley said.

"Enrique informs me that, according to the legend, the "Sky People" crashed here and were later rescued by another ship after a prolonged stay. There should be record of this in the archives."

"The Trochinids could have surprised them on the way home," Ridley offered.

"If the Trochinids were anywhere near this system, this planet would not be here now."

"It was said the great ship of the Sky People crashed on top of the mountain on *Isla Tiburón*," said Enrique. "Over time, many have searched for the fallen ship. They all came back empty handed."

"I wonder if their ship was able to self-destruct like yours did."

"That could provide an explanation as to why more of the ship was not found," Azrnoth-zin said.

"When the rest of the village elders are gathered here, we will ask them if they know anything that can help you," said Enrique, sensing Azrnoth-zin's frustration.

Suddenly, Ridley felt the overwhelming pull of gravity on his fatigued body. Puzzle or no puzzle, he was beyond all forms of reason now. He found a mat in a corner near some of the baskets that Maria had woven, baskets that would be sold to the tourists in Kino. In the past forty-eight hours, he had amassed less than six hours of sleep. Unconsciousness came to him as soon as his head touched the mat.

If Ridley dreamed, he never remembered it. Several times he stirred, hearing far off voices that were speaking in a foreign tongue. He awakened hearing the muted murmurings of several men. Opening his eyes, he saw shadows dancing across the ceiling, exaggerated gestures emanating from fantastically elongated appendages and heads. Turning on his side, he saw the source of these apparitions.

A rusted out Weber barbecue grill without legs, sat in the middle of the room, the warmth from its flames Ridley could feel even where he was lying. Around it a circle of men were gathered, talking quietly. Azrnoth-zin and Enrique were sitting almost shoulder to shoulder. Ridley guessed the others to be the elders of the village, judging by their ages and the air of somber formality of the meeting. Right about now, they were probably discussing the stranger's fate and their options. Azrnoth-zin listened intently.

Enrique looked up and noticed Ridley was awake. He got up quietly and came to where Ridley lay.

"You must try to sleep more, my friend," said the older Seri man. "You have much dangerous work to do soon."

"What?" Ridley whispered. "I don't understand."

"The elders have decided that it is not safe here for the stranger or our people as long as the *federales gringos* are looking for him. They believe you have been chosen to guide the stranger back."

"Chosen? Me? By whom?" Ridley said, rubbing the sleep out of his eyes.

"Tomorrow, at first light, I will drive you both to San Carlos where you can get your truck. It is most important that you and the stranger get away from here and cross the border as soon as possible. We have information from *Disemboqúe* and *Puerto de la Libertad* that these men will stop at nothing to capture the stranger."

"Are the other villages all right?"

"For now. For now," said Enrique. "But the stranger's trail must not be traced through our villages. The other elders fear reprisals from the government."

Ridley propped himself up on an elbow. "I still don't get it about this chosen thing. I mean -."

"Sleep now, Ridley. Come tomorrow, you will need all of your senses sharp as knives." Enrique touched Ridley lightly on the shoulder, rose and went to join the others.

Ridley saw that some of the other elders were staring at him. He felt a twinge of discomfort at being the focal point of their gaze. They quickly turned back to the discussion.

Rolling onto his back, Ridley watched the flickering shadows play out their bizarre patterns on the ceiling. *These events just kept getting weirder and weirder*, he thought. He tried to fit pieces of the puzzle into place: the limited bits of information the alien provided coupled with the strange relationship to the Seris. A rapport established quickly between the alien and these people of the desert sea. Ridley wondered if Azrnoth-zin's people had actually visited here a long time ago, back when history was passed on through oral tradition.

At some point in time, Ridley's brain shut down and he dropped into deep, uninterrupted slumber.

Ridley awoke to a hand gently shaking his shoulder. The outline of Enrique's face was highlighted by the gathering dawn filtering in the doorway. The air inside the house was chill, smelling of last night's meal and the essence of burnt wood.

Azrnoth-zin was already up and moving about. Perhaps he had never gone to sleep. Delfinians did not appear to require the same amount of sleep that humans needed. He had exchanged his tunic for a pair of worn jeans and a faded cotton shirt. In a tattered cordura knapsack, he was arranging the items he brought with him from the fallen ship. The clothes hung loosely about Azrnoth-zin's delicate frame. *He'd be passable though,* thought Ridley.

Ridley crawled out from under the tangle of blankets and made his way to the boat. Everyone was up except the children. Maria was already preparing the morning meal. Stepping outside, the air felt cool and damp, with a sweet smell of ocean greeting his nostrils. In the rear compartment of the kayak, he found a pair of jeans and an old flannel shirt to ward off the morning chill. On the side of the house, Ridley washed himself from a cracked porcelain bowl resting on a rickety wooden table.

Ridley cleared the rest of his belongings from the kayak and threw them into the bed of Enrique's rusty 1982 Ford pickup. Stepping back inside the house, Ridley observed Maria speaking quietly to the alien. He walked over to where Azrnoth-zin and Enrique sat on the floor.

"We must leave soon," said Enrique, "before the rest of the village awakens."

"I'm set," said Ridley.

Azrnoth-zin nodded.

Maria handed each of them a plate of *chorizo* with more freshly made tortillas. Ridley wanted to savor the rich spiciness of his breakfast, but was forced to eat quickly.

"Enrique, I want you to sink the kayak for me," Ridley said between bites. "If the *federales gringos* trace my boat to you, there'll be hell to pay."

"What boat?" said Enrique smiling, the gaps in his teeth evident. "Do not worry, Ridley. It will be hidden for you if you return."

"I'm not sure when I'll be ba- what do you mean "if"?"

The old man looked at Ridley momentarily as if he were looking straight through him. The way that Enrique met his gaze gave Ridley a chill. Enrique got up and went to speak with Maria. She looked over at Ridley and Azrnoth-zin. Finally she came over to Ridley and gave him a hug.

"*Buena suerte,* Ridley." she said and kissed him on the cheek. "I will kiss the children for you." Turning to Azrnoth-zin, she spoke to him in Seri.

Ridley and Azrnoth-zin went outside to wait for Enrique while he said goodbye to his wife and children. Standing next to the pickup, Ridley turned to Azrnoth-zin. "What did Maria say to you in there?"

Azrnoth-zin was gazing at the light growing in the east. "She said I was to take care of you."

Ridley squinted at the alien. "Is that so? I sure wish everyone would stop speaking in riddles. I feel like I've been left out of a really good joke."

"No joke. Not funny," said Azrnoth-zin, making direct eye contact.

Enrique strode out of the house and got in on the driver's side while Azrnoth-zin, followed by Ridley, climbed into the cab from the other side. It was not until the third try that the engine turned over and roared to life, belching smoke out the back.

"Remind me to bring you an exhaust tailpipe next time I'm down," Ridley said loudly.

"What do you call this mode of transportation?" Azrnoth-zin said above the grumbling of the motor.

"Iffy," said Ridley. "It's called an automobile. This particular model is a 1982 Ford pickup."

Azrnoth-zin repeated the words. "Interesting. This is what humans use for terrestrial travel?"

"Yep. And you have the privilege of riding in one of the finest pieces of machinery made by man."

The alien was quiet for a moment. Finally he looked at Ridley and Enrique and said, "I am surprised your race was successful in leaving the planet's atmosphere at all."

Within minutes, they were following a sandy track away from the village and toward the east. The washboard road was not well maintained. Even though it would take them longer, Enrique had decided to take the back roads to avoid any encounters with the agents. Ridley wondered if his teeth or his ears would ever be the same after the bumpy three to four hour ride to San Carlos.

No one spoke for quite a while. Ridley felt the cool morning breeze against his face, the fragrance of creosote and brittlebush strong. Reaching down into his pack on the floor between his feet, Ridley produced a long-billed fishing cap and dark sunglasses and handed these to Azrnoth-zin.

"No offense, but I think you should wear these, just in case," said Ridley. Azrnoth-zin examined the hat and glasses. The front of the cap had an embroidered kayaker with the words, "Pilots of the Waterways - Mexico - U.S. - Canada." The alien fitted the hat over his prominent brow ridge, then slipping on the glasses, turned to Ridley.

"How do I look?"

Ridley laughed loudly. "Just pray we get stopped by only blind or stupid agents, that's all."

Azrnoth-zin adjusted the rear view mirror to look at himself. Turning to Ridley, he said, "I think I make a good human."

Ridley tried to contain himself, but again he laughed out loud. "Women of earth, watch out. There's a new kid in town." Ridley wiped his eyes, trying to regain his composure. But every time he looked at Azrnoth-zin, he broke into fresh gales of laughter. Enrique was smiling broadly over the whole exchange. The alien's expression never changed.

"We still have to do something about those ears," Ridley said, finally catching his breath. "Or should I say, lack of them."

"There is nothing wrong with my ears," Azrnoth-zin said indignantly. "They are the culmination of thousands of years of the most sophisticated natural selection."

"Right." Ridley fished a red bandana from his hip pocket. "Here. Tie this around your head so it covers your marvels of evolution."

It took Azrnoth-zin several tries before the bandana covered below the levels of his lobes. Finally, he looked in the mirror once more and turned to Ridley, "Is that satisfactory?"

"It'll have to do. I'm not sure what I'm going to tell people when they get a close look at your skin. Maybe I'll just tell them you have a rare skin disease."

"I think I like becoming human less and less," said the alien.

"Look. Another thing. I can't keep calling you Azrnoth-zin in public. People don't understand names like that, and frankly, I have a hard time pronouncing it myself. You need a handle that doesn't sound like you have a mouthful of marbles and doesn't draw attention to - uh - your other features."

After several moments of contemplation, Ridley announced, "I've got it. For our purposes and as long as you're here on good ol' planet earth, you will be Arnold Zinn. Arnie for short." Ridley nodded, pleased with himself.

"Arnold Zinn," repeated the stranger slowly. "I am not sure I like this new name."

"You'll get used to it. Besides, what's in a -."

Ridley stopped in mid-sentence as Enrique began slowing the truck. Ahead, two federal vehicles were on either side of the road. Two uniformed men were standing in the middle of the dirt road. In the early morning light Ridley could see they were armed. The two *federales* waved them forward.

"Shit," whispered Ridley. "Roadblock."

CHAPTER NINETEEN

"Be cool," Ridley said, staring through the pitted and dirty windshield. "As far as they're concerned, we're going to San Carlos to pick up some truck parts. Don't speak unless you're spoken to."

They pulled to a stop in front of the two federales. One sauntered around to the driver's side and ordered Enrique to produce his registration for the truck. The other one approached the passenger's side and stuck his head in the window, staring at Ridley and Azrnoth-zin. Azrnoth-zin focused his gaze ahead, while Ridley nodded and smiled slightly at the official.

"Where are you going?" the second federale demanded.

"Our friend is taking us to San Carlos to look for an alternator for our truck which broke down in Kino," Ridley said in his best Spanish. "There are no automobile supply stores in Kino that carry this type of alternator."

"You are both Americans?"

"*Si.*"

"Do you have your travel visas?"

"No," said Ridley. "They're with the rest of our belongings back in Kino. We did not think we would need them for such a short trip."

"How long have you been in Mexico?" the first federale said while still holding Enrique's papers.

"Three weeks. We came down to do some fishing. We have to get back to the states by the day after tomorrow. Work, you know."

"How is it that you come to be in the truck of this *Indio?"* the federale said, an air of contempt in his voice.

"He's the best fishing guide in northern Mexico," said Ridley. "I've been using him for the past ten years."

The federale snorted and moved around to the other side of the truck, where he conferred with his cohort. They spoke in low tones, but their gestures were animated.

The first one handed Enrique back his papers. "This truck is not legal," he said. Pointing to the rear of the truck, he said, "no tailpipe."

Ridley could see it coming. "What do you mean, no tailpipe? Every other vehicle in this part of Mexico is missing a tailpipe."

"It is grounds for impoundment of the vehicle, until the problem is fixed," said the federale, shrugging his shoulders.

Ridley sucked in a deep breath. "How much would the fine be?" he said, barely able to hide the irritation in his voice.

The federale looked at his partner. "In Hermosillo, this would be a hundred dollars, American." He flashed a greasy smile. "But Hermosillo, my friends, is a long way off."

Normally, Ridley would have argued with the crooked officials all day long. He fumbled for his wallet and fished out two worn twenties.

"This is all I have," Ridley said.

The federale snatched the money out of Ridley's hand. Pointing a finger at Azrnoth-zin, he said, "What about you, silent one?"

"I cannot be trusted with money," Azrnoth-zin replied in deadpan Spanish. "He carries it for me."

The federale laughed. "Then I think his wallet is very shallow." Ridley ignored the jibe and hoped the federales would not persist in asking Azrnoth-zin more questions.

The two federales conferred once more away from the truck. After a few minutes, the first one walked up to the driver's side and said, "You may pass, but get a work order for that tail pipe."

"*Gracias, señor,"* said Enrique, turning on the ignition. He engaged the gears and the old truck lurched past the two smirking officials.

Once they were safely away, Azrnoth-zin was the first to speak. "They were part of the searchers?"

"Only thing they could be," said Ridley, irritated. "No one would set a drug checkpoint out here. I can't believe they wanted a hundred bucks from you, Enrique. What a bunch of grifters."

"My disguise appears to have worked," Azrnoth-zin said, pleased with his appearance.

"Yeah, how about that," said Ridley. "I guess they were more interested in how to fleece us out of our money than to give you a really good look."

Enrique smiled. "I think it is because all of you *gringos* look the same to us when you dress like that. That was good information they passed on, although they did not realize they did so."

"How's that?" said Ridley.

"They did not know what they were looking for. The *federales gringos* must have told them very little."

"Well, that may be our one miracle," said Ridley. "We were lucky enough to go through a checkpoint manned by Heckyl and Jeckyl. Let's hope we don't have to do that again."

The truck rattled and bumped along the worn sandy track. Every now and then they would turn a corner and the Gulf of California would appear as a dazzling blue gem between the hills of creosote and cardon cactus. The sun was climbing in the sky, warming the inside of the truck. Whenever Enrique slowed the truck to avoid a rut or decelerated down a steep grade, the cab was awash in dust. Soon, all three of them wore a fine coating of dust on their faces and clothes. After topping a series of low-lying hills, Enrique turned the truck onto another dirt road, this one more substantial, that skirted several large *ranchos*.

They pulled into San Carlos around nine-thirty without further incident. Most of the local businesses were just starting to open their doors. The main road was quiet except for the occasional Chevy Blazer filled with divers on their way to the marina. Even at the marina, there were only a few scattered boats moored at the slips. It would be several weeks yet before the winter boaters invaded. The dive operations were already winding down for the year.

Enrique eased the truck next to Ridley's old white Toyota pickup. Ridley jumped out and worked at unfastening the kayak racks from the roof of the camper shell. He tossed these into the back of

Enrique's truck, then opened the back of his own truck, throwing in his backpack. From the back, he grabbed a worn, brown leather flight jacket and put it on. The name B. RIDLEY was stenciled over the left breast pocket. The faded jacket had belonged to Ridley's father.

Azrnoth-zin and Enrique were still in the cab, speaking Seri when Ridley approached.

"Enrique, that rack may come in handy. Sell it for whatever you can get and use the money from it and the kayak for your family."

Enrique nodded. *"Gracias, mi amigo."* The old man's face grew more lined and severe. "I had a dream in the early morning hours. In it, there were many strange creatures, none like I have seen before. In one part of the dream, you were surrounded by many small, bear-like creatures. They had hands like men but they were not harming you. Later, there was a vision of you bleeding, dying in a desolate place. I am not sure of the meaning now, but I believe it is a warning. You must be careful in your deliverance of our visitor. You are dealing with very dangerous men. Do not underestimate them."

Ridley smiled his crooked smile and grabbed Enrique by the shoulder. "Hey, you know me. I'm always careful. Okay, so I'm not always careful. It's going to be all right. Once we can get Azrnoth-zin to a safe place to make the signal, his people will pick him up, and we'll be left with some great tall tales to tell our grandkids while Jenks and company will still be fondling themselves out on the ocean."

"Still, my American friend, please be careful."

"Enrique, I promise. And I am not taking any of this lightly. I'll be back in a few weeks."

Azrnoth-zin and the Seri elder stepped out of the truck. They clasped forearms and spoke in Enrique's native tongue, Azrnoth-zin nodding solemnly while Enrique spoke in a rapid cadence. Finally, the alien went around to the passenger's side of Ridley's truck and got in.

"Do not linger here in San Carlos," said Enrique. "I fear the *federales gringos* are not far behind us.

Ridley hugged his friend and jumped into the front seat. *"Muchas gracias, mi amigo.* Next time I get down, I'll bring some bolts of cloth for Maria and truck parts for you."

Enrique nodded and waved a final time. Ridley fired up the old, but dependable Toyota. Pulling out of the parking lot, he was struck by the look of sadness on Enrique's face.

The Seri watched the truck roll out of the marina and turn onto the highway, overwhelmed by the feeling that he would not see his American friend again.

CHAPTER TWENTY

It was shaping up to be another bad day for special agent Richard Jenks. Into the third day of the search they hit a dead end. The first few hours were promising; part of the alien ship had been recovered along with some other debris. The salvaged items were now resting in a makeshift lab on board the recovery vessel, sealed and protected from contamination. The team of microbiologists sent by the Phoenix Project were already insuring no extraterrestrial vector could be spread. What appeared to be part of the command console and internal workings of the ship, as well as fragments of the ship itself, had been identified. Someone, or something had piloted that ship to the earth's surface and Jenks was no closer to finding it this morning than he was yesterday.

The chart which lay spread before him was now as familiar as a city map of the District of Columbia. Over the past two days, they had covered an area of nearly two hundred square miles, running transects and chasing down any and all leads. Nothing out of the ordinary had shown up, unless you wanted to count the occasional Mexican fisherman, the two women biologists, and Ridley.

Ridley. The last person he expected to see in the middle of this God-forsaken place was his former subordinate. Ridley was indirectly the reason why Jenks was passed over for promotion to Captain. That and the loss of two valuable project assets while under his command. A smoldering rage rekindled inside of him. He thought for a second that he might be losing his killer instinct. He should have dealt with Ridley once and for all in their last encounter.

Another agent dressed in a white muslin shirt and khaki shorts stepped inside the galley and approached Jenks. He held a cup of coffee in one hand and a sheaf of papers in the other. Jenks did not bother looking up from the chart.

"Morning, sir," said the man in muslin, a bit too cheerily. "How are you today?"

Jenks cast a sideways glance at the agent. "Carlisle, you had better have some good news for me this morning with that tone of voice or I will be forced to feed you to the sharks."

"Just got in the latest data analysis on that ship. There are three metallic elements that are identifiable. The rest, well…"

"The metallurgical team will arrive today," Jenks said. "We should get a better idea of the composite after they run their tests. Any other news?"

"Sorry, sir. All the other ships reported in within the last twenty-five minutes after their last sweep. Nothing to report."

"It's out here somewhere," Jenks said, staring intently at the chart. "And I think it knows we're after him. There's got to be something I'm missing, something that's probably sitting right in front of me."

Jenks dismissed Carlisle and went for his third cup of coffee of the morning. There was going to be hell to pay today, he thought. He expected Number One to be calling anytime now to check their progress. The old man expected results. Jenks hated the idea of telling the head of the Phoenix Project that they had reached a dead end.

Roberson burst through the doorway, a look of excitement on his face. "Sir, I think we may have something."

"What have you got?" Jenks said, looking up at his second in command.

"The *San Felipe* picked up a fisherman a few moments ago not far from Punta la Gorda. It seems he discovered a cache of equipment that has been stashed in a subtidal cave where he fishes for octopus."

"What kind of gear?"

"He didn't know. He wasn't able to identify it to the Mexican officers. It sounds like someone was trying to hide something."

Jenks looked at the chart, tracing the coastline with his finger. When it stopped on Punta la Gorda, he said, "Give me an ETA."

"About an hour at full steam. The *San Felipé* will be there in twenty minutes."

"Tell them to not disturb anything until we arrive. Is that clear?"

"Yes sir. I'll make sure they wait on us." Roberson ducked out of the room and went forward to communications.

Just under an hour later, the gunboat made a rendezvous with one of the trawlers. The trawler was anchored about a hundred yards off a precipitous series of cliffs and outcroppings that appeared to extend for several miles. The gunboat anchored close to the trawler and no sooner had the anchor been set than an inflatable launch motored over to pick up Jenks, Roberson and Carlisle.

On board the trawler, Jenks was led to the forward salon where a contingent of other agents sat with a Mexican fisherman. They all rose when Jenks entered the room. The Mexican fisherman stood and nodded nervously toward Jenks, his soiled baseball cap held in his hands.

"You made good time, sir," said one of the agents stepping forward. "Didn't expect you for another fifteen or twenty minutes."

"Talk to me, Owens. What have you got?"

"This is Guillermo," said Owens. "He's been fishing this part of the coast, from San Pedro point to Punta la Gorda, in his panga for three years. It seems he has a secret place where he gunkholes for octopus - a subtidal marine cave. At high tide, it's invisible. At low tide you can't see it unless you're right on top of it, and then it's too narrow to get any boat in there wider than six feet."

"How does he get back in there?" said Jenks.

Owens fired off some Spanish and Guillermo responded. Jenks could see the fisherman's clothes were tattered and when he opened his mouth, a great many of his teeth were missing. His eyes were reddened and his skin sun damaged.

"He says he swims in with his gear sitting in a mesh bag inside of an inner tube. He's what they call a Hooka diver. A small compressor and several hundred feet of tubing is kept inside the inner tube. He dives with this system. Says he can stay down for hours. He's never seen another boat inside of the cave while he was diving"

"Ask him again what he found in there," said Jenks.

Owens repeated the question in Spanish. Guillermo answered excitedly, gesturing with callused hands.

"He says he found several brightly colored bags that keep out the water. He put most of what he found on a ledge inside of the cave. He swears he did not take any of it. He heard the *federales Norte Americanos* were looking for something on the sea. He wants to help and hopes there will be a reward."

Jenks' lip twitched slightly. "Tell him if we like what we see, there will be something in it for him. I want a team of salvage divers assembled and ready to penetrate that cave in thirty minutes. I'll be needing a wetsuit and scuba set-up."

"We've got flotation tubes ready to haul in the salvage equipment," said Owens. "There's tanks, regulator, BCD and wetsuit laid out for you below. We're ready to go in as soon as you get suited up."

Twenty minutes later, Jenks, Carlisle, and three other agents were finning their way through the cave entrance. The tide was ebbing, but the opening would not allow the passage of any vessel yet. Switching on halogen lights attached to their dive helmets, they dove down and followed the bottom until it opened up into the great room. The surge was powerful; they were able to ride it in during the flood cycle, but quickly learned to grab onto any outcropping to avoid being flushed out during the backwash. After the surge calmed, Jenks signaled for the team to surface and ascend the short distance. On the surface, he turned in a 360-degree arc, his lamp reflecting off the moist walls. It did not take him long to spot the ledge at the back of the cave Guillermo described.

Jenks finned to the ledge and pulled himself onto the rocks, then removed his fins. He lumbered over to the pile of recovered drybags. Some of the items had been pulled from their watertight containers by the fisherman. Jenks wondered how much of the recovered items had been removed and hidden by Guillermo. He was going to make a point of asking him when he got back to the boat.

"Start a standard search grid, two by two," ordered Jenks. "Carlisle, you and Harris begin over at the far wall and work your way back to the middle. Beatty, you and Metzger start near the ledge and work outward. If one of you finds something, bring it to me while the other one holds the position."

Jenks looked at his watch. It would still be another hour before the low tide would allow them to bring in the float bags with the heavier recovery equipment. Jenks spoke into the microphone that was wired into the front of his dive helmet.

"Roberson, do you copy?"

There was static, then, "I copy you, sir, but the signal is a little weak."

"There's a lot of rock between you and me right now. We're in the cavern. We've started a search grid and I'm going through the bags already on the ledge. Stay close to the radio and as soon as the tide is out get that equipment in here. So far, the only thing I'm seeing is a lot of camping gear. Although judging by the looks of it, it hasn't been down here long."

Slipping out of the cumbersome equipment, Jenks donned a pair of sterile gloves he removed from a small waterproof case. He knelt down and began sorting through the contents of the drybags. In one, he found freeze-dried foods and utensils. In another, cookware. All of the equipment was designed not to take up a lot of space.

Something gnawed at Jenks, something about the placement of all this gear. Why would someone leave all of this here? If the pilot of that ship left it, then he must have done his shopping at one of the local outdoor stores. That did not add up to the other discovery so far.

Jenks radio crackled. Picking up the mask and detaching the microphone, he said, "Go ahead, Roberson."

"Sir, the seas are picking up out here. I have been informed that we need to back the boats farther away from the rocks."

"Just make sure I get my equipment in here as soon as there's clearance."

"That's affirmative, sir. It may be a bumpy ride in and out judging from the looks of things."

"Keep me informed. Jenks out."

The divers surfaced with another cache of drybags. They brought over the four bags and set them on the ledge. Jenks retrieved them and began systematically sorting through the contents. More of the same - camping gear and some odds and ends of clothing, American-made. He found another bag labeled "lunch" and opened it to find more of the freeze-dried items. To Jenks, the packets resembled the rations he remembered eating in the Navy.

The last bag brought up was medium-sized and blue. The seal had been broken while underwater as evidenced by leakage into the dry compartment. Jenks emptied the contents onto the cave floor. He stared at soggy, bloodied bandages and a swatch of material the likes he had never seen before. He picked up he fabric and held it between his fingertips. It possessed a luminescent sheen that shed the water droplets. The material had an almost metallic feel to it, but was soft to the touch. Along the frayed borders, the material appeared to be singed.

Jenks' heart started pounding. He picked up the microphone and contacted Roberson.

"I think our pilot's been here," said Jenks. "And he sustained some damage during impact. There's some bloody dressings and a piece of what looks to be some type of clothing material, but nothing like I've seen in Nieman Marcus."

"No sign of the pilot in the cave?" said Roberson.

"That's a negative. The cave is clear."

"I think we can start moving the floats in with the equipment. It's going to take us a few minutes to compensate for the sloshing out here. The waves are really piling into the rocks now."

An hour later, a half a dozen men were scouring the bottom and taking air and water samples. Several more were on the ledge, bagging the items from the drybags and dusting them for fingerprints. Jenks was growing impatient. Nothing more had been brought to the surface in the last forty minutes. The pilot, if he was still alive, could be slipping away from them with each passing moment.

Out in the water, near the far corner of the cavern, one of the divers called out excitedly. Jenks looked up to see the diver waving something over his head. He went to the water's edge while the diver swam quickly to him. It was one of the salvage divers who had been operating the underwater metal detector.

"Sir, I was performing one last sweep in section six when the detector came in with a winner. Thought you might find this interesting," the diver said, catching his breath and handing a mesh bag up. Jenks pulled the object from the mesh bag and stared at what was once a semi-automatic pistol. The muzzle and leading portion of the barrel were fused and turned upward at an angle. Jenks examined it from all sides.

"What in the hell could melt the barrel of a semi-auto out here?" He looked closer and realized the serial numbers were still intact on the underside of the grip.

"Roberson," he said, picking up the microphone once more. "Get me an I.D. on this semi-auto. Let's see if we can find out whom it's registered to. Serial numbers Alpha, Omega, 4782269, appears to be a Sig Sauer, forty caliber. And I want that yesterday."

Roberson repeated the numbers and signed off. Jenks was distracted by a commotion occurring in the middle of the cave lagoon.

"Jesus Christ!" the diver exclaimed. "Get it off him!"

It took Jenks a moment to realize what was going on. All he could see was foaming water and several divers converging on the area. In the middle of it all, one of the divers had a large, slick, green form wrapped around his neck.

"What is it?" Jenks yelled.

Two of the divers moved in and began slashing at the coiled moray with their dive tools. The water was churning with red as the divers worked feverishly to free their hapless comrade. Suddenly, the struggle was over as quickly as it had begun. The diver was brought to the surface by his colleagues and was being carried, rescue-fashion, toward the ledge.

Jenks could see the diver was in shock. There was a large gaping laceration on the left side of his neck, the blood flowing freely from the wound. The other divers pulled him up on the ledge and began treating him.

"He's lucky it didn't hit the carotid," said Harris. "Keep applying pressure until we can get him back to the boat. Any one else get hit?" The rest of the team shook their heads.

"That's the biggest fuckin' moray I've ever seen," said one of the divers. "It happened so fast. Smiley was reaching inside of the rocks and the next thing I see, he's got that damn thing wrapped around his neck."

"Can he be moved?" said Jenks.

"He's lost a considerable amount of blood, and he's in shock," said Harris. "But I think we can take him out of here on the floats."

Jenks spoke into the radio. "Roberson, we have wounded in here. I want a launch waiting outside of the cave and find out what kind of medical abilities the Mexican crew have."

"Who is it, sir?"

"It's Smiley. He was bitten in the neck by an eel."

A pause, then, "Jesus," said Roberson. "Those things are nasty. We'll get a sick bay set up now." Jenks heard Roberson ordering the other members of the crew in Spanish.

Turning to the divers on the ledge, Jenks said, "Clear some room on one of the floats and load Smiley onto it. Gather up the rest of the gear and start making for the entrance."

"I'd like a little payback on that eel," said one of the divers.

"You can come back on your own time," said Jenks.

"I think I got a few good rips at it" said the other diver. "If it doesn't die from the injuries, then it will be left with a lasting memory of the encounter."

"So will Smiley," said Jenks, turning to pick up his equipment.

Half of an hour later, the team was safely back on board the trawler. Smiley was rushed to the galley where a nervous young Mexican officer was to tend to his wounds. The officer concluded that the injuries were too serious to treat other than superficially. Smiley would have to go to Guaymas. Fluid electrolytes were started on the diver and the wound was cleansed as effectively as conditions on the boat would allow. All of the contents recovered from the cave were taken below deck and examined. The material and the bloody bandages were being analyzed by a team of scientists in a clean room that had been established below.

After Jenks went to check on Smiley, he made his way to the bridge. Stepping inside, he saw Roberson, a strange look shadowing his face.

"What's up?" said Jenks. "Did you get an ID on that semi-auto yet?"

"Yes, sir," said Roberson. "But you're not going to believe it when you hear it. The Sig was sold in Tucson, Arizona, on May 9, 1998 to one Cooper M. Ridley."

"What? Did you say Ridley?"

"Uh, yes, sir. Turns out some of that gear can be traced back to Ridley as well. His fingerprints were all over the cookware."

Jenks slammed his fist down into the table. "Son of a bitch! Ridley had the pilot in his boat right under our noses the whole time." He stared out the wheelhouse window. "Why didn't I see it? I thought that boat was riding low in the water. I must be going soft. I let him distract me."

Jenks wheeled around suddenly and spoke to the captain. "I need you to call in to the federal jurisdiction. We need roadblocks set up immediately at the border. I want those border crossings closed. Do you understand?"

"*Señor* Jenks, that will take time to coordinate -."

"Do it!" Jenks said sharply. The captain nodded and spoke to his next in command in rapid-fire Spanish. Several moments later he was talking to the district supervisor for northern Sonora.

"Get in touch with our people on the other side of the border. Make sure a net is established at all available outgoing roads, bus stops, and train stations. Get me a list of all known and used airfields between here and Guaymas. Find a picture of Ridley and post it to all agencies. Make up something, but make them believe he is armed and dangerous."

Roberson nodded and went down to the communications center the Phoenix Project had established on the trawler. At the moment Jenks very badly wanted to hit something. The pilot had been in his grasp, but he had let him slip away. Slip away with Ridley.

"Where's the nearest settlement?" Jenks said to the Mexican captain.

"That would be Kino Bay, *señor,*" the captain said matter-of-factly. The captain was hoping this foolish chase would be over soon. The sooner he was rid of the arrogant Americans, the better.

"Turn this boat around and head for Kino bay. Tell your people I want Kino Bay bottled up. Nobody goes in or out that we don't know about."

The captain nodded compliance once more and spoke into the radio.

Jenks turned to one of the subordinate agents and said, "Tell Roberson to put out a message on channel sixteen. Any and all boat traffic is to be on the lookout for a red sea kayak paddling along the coast. Tell them the man in the kayak is wanted by authorities for suspicion of terrorist activities in the United States and Mexico."

"What about the fisherman, Guillermo?" said the agent.

"Escort him off the boat. Now."

A moment later, the complaining Guillermo was shoved roughly into his panga and cast away from the trawler. Jenks tried to order his thoughts. Pulling out the chart of the coastline, he plotted where they had seen Ridley yesterday and projected how far he could have gotten today. They could have made Kino, probably no further. Jenks knew he was overdue to make the call to Number One and inform him of their progress. The old man was going to have to wait just a little longer. Jenks did not relish the thought of telling the director of the project that the most important find of the twenty-first century had just slipped through his fingers.

"Come on, you bastards," he said through gritted teeth. "Be in Mexico."

CHAPTER TWENTY-ONE

Ridley turned the white Toyota pickup into the Pemex station and pulled up to the pump. It was going to be a long haul back to the border and the gas tank was half full. He surveyed the premises, then looked across the street. Although it was approaching midmorning, the traffic was still light; only a few pedestrians were moving up and down the main artery of San Carlos.

Ridley stepped out of the cab and checked the surroundings again. Satisfied they were not being observed, he signaled to the attendant who began pumping gas into the Toyota. After Ridley paid the attendant, he stuck his head in the window.

Azrnoth-zin was adjusting quickly to his *persona incognito*. The alien's head was covered by Ridley's old cap; a worn bandanna was tied around his head under the hat to conceal his distinctive ears. Ridley's Ray Bans rested comfortably on the smallish nose. The only giveaway was the alien's almost translucent bluish skin and the thin webbing between his fingers. Ridley found himself smirking when he gazed down and saw the red Converse sneakers on the alien's feet.

"I think I have an idea," said Ridley, popping the hood latch under the dashboard. He went to the front of the truck and scraped a glob of grease from the engine with his finger. He came back to the truck cab and began to apply the goo to the alien's face. Azrnoth-zin balked at first, then acquiesced as Ridley blended the grease in with the lighter skin tone.

"There. That's better. Now you look like just another dirty camper coming home from Mexico."

Azrnoth-zin looked at his face in the mirror. "Now I look like you, Ridley."

"That's not funny," said Ridley. "It seems to be all clear here. I'm going to pick up a few things for the road at the market across the street. I think it would be a good idea if you stayed in the truck."

"I would like to see this market," said the alien. "I am curious about the things in it."

"No. Just stay here. I have enough to worry about without you wandering around the aisles of a *mercado*." Ridley held his hands in a palms-forward gesture. "Stay." He turned and walked quickly across the street.

Azrnoth-zin waited several minutes, adjusted his costume and headgear, then walked the short distance to the market. Passing through the glass door, his nostrils were assaulted by a myriad of strange and exotic odors. Several times, humans looked at him but continued going about their activities. His disguise appeared to be working. Pleased with himself, Azrnoth-zin turned his attention to the multitude of items lining the shelves.

He took some glass jars down off one of the shelves and studied them. Inside were small green cylindrical objects. After a moment or two of trying to figure out how to gain access to the contents of the jars, Azrnoth-zin discovered the screw-top lid. He reached inside and popped one of the jalapeño peppers in his mouth, chewing contemplatively. Suddenly, the alien's eyes grew very wide. In a panic, he looked for something to stop the burning.

On a shelf was a large brown bottle with the encryption "Vanilla" on the front. Azrnoth-zin, a quick study in the opening of jars, uncapped the bottle and put it to his lips, taking a long draught. He coughed and then took another taste. The burning in his mouth was a little better.

When he came to the refrigerated section, he found himself standing before row upon row of slender canisters with brightly colored labels. Reaching inside of the refrigerator, he came out with one of the canisters and eventually figured out how to remove the top. This one was different. A slender nozzle lay under the white plastic lid. Azrnoth-zin studied it, then tried to remove it, but to no avail. He pointed the nozzle at his face, looking down into it, trying to find a release for the contents. Inadvertently, his finger pressure forced the nozzle to one side. A stream of whitish substance erupted from the canister, covering his face in a sickly sweetness. It was just about then when Ridley came around the corner.

"Oh no," Ridley said.

The alien stood in the middle of the floor with whipping cream on his face and half a dozen opened jars and cans gathered at his feet. Regaining his composure, Ridley strode over quickly to where Azrnoth-zin stood.

"I thought I told you to stay with the truck," Ridley said. "What the hell are you doing here, anyway?"

"There are many strange food sources here, Ridley. I am experimenting with the many tastes."

"You can't go around in a store and open packages up without paying for them first." Ridley reached into his back pocket and produced a handkerchief and started wiping the whip cream off the alien's face. "This is not what I call keeping a low profile."

Ridley bent down and began combining the items Azrnoth-zin had picked up with the groceries he had placed in the hand basket. As he was about to stand up a voice behind him spoke.

"Ridley, is that you?"

The voice belonged to a woman.

Ridley spun about and was looking up at Darcy Billings.

"Oh, hello," Ridley stood awkwardly. "Had a little accident here."

"I guess so," said Darcy, a quizzical look on her face. Her gaze shifted to Azrnoth-zin, who was licking the last remnants of the whipping cream off his fingers, then back to Ridley. "What are you doing in San Carlos? Cabo San Lucas is the other direction."

"Well, ah, I had some difficulties after I left you. I hit a rock while traveling at night. Tore the bejabbers out of the bottom of the kayak."

"Who's your friend here?" Darcy said with amusement. "Looks like he crashed into a whip cream truck."

"Oh, this is Mr. Arnold Zinn," Ridley lied. "He was with one of those foreign tour groups and got separated from his party. I'm giving him a ride to Hermosillo to make his connection."

"*Mucho gusto*," said Darcy extending her hand. Azrnoth-zin was about to extend his hand but stopped himself abruptly. He muttered something unintelligible and bowed awkwardly.

"He's not from around here," Ridley said with a shrug. "We've been having a hell of time communicating."

Darcy eyed Azrnoth-zin suspiciously. "Well, good luck finding your people."

"Thank - you - very - much," came the alien's stilted reply. Darcy smiled at the foreigner's attempt at English.

"Yeah, I guess you're not the only one who's had a bad time of it. Ever since that meteor went down the other night, this whole area has been turned upside down by federal agents, both Mexican and American. We had a very unpleasant experience with some feds who wouldn't identify themselves. They ransacked our boat."

"I heard there's a lot of people around asking questions and doing some general bullying," said Ridley.

"If the boat wasn't enough, when Teresa and I got back to our house, we came home to the entire place in shambles."

"Boy. That sucks. Was anything missing?" said Ridley.

"Not as far as I can tell," said Darcy. "They, whoever they are, must have been looking for something specific, but what? I can't help but think that it's all tied in somehow to that meteor."

"That could be. It's not every day -."

Walking in the front door of the *mercado* were two men. Both wore aviator style sunglasses, light field jackets and khaki trousers. Their hawk-like glances around the market gave Ridley all the information he needed.

"Um, Darcy, I need a favor from you," Ridley said, as calmly as he could. "There are two men in the front of the store who want to ask my friend and I some questions. I don't feel very inclined to speak with them right now."

Darcy turned her head slowly and saw the two agents moving around the front check out stands. "What do they want to talk to you about?"

"I don't have time to discuss it now. My favor is this: can you distract them away from the front window long enough for us to reach my truck? This is very important."

"If you would just tell me -."

"*Please*."

"Okay, Ridley. Just tell me this. You didn't kill anyone, did you?"

Ridley cast a hard glance at Azrnoth-zin. "Not yet."

"Slip through those back doors. I'll distract them. As soon as you see them move away from the front of the store window, that's your cue to move."

Ridley nodded. "Thanks, Darcy. I owe you one."

Darcy smiled at Ridley. "No. That makes us even. Sometime, though, I'd like an explanation."

As Ridley and Azrnoth-zin turned toward the back door, Darcy whispered loudly, "Hey! What about all this stuff?"

Ridley shrugged. "Enjoy. I'm not crazy about *habañero* chilies." They disappeared behind the set of swinging green doors.

Darcy spread the items on the floor and sprawled out on the tiles. Waiting for a full minute, she took a deep breath and began yelling at the top of her lungs. "Help! Help! Someone please help me!"

As she had hoped, the two agents came sprinting around one of the aisles and saw her.

"Please, you must help me! A man grabbed my purse and took off through those doors. I think he's going out the back door. You have to help me get it back!"

One of the agents stopped briefly, and then ran through the double doors. The other knelt down beside Darcy.

"Are you all right, miss?" he said. "Are you hurt anywhere?"

"I don't think so," Darcy said, feigning anger. "One minute I'm about to pick up a liter of milk and the next I'm on the floor."

"Can you describe him?"

"I never even saw his face. All I remember seeing was the back of his tank top. It said something about Harley Davidson motorcycles. He was a heavy-set guy and I think he had on plaid shorts. I think he was an American. Dammit! He got all this month's rent money not to mention my credit cards and license. I hope your friend is quick on his feet."

By now, a small crowd had gathered around Darcy and the agent. She was hoping the agents would leave so she could pay for the damages and get out of the store without further incident. The agent in pursuit returned, out of breath and sweating profusely.

"Any luck?" said the agent kneeling next to Darcy.

The other agent shook his head and was finally able to gasp, "No…never…saw him. And I ran down…several alleys. He is one fast thief."

The kneeling agent eyed Darcy suspiciously. "Are you sure of your description of this character?"

"I - I think so," said Darcy. "It happened so fast, but I'm pretty sure of what I saw."

"Well, then he must be one of the fastest fat people around these parts," said the breathless agent. "Do you need some help up?"

"No. No, thank you. I think I can manage." Darcy stood up, slowly brushing herself off. Thanks for trying, anyway."

"I suggest you contact the local authorities as soon as possible regarding your loss," said the agent who had attended her. "Good luck."

With that, they turned and headed for the front door. Darcy looked around sheepishly at the now dispersing crowd. It was going to be a while before she would feel comfortable entering this store again. She hoped she had given Ridley enough time to make his break. Next time she saw him, if there was a next time, he was going to come clean.

Outside, Ridley peered around the corner of the front of the store until he saw the agents move toward the back of the store. He and Azrnoth-zin walked quickly across the street, got into the truck and pulled out onto the highway before they were noticed.

Ten miles down the road, after Ridley was sure they weren't being followed, he looked over at Azrnoth-zin.

"That was not cool back there," he said. "You were almost a lab rat before we even got out of San Carlos. Next time you pull something like that, I'll turn you in myself."

It was several moments before the alien spoke. "I am sorry, Ridley. I know you are placing yourself in great danger to assist me. But I must learn as much as I can about your world before I leave it. After meeting with the Seris yesterday, I have many unanswered questions."

"Like what kind of questions?"

"It is most disturbing that those people have an oral record of my people being here before. No where in our history is there any reference to earth or the Seris. I do not understand this series of events."

"Could earth be one of the planets that was a forgotten chapter in your history?" Ridley said.

"That is highly unlikely," said Azrnoth-zin. "As explorers, we create vast systems of information on every new world we encounter. A planet as richly diverse as earth would not be overlooked in the annals of Delfinian exploration."

"Yeah, I know. So many planets, so little time."

The alien gave Ridley an odd look and turned back to staring out the windshield.

Ridley turned his thoughts inward for a time as well. He thought back to the second encounter with the marine biologist. *If Darcy hadn't happened along when she did,* he thought, *Azrnoth-zin would be on his way to some clandestine destination, probably to be subjected to endless testing in a government laboratory. And me? Well, who knows? If Jenks has anything to say about it, I may just wind up being another face on the back of a milk carton.*

What was it that Azrnoth-zin had said? That Jenks had the mental fingerprint of someone who enjoys killing for killing's sake.

Ridley decided two things at that moment: first he would look up Darcy Billings the next time he was back down here; second, he would make it a point to avoid Richard Jenks.

"Hey, Arn," Ridley said, breaking the silence. "I have an idea. Maybe if you tell your people that we are somehow connected to the Delfinians, they'd help us out when the Trochinids come to turn us into Alpo."

The alien turned slowly toward the human, staring through the darkened Ray Bans. He turned his gaze back to the road.

"You know, there are several groups of people on earth that have been around a very long time," continued Ridley. "Besides the Seris, there's the Aboriginal people of Australia. They've been around for fifty thousand years. Perhaps you should have a conversation with them before you leave."

"I do not think I should discuss this matter further with an off-worlder. There are strong edicts among the Delfinians concerning the discussion of our history with other species."

Ridley slammed on the brakes, causing the truck to fishtail around and almost spin out in the dirt. Azrnoth-zin lurched forward, barely missing the dashboard with his head.

"Goddammit! I want some straight answers from you or this truck stays here. I'm risking my neck to get your sorry ass out of Mexico and all you do is tell me half-baked stories of Armageddon and go on and on about how superior you Delfinians are."

Azrnoth-zin stared at Ridley, momentarily taken aback by the forcefulness of the human's dialogue. He turned back and shifted his gaze down the shimmering ribbon of blacktop, a great sigh registering from his chest.

"We Delfinians believe it is a violation of our laws of exploration to contaminate alien species who do not possess the same level of technology. By doing so, we interfere with the natural progression of events that the society must endure on its own." He paused for a moment. "I violated those rules when I crash landed on your planet."

"You couldn't help that. It was a legitimate mistake," said Ridley.

"You do not understand. I was not supposed to be in this sector of space."

"What do you mean, you -?" Ridley's mouth dropped open as the realization sunk in. "You deserted your fleet. That's why you're so far off course. That's why you stumbled onto planet earth. You really had no idea we were here, did you?"

"That is also the reason I cannot help you," said Azrnoth-zin. "I have committed the ultimate crime in Delfinian society. When I return to my people, I will be punished severely. If I am fortunate, I will be put to death. In all probability, I will be shunned and stripped of my thought processes. No other Delfinian will be allowed to hear my spoken or unspoken thoughts. I prefer the first alternative."

"That's a pretty hefty penalty. What made you leave?"

Azrnoth-zin looked down at his hands, flexing the long delicate fingers. "I do not remember a time of peace in my lifetime. From the time of my childhood, I have known nothing but death and destruction. All of the people I was close to, my mother and father, siblings, friends from the Institute of Defense and Sciences. All are gone. They were casualties of the Great War, the endless war. There was a time, a brief moment in time that I experienced the closest thing to happiness any Delfinian can. It was when I chose Resar-dan for my mate. She too, was a warrior and a star fighter commander. We talked of leaving together, trying to hide among the countless systems for as long as we could avoid detection. She was to fly one more mission and then we were to make our escape. Her attack group was ambushed by a Trochinid battle squadron. I was told she died bravely and quickly." The alien turned back toward Ridley. "You see now why I must go back."

"Not much of a choice the way I see it," said Ridley.

"I must not let Delfinian technology get into the hands of those who pursue us," said Azrnoth-zin. "I fear it will be used against your people."

"Well, whoever is bankrolling that operation apparently isn't worried about the cost of bringing you in."

"I must transmit another signal, Ridley. The sooner I leave your planet, the better it will be for you and the others of earth."

"Okay, but I think we'll get out of Mexico first. I'll feel a little more comfortable if we can put some distance between Jenks and his band of sphincter boys."

Ridley eased the truck back out on the highway and was soon cruising northward at seventy miles an hour.

They traveled in silence each swept up into their own thoughts. The afternoon passed and the shadows grew long over the September desert. Ridley hoped to reach the border by dusk, barring any further incidents. His mind was full of questions, things he wanted to ask the alien. How had they solved the problem of intergalactic travel? Were there any diseases on Delfinus? What were other alien species like? Any one of these questions set Ridley's mind to spinning. He thought of Azrnoth-zin and what drove him to leave his people, to travel such a great distance across the galaxy.

Outside of Santa Ana, they were stopped by a group of Mexican *federales* dressed in camouflage and hefting automatic rifles. Most of them did not look much older than sixteen. After detaining the truck for a few moments, taking time to see Ridley's drivers license and visa, they let Ridley and Azrnoth-zin pass through.

"They're getting younger all the time," Ridley said as he carefully brought the truck up to speed. "But once again, I think the universe is on our side."

"Why do you say that?" said Azrnoth-zin.

"Because, they let us pass. Apparently, word has not gotten out yet. They took us for just another couple of grungy *gringos* making our way back to the states. I don't want to jinx this party, but I'm actually beginning to think we're going to get you out of Mexico."

They arrived at the border in Nogales after dark, the traffic gradually increasing, the pace slowing as they approached the international border. Soon, all Ridley could do was to inch along at a snail's pace as the cars attempted to merge from the side streets. Throngs of people were out on the sidewalks. The city came alive after dark. Azrnoth-zin focused his attention on all of the sights and sounds of the busy border town. He took particular interest in the roadside stands, where the smell of tacos, *birria*, and cooked chilies floated on the night breeze.

"Come on, come on," Ridley said anxiously, tapping his foot.

Finally, Ridley could see the illuminated white arches that defined the border. When he got within twenty yards, he saw an armed guard and a dog tethered on a leash stationed at every booth. Ridley had never seen such a concentration of *federales* at the border before. While the cars were waiting to cross over, an officer and a dog would move out among the cars, the dog sniffing as they went. Ridley hoped the alien's body chemistry wouldn't draw the dog's attention. As far as he knew, there were no space alien sniffing dogs in use.

The passenger van in front of them was waved through and proceeded to the American side where it stopped. Ridley was next. When the light changed to green signaling for him to move ahead, Ridley drew a deep breath and inched the truck forward.

"One more time, please," he said under his breath.

"Both U.S. citizens?" inquired the border agent.

"Yes, sir," said Ridley. He hoped the customs agent would not notice that Azrnoth-zin still had his sunglasses on.

"Where are you coming from?"

"San Carlos," said Azrnoth-zin, in almost perfect diction. Ridley shot him a glance.

"We were down there at the Club Med," continued Ridley. "Always wanted to check it out."

The agent leaned down and peered in the window. "Got any plants, animal by-products, liquor, or pharmaceuticals that you purchased in Mexico."

"No, sir," said Ridley. "Just a couple of tee-shirts we bought at the resort."

The agent went to the back of the truck, taking note of Ridley's license plate. He returned to the booth and punched in the numbers. The seconds it took to come up on the screen seemed like an eternity. The agent pulled on his mustache and entered something into the computer.

"Sure are a lot of agents and dogs as you come across," said Ridley, trying to sound nonchalant. "What's the occasion?"

The agent looked over his glasses at Ridley. "Someone received an anonymous tip earlier to be on the lookout for two individuals who may be trying to traffic illegal contraband through this checkpoint. I don't think it's going to happen here." The agent turned back to the computer as the reading came back to him. "Okay, gentlemen, you can pass. Please drive safely on your way home."

"Thank you, sir. We will." Ridley pulled the truck slowly and merged with the traffic moving up the four-lane street of Nogales, Arizona. Just to be on the safe side, he opted to take the old Nogales Highway instead of the heavily traveled Interstate 19. When he came to the exit, Ridley took the off-ramp and followed the worn, two-lane road into the darkness.

Ridley breathed easier. He suddenly realized he was very hungry and his stomach was not about to let him forget it. He looked over to Azrnoth-zin who had removed the sunglasses at last, his eyes reflecting deep blue from the dashboard lights.

"I think I could eat a picture of the Last Supper," Ridley said. "Are you hungry?"

Azrnoth-zin turned to him. "Yes, Ridley. I would like to take nourishment."

"Arnie, I think it's about time to introduce you to one of earth's greatest pleasures. This is the stuff that will make intergalactic travelers go light years out of their way."

"What is this food source?" the alien asked, his interest obviously piqued.

"About twenty minutes from here, there's a little Mexican restaurant that has the best chicken enchiladas and molé in the world, probably in the entire universe. I always make it a point to stop there when I come back home."

"The universe is infinite. Will it taste like the food in the cave?"

"Hell, no. It will be similar to Maria's cooking, only spicier. You have to try it to believe it."

"That is good, then," said Azrnoth-zin. "I was not looking forward to experiencing your cooking skills again."

Ridley shook his head. "From what I've seen, if the rest of your species has the same taste in foods as you, then I may just enlist as the first gourmet chef in space."

The burly customs agent checked his watch. Only thirty more minutes to go before shift change. It had been an unusually busy, yet uneventful night. The traffic coming through the border did not appear to be letting up much. After he spoke with the owners of a Jeep Cherokee, a family on their way back to Phoenix, he went to the rear of the vehicle to perform the standard check on the plates. As he waved them through, the telephone inside of his booth started to ring. He motioned for the next vehicle to stay while he went for the phone.

"This is Ellis. Can you give me that description again? Okay. License number? Well, nobody with a kayak on top of a white Toyota pickup has gone through this checkpoint. I'm running the plates now. Hold on...Damn! The vehicle, 1990 white Toyota, license GTC 344 passed through here not twenty minutes ago. Yes, there were two males in the truck. Nothing significant except one kept his sunglasses on the whole time. No. They merged with traffic heading toward the interstate. What are they suspected of?" The agent held the phone away from his ear as if it had been seared. "Yes, sir. I'll take care of it right away." He replaced the phone back onto its cradle and wondered why his supervisor had gone off on him like that.

Within minutes, every law enforcement officer from the border to Tucson had been notified to be on the lookout for a white Toyota pickup carrying two males, possibly dangerous, wanted by federal authorities for questioning. It was to be the largest manhunt ever mobilized in Arizona history since the search for Geronimo and it had begun in earnest.

CHAPTER TWENTY-TWO

Richard Jenks stared at the phone sitting on the desk in the makeshift command station in San Carlos, Sonora, Mexico. Next to it lay a thick folder that had the words "Cooper M. Ridley," and underneath the word "confidential" stamped across the front of it.

His last conversation with Number One had not gone well. Five minutes ago, he received confirmation that a white Toyota pickup registered to Ridley had passed through the international checkpoint in Nogales at 7:14 PM. Of all the dumb luck. Ridley and the alien were just half a step faster than the dragnet that was attempting to encircle them. The Toyota had made it past the two federale checkpoints and then slipped by the customs agent at the border. A tip that Ridley was seen in a *mercado* in San Carlos turned out to be dead end. And now, Ridley and the alien were somewhere in southern Arizona.

Jenks picked up the phone and punched in a series of numerical codes. He heard the familiar scrambling over the line and then a click. A soft-spoken male voice with a definitive southern drawl came on the line.

"What do you have for me, Number Two?"

Jenks cleared his throat. "Sir, they slipped through the net. I just received word that they passed through the border at Nogales at 7:14 this evening."

A painful silence ensued. "That is most unfortunate, Number Two," said the voice. "Covert operations are much more hazardous in our own back yard. Twice now, this Ridley has eluded you and your task force. You told me he is not a factor in this equation. Perhaps you have underestimated him. Perhaps I have overestimated your capabilities."

"Sir, I assure you. Ridley has just been lucky up to now. We have established a major dragnet across all of southern Arizona. As we speak, various branches of law enforcement at our disposal are bottling up every highway and side road from Nogales to Tucson. We'll catch them, sir. You have my word on it."

"Please do not disappoint me again, Number Two."

"Did you get the bio on Ridley?" Jenks said, hoping to avoid any further browbeating.

"I have received the dossier on Mr. Ridley," said Number One. "And I have reviewed it. I find it most interesting that you and Mr. Ridley have a certain history. Hmmm. Let me see..."

Jenks could hear momentary shuffling of papers on the other end of the line.

"Cooper Mathias Ridley, born November 23, 1982. Father, Benjamin J. Ridley, captain, marine pilot killed in Gulf War of 1991, flying covert mission over Baghdad. I remember him. War hero. Very charismatic. Mother, Janice, died of ovarian cancer in 1989. Ridley raised by uncle and aunt, Jacob and Marjorie Holtzman of Three Points, Arizona. I see they have a substantial ranch there, raising cattle and some strange breed of horses of Spanish descent. I assume you are sending personnel to pay a visit to Mr. Ridley's relatives, Number Two?"

"They're on their way there now, sir. A chopper is sitting out on the tarmac, fueled and ready to go. I will be personally overseeing the visit."

"Good. I expected no less. It seems our young friend has led somewhat of a ne'er-do-well existence since his untimely dismissal from the Navy. He has worked on and off for Greenpeace and the Sea Shepherd. A bona fide tree hugger. His psych profile reveals an intelligent, non-conformist persona. It says here he is three credits shy of a college degree. All throughout his file, he shows a distinct contempt for authority."

"That's Ridley, all right. He took a section eight over striking a superior officer and losing a couple of dolphins he was training in Special Projects. Definitely unstable. Unfortunately for me, I was the supervisor for that project."

"Ah. Now I remember. Be careful in your estimation of him, Number Two. Apparently, Ridley likes to side with the downtrodden. He may have taken on hiding this visitor as a personal mission. Since he is a sympathizer for the underdog, we may be able to capitalize on his emotional ties to the remainder of his family."

Roberson stuck his head inside the door and mouthed, "Ready."

"I understand, sir," Jenks said, nodding to Roberson. "I'll have men posted on the Holtzman property tonight and we will pay them a visit first thing in the morning."

"Keep me informed, Number Two. Ridley has an asset we cannot afford to lose. I don't want to have to call up some old favors if I don't have to, but with the proper amounts of leverage to some of my esteemed colleagues on the hill, any and all resources and manpower will be at your disposal."

"Thank you, Number One. I know with this amount of support, we won't fail in our mission."

"The arm of the Phoenix Project reaches into a great many pockets," said the voice, and the line disconnected.

Jenks replaced the phone on its cradle, gathered up the papers strewn about the desk, and stuffed them in his briefcase. He met Roberson in the hall and the two men strode quickly outside toward the waiting helicopter.

"I want constant communication from the first surveillance team at the Holtzman place. Anything or anyone that goes in or out I want to know about it stat," Jenks said, climbing into the helicopter.

"It's going to take another hour before we can get a tap on their phone line," said Roberson. "Hopefully, our targets have not communicated with the Holtzmans as of yet."

"Get that tap established in the next thirty minutes," Jenks said. "I don't want any more screw ups from here on."

Roberson could tell from the tone in Jenk's voice that mistakes from here on were going to be a career, if not a life threatening mistake.

"I'll make it happen, boss," Roberson said assuredly.

"Start a data search. Get me names and addresses of Ridley's recent contacts. We have the manpower at our disposal, so any former girlfriends, co-workers, acquaintances, enemies - put a tail on them until he makes his next move. He's going to have to surface sometime."

Roberson was already on the phone and speaking loudly over the helicopter noise. Jenks settled into the chair, strapped himself in, and began to contemplate how he was going to handle the interrogation of the Holtzmans.

CHAPTER TWENTY-THREE

Ridley pushed the empty plate away and drained the last of his *Dos Equis* beer. He looked across the table at Azrnoth-zin and shook his head in wonder. The alien was wiping up the last of what was earlier a very substantial plate of chicken enchiladas, beans and rice. It was the alien's second order of food. Five empty beer bottles stood between Ridley and Azrnoth-zin.

"You know, you may want to be careful about the food," said Ridley, stifling a belch. "This stuff has been known to come back on you with a vengeance later on."

Azrnoth-zin appeared to be in a trance, his eyelids half closed behind the Ray Bans, his mouth moving slowly and rhythmically, savoring every nuance of spice.

"Ridley, never before have I experienced such a sensation of tastes. Your people may be technologically backward, but your foods are unparalleled." He reached over and took another generous spoonful of salsa and mixed it with the unrecognizable array on his plate. Azrnoth-zin then placed the mouth of the beer bottle to his lips and tipped his head back. He set the empty bottle next to the others.

"This beverage, beer you call it?"

Ridley nodded.

"It is most refreshing."

"You're not feeling anything yet?" Ridley asked.

"What should I be feeling?"

"Well, you should - never mind." Ridley looked around the large dining room, empty except for a white-haired foursome in the booth across the room and two bearded men wearing motorcycle leathers sitting at the bar. Ridley was glad they came through on a Tuesday night. The waitress, a stocky, middle-aged woman who looked like she wanted to be anywhere else besides slinging *chimichangas* to the Green Valley crowd and road derelicts, was looking bored standing at one corner of the bar.

Ridley took his wallet out of his back pocket and peered into it. "This is not good," he said, sliding out of the booth and standing next to the table. "I need to contact some people. We're running dangerously short of cash and if you keep up your present pace, I'm going to have to sell my truck."

"What is cash, Ridley?"

"Oh. Sorry. It's a means of exchange we use here on earth to barter goods and services. There are many forms and denominations the world over. Presently, the U.S. Dollar is the third most stable currency, last time I heard. Unfortunately, my cash flow is not very stable at the moment and I need to call ahead for replenishment." Ridley looked at the mass of destruction on the table. "Do you want anything else?"

"I would like another one of these," Azrnoth-zin said, holding up the empty *Dos Equis* bottle.

"Now I know where black holes come from," Ridley said. "Do not, I repeat, do not venture from this table until I get back. Are we together on this one?"

The alien nodded solemnly. *"Mas cerveza, por favor."*

Ridley walked to the back of the restaurant toward the phones and rest rooms. On the way, he stopped by the waitress station and ordered another beer for Azrnoth-zin. Ridley checked his watch. It was almost 9:00. He hoped Jake and Marjorie weren't in bed yet. After Jake's minor stroke last year, the old man had definitely slowed down.

"Hello?"

Ridley recognized his Aunt Marjorie's voice. There was an odd click that occurred just as the receiver was picked up.

"Hi, Marjorie, it's Cooper. I hope I didn't wake you or Jake."

"Cooper? Where are you? Did you run into trouble during your trip?"

"No, nothing like that. Something else came up, that's all. I'm fine. How are you and Jake doing?"

Oh, we're fine on this end." Ridley could hear Marjorie moving away from the receiver and yell, "Jake, it's Cooper. Can you pick up in the bedroom?"

"How ya doin', son?" came the gravelly voice of Jake Holtzman, seventy-six year old rancher.

"I'm good, Jake. How are you?"

"Fine, fine. As long as I stay away from those goddamn doctors, my life's a walk on the beach. So, speaking of the beach, I guess Mexico didn't pan out the way you had hoped, eh?"

"Let's just say that something else needs my attention right now. Jake and Marjorie, I need a favor from you," Ridley said.

"What's wrong?" said Marjorie.

"Nothing's wrong," Ridley lied. "Look, there's a possibility that some men will be coming around, asking questions. They may conjure up some stories about me being in some sort of trouble with the federal government and wanting to locate me. It's just a ruse. Don't believe them. Tell them you haven't seen me since I left for Mexico two weeks ago."

"Are you in some sort of trouble, son?" said Jake.

"It's not what you think, Jake. I need to keep a low profile for a few days, then I'll explain the whole thing to you both."

"Is there anything we can do?" said Marjorie.

"I'm running a little short on cash," said Ridley. "There's about four hundred dollars in a coffee can in the back of the closet in the bunkhouse. I'm going to need the spare sleeping bag and several changes of clothes, including a couple of sweaters or light jackets."

"Consider it done," said Jake. "How do we get it to you?"

"I'll contact you in the morning. We'll set up a meeting place and have Carlos bring it."

"Are you sure that's it?" said Marjorie. "We're worried about you, Coop."

"Everything's fine," said Ridley. "Please don't worry about me. You both know - better than anyone else - that I wouldn't get involved in any kind of nonsense. If these men come around, be careful. I know one of them. He's not one of the good guys."

"We'll take care of our end of things here," said Jake. "You just keep out of trouble, you hear?"

"Loud and clear. I'll talk to you in the morning. Thanks to both of you."

"Take care of yourself, Cooper," said Marjorie.

Ridley hung up the phone and walked back to the booth where Azrnoth-zin was sitting, finishing off the last of his beer. Ridley slid into the other side and picked up the check the waitress had left. He winced when he read the total. Reaching into his wallet, Ridley laid the bills on the check and pushed it to the edge of the table. His attention was drawn to two couples who moved into the booth behind Azrnoth-zin. They both appeared to be in their late thirties or early forties.

"I thought we'd never get here," said the blonde woman, who sat directly behind the alien.

"I can't believe the search they were doing at the border," said the brunette opposite her. "They were tearing everyone's cars apart."

"Did you ever get any explanation?" said the man next to her.

"Just that they were looking for two fugitives who might be dangerous," said the man next to the blonde. "Whatever was going on, those guys at the border looked like they weren't to be messed with."

Ridley looked at Azrnoth-zin and motioned toward the door. As he slid out of the booth, a bizarre, high-pitched sound filled the room. Suddenly, light fixtures exploded in showers of sparks, the bulbs popping all around the dining room, plunging the restaurant into total darkness. The Wurlitzer jukebox in the corner sputtered and shorted out. One of the elderly ladies in the corner shrieked.

The man at the next table said, "What the hell…?"

Ridley felt Azrnoth-zin ushering him forcefully toward the door. A strange buzzing sound seemed to be coming out of the walls. Ridley felt like he was in the epicenter of the vibrating sensation. He realized the sound was emanating from inside Azrnoth-zin's backpack. Just as quickly as it had started, the humming ceased.

Outside the restaurant, Ridley said, "Was that your way of skipping out on the check?"

"I have just received a sub-space signal from my people," said Azrnoth-zin. "We must find a place to set up the array and to receive the complete transmission. I will need to transmit my location and await instructions."

"That message blew all the circuits in that restaurant," Ridley said. "That gives a whole new meaning to "E.T., phone home"."

"It is necessary that we find a location where there will be no interference from electrical, microwave or radio transmissions," said the alien.

"Looks like we're camping out for the night," said Ridley, as he started up the truck. "I think I've got a place that may suit our needs."

They followed the access road for several miles, then turned off on a little used dirt road that would lead them to the base of the Santa Rita Mountains. It had been several years since Ridley had explored these back roads and at night, he had no familiar landmarks to guide him. Two hours and three wrong turns later, they emerged on the backside of the Santa Rita Mountains. Ridley found the turnoff for Gardner Canyon and soon they had passed the last ranch fence and were on national forest land.

The harvest moon, glowing large and luminous orange-yellow, cast a silvery sheen on the trunks of the sycamores and cottonwoods, creating circles of dappled light on the ground. There was a chill to the air, the first hint of winter's embrace in the mountains. *Tonight might not be a bad night to sleep in the back of the camper*, Ridley thought.

Ridley walked on a carpet of fallen leaves that swished with each step. He carried an armload of dried branches and approached the small fire. Azrnoth-zin was off to one side of the fire, hunched over something, his head cocked in an attentive posture. Nearing the fire, Ridley felt the hairs on his arms and the back of his neck begin to tingle. The humming sound grew louder. Ridley felt the firewood vibrating in his arms and dropped the load when he thought the branches would vibrate from his grip. He approached Azrnoth-zin and hunched down several feet from the alien and watched.

Azrnoth-zin was kneeling before an oddly shaped metallic device. Attached to it was the horseshoe that Ridley had used on the alien to treat his injuries in the cave. The display on the device was lit up, humming with a strange resonance. Azrnoth-zin's face was highlighted by the glow of the campfire as he concentrated on the device. Suddenly the humming ceased and the device went dark.

"Did you contact your people?" Ridley said when he felt sure the transmission was over.

"Yes," said Azrnoth-zin. "A ship will come in five of your planet's rotations. I have received the coordinates where they will meet me. It is…in that direction." The alien pointed toward the southwest.

"That direction? That could be from here to California or any place in Mexico for all we know."

"If I could study some of your charts of this region of earth, I could extrapolate the coordinates where I will need to be."

"Okay," said Ridley. "First chance we get tomorrow, we'll pick up some topo maps and give them a going over. Maybe I can help you by explaining the meridian lines by which we plot points on our maps."

"That would be most helpful, Ridley. Thank you."

Ridley shivered slightly. "It's going to get cold tonight. Probably down into the thirties. "We only have one sleeping bag. You take it. I'll use the emergency survival blanket."

"I could deploy the personal force field," said Azrnoth-zin. "It can be adjusted to a constant temperature."

"Better not, Arnie," Ridley said, turning his head to listen to some twigs snapping somewhere off in the darkness. "Hmm…Raccoons, I'd bet. No, it's better if we keep the high tech gadgetry to a minimum right now. Besides, the inside of the truck is a good buffer against the cold - just a little cramped, that's all." Ridley stood up, walked to the back of the truck and opened up the camper. After several minutes of rummaging, he located two warm bottles of Pacifico beer that were left in the ice chest. Walking back to the fire, Ridley opened the bottles with his Swiss Army knife. The alien was staring into the campfire when Ridley thrust the bottle in front of him.

"I just remembered I had these in the ice chest. Sorry they're not cold, but given the circumstances they'll still probably taste just fine."

They drank without speaking, each turned inward to their own thoughts as they stared into the flames. It was Azrnoth-zin who finally broke the silence.

"It is strange. Tonight, I have been thinking of Resar-dan more than I normally allow myself to. I do not know why these thoughts are so strong here. Perhaps, it is because I am a very long way from my people."

"I'm sorry to hear about your mate," said Ridley. "She must have been one special lady."

"She was..." The alien never finished the sentence. A troubled look darkened Azrnoth-zin's face, like nothing Ridley had witnessed there before. Ridley felt awkward. He didn't have the words to console the visitor.

Ridley held the beer bottle up and clinked it to Azrnoth-zin's. "Here's to Resar-dan."

"To Resar-dan," Azrnoth-zin said, comprehending the meaning of the gesture. They both took a long drink from the bottles.

"Do you have a mate, Ridley?"

Ridley squinted at the night sky as if he were hoping for some illumination. "I was married once. For about five years. She too, was a one-of-a-kind woman. I screwed it up. Because I couldn't or didn't know how to be truly intimate and tell her what went on in my head, she found it impossible to live with me. I had few bad years where I put her through hell. I was doing too much of this." He indicated the nearly empty beer bottle. "Only a lot stronger and more poisonous. I got word she remarried last month. To a nice, stable guy. Insurance broker, I think. I guess that's part of the reason I was in Mexico when I was."

Azrnoth-zin drank down the last of his beer. "Interesting. We were both running away from something when our paths collided."

Ridley smiled. "Yeah, but you get the prize for coming the longest distance."

The alien's face contorted into a facial gesture Ridley didn't recognize. He realized the alien was trying to smile.

"Ridley, sometimes I find you to be an amusing human."

"Well, I'll take that as a compliment."

Azrnoth-zin turned back toward the fire. "Will we go back to Mexico tomorrow?"

"Judging by what those people back in Velasquez's were saying, I think it would be a good idea to stay away from Mexico for a few days. At least until things cool off. If they didn't pick up our trail yet, we have to find a place to lay low for a few days and figure out exactly where the rendezvous point is. Before we can go anywhere, I need to get some money and provisions to tide us over. These friends of mine live about an hour and a half from here."

"What will happen to you after I leave, Ridley?"

"Oh, I don't know. I think Jenks and his gang of chuckleheads will lose interest after you can't be found. I doubt they'd have much use for me. Hey! Maybe I can go on the talk show circuit and tell the world about my own personal close encounter of the third kind."

"Ridley, I am coming to understand the English language better with each passing day, but there are word combinations in your vocabulary that do not translate."

Ridley rolled his eyes. "Sorry, Arnie. Some of the stuff that comes out of my mouth you don't want to learn. Stick with the direct translations for now."

They were silent again for a time. Finally, Ridley stood up and stretched. "Well, I'm about done in. I think I could use two or three days of uninterrupted sleep. But I'll have to settle for six hours. I'll see you in the morning." Ridley turned to walk toward the camper when he heard Azrnoth-zin in a low voice say, "Ridley."

He turned and lifted his chin toward the alien.

"I do not know if it will be of any benefit to earth or not, but I will speak to the Water Council when I return."

"Thanks, Arn. I can't speak for eight billion others, but I do appreciate it."

CHAPTER TWENTY-FOUR

Jake Holtzman saw the dust forming over the low hills before the cars came into view. He was down by the corral where Carlos, the foreman, was separating out the choice brood mares. After the stroke last year, Jake's lack of balance and decreased reaction times prohibited him from participating in his favorite of ranching duties. He leaned on the cane and tried to see how far off the vehicles were.

"We got company, Carlos," Jake shouted. "Better come out of there."

Carlos came running up to the fence and looked in the direction Jake was pointing. Carlos had been working for the Holtzman's for seventeen years. He and Ridley had practically grown up together and were like brothers. Carlos had moved his family up to the ranch on Jake's and Marjorie's urgings. Now, three generations of the Hernandez family lived and worked on the twenty thousand acre ranch.

"Is it the men Ridley warned us about, *Señor* Jake?" Carlos said, dusting off his hat.

"I reckon so. I can't think of anyone else coming out here this early in the morning," said the old rancher. "You'd better make yourself scarce for a while, son. Get your mother and aunt out to the line shack for a spell."

"Okay. Are you sure you will be all right?"

"I'll be fine. Dammit. I sure wish you would go ahead and get naturalized so we wouldn't have to go through this nonsense every time some bureaucrat comes poking around."

"You keep me too busy, *Señor*," Carlos said with a laugh. "I have no time to study for the test."

The old man smiled. "You're not going to be able to use that excuse much longer. Now get going. The missus and I will be all right."

Carlos ducked under the corral and disappeared around the corner of the bunkhouse which served as Ridley's quarters when he was home. Jake hobbled up to the sprawling ranch style house and sat in his favorite old rocker on the porch. Marjorie came outside, removing her apron from breakfast.

Jake nodded toward the three black sedans now visible, churning up the dusty road a mile away.

"Looks like we're about to get paid a visit from some officious types," he said.

"Are these the ones looking for Cooper?"

"Who else. Who else would be stupid enough to be driving black Lincolns on that road." Jake continued rocking, as if he were watching a late afternoon monsoon rolling across the valley.

The three vehicles pulled up in front of the house on a cloud of dust, causing the horses in the corral to become agitated. Almost simultaneously, the doors of the cars opened and a small armada of men poured out.

"Jacob Holtzman?" said the large man walking toward the porch. He had crewcut blonde hair and wore aviator glasses.

"You're looking at him. Who wants to know?"

"Special agent Jenks. Department of Internal Security. We have a warrant out for one Cooper Ridley. We understand he uses this place as a residence."

"I can't recall ever hearing of the Department of Internal Security," Jake said.

"There are branches of the government that most people know nothing about." Jenks quickly flashed his I.D. and slipped it back into his pocket. "Have you seen Mr. Ridley?"

"Last time I spoke with him, he was headin' to Mexico. That was over two weeks ago."

Jenks stopped at the base of the porch steps, sighed, and then walked slowly toward Jake and Marjorie. He removed his glasses and wiped them on his shirt sleeve.

"Mr. Holtzman. May I call you Jake?"

"Call me Mr. Holtzman."

"Very well, Mr. Holtzman. I won't waste our time mincing words. We happen to know Ridley is back in the states as of early last evening. We also know that he placed a call to you from a pay phone from Velasquez's Mexican Restaurant. So, I'm afraid you and your wife are guilty of aiding and abetting a known fugitive wanted both here in the states and in Mexico."

Jake Holtzman had stopped rocking. "What, you bastards are tapping my phones now? What is he charged with?"

"Crimes against the state is all you need to know, old man. I am prepared to do whatever it takes to bring this fugitive to justice." Jenks leaned toward Jake and said in a low tone, "Whatever it takes. Do we understand each other?"

Jake began to feel uneasy, realizing this was the one Ridley warned him about.

"I don't know what you want from us," said Jake. "He's not coming back for a while."

"Ah, but you were going to arrange a meeting to supply him with money and clothes. Come on, old man, the conversation was just last night. Surely you can't be that senile."

Jake found himself bristling. It was only the touch of Marjorie's hand on his shoulder that stayed him.

"Mister, he had a stroke last year. You could likely cause him to have another one."

"That would be too bad," Jenks said. "Perhaps if your husband and you were to cooperate, things could go a bit easier for you."

"You won't get any cooperation from either of us," said Jake. "I do not believe for one minute that Cooper is guilty on any of the bullshit charges that you've trumped up. And I don't think you are who you say you are, either. So why don't you and your boys go pound some sand."

Jenks lashed out and backhanded Jake with a powerful slap across the face. Marjorie cried out and Jake slowly turned back to face his assailant, blood oozing from a small split in his lip.

Jenks leaned in close to Jake and said, “I don’t expect you to cooperate for your own sake, but if you want to keep your lovely bride healthy, I suggest you work with us. You don’t have to do much. Just answer the call when Ridley checks in and act like nothing’s wrong. We’ll take care of the rest. Ridley will be treated fairly. You have my word on it.”

“Just leave her out of this,” Jake said. “She doesn’t need to be involved. I’ll help you bring in Ridley.”

“Jake! What are you saying?” Marjorie said. “You can’t turn him in any more than I can.”

“Margie, if Coop’s got himself in a jam, maybe the best thing for him would be to give himself up. We can better help him by providing him good legal counsel than to perpetuate his running away from his responsibilities,” Jake said evenly.

“Jake Holtzman, I thought I knew you better than that. When were you ever intimidated by the likes of these hoodlums?”

“Maybe I’m worried about you!” Jake snapped. “And maybe I’m just plain wore out - I got no fight left in me.”

Tears were welling in Marjorie’s eyes as she turned away from her husband and stared beyond the corrals.

“You made a wise choice, Jake.” Jenks said. “You could be saving Ridley’s life, not to mention allowing both of you to be able to enjoy the rest of your golden years together.”

The old rancher choked back tears of his own. “Tell me what I have to do.”

“Just continue on with your original plan. When Ridley calls, you ask him where, when and how he wants to pick up his supplies and money. Remember, Jake, I’ll be on the other line, so you’d better watch your p’s and q’s. You’d better round up your delivery boy, Carlos, too. That’s his name, isn’t it?”

The phone rang at 8:42. Jake answered it on the second ring.

“Mornin’ Jake, it’s me, Cooper.”

"How you doin', son?" Jake looked at Jenks who gave him the thumbs up sign.

"I'm a little worn around the edges. Could use a hot shower and a shave, but otherwise, life's good. Had any visitors?"

Jake bit his lip. "No, not yet. Nobody's come by."

"That's good. Maybe they won't, then. Did you find the cash and supplies?"

"Right where you said they were. Where do you want Carlos to bring them?"

"I was thinking Sendario wash, near the entrance to the Buenas Aires Reserve. How about two hours from now?"

Sendario wash. Where we stumbled on that rattlesnake den during spring roundup, right?"

"Oh - yeah. Right. I almost forgot about that. You came real close to landing right in the middle of those damn snakes."

"Yeah, damn snakes. Carlos will be there in two hours. You take good care of yourself, son. We love you."

"I'll see you soon, Jake. Thanks a lot." Ridley disconnected.

Jake slowly hung up the phone and then glared at Jenks. Jenks smiled at the aging rancher. "You did real good, old man. Smooth as silk. I'll bet even the missus didn't know you could be such a good liar."

"Nothing better happen to that boy, between now and after you bring him in." Jake's threat rung hollowly in the morning air.

Out of the corner of his eye he caught Marjorie's hard stare and suddenly felt very old.

CHAPTER TWENTY-FIVE

Ridley placed the receiver in the cradle and stared at the black pay phone. Something was wrong. Either Jake had gone batty or else...

Ridley stepped out of the booth and walked back to the truck where Azrnoth-zin stood leaning against the fender. He appeared to be absorbed in observing the traffic at the Circle K in south Tucson. He finished the junk food that Ridley had bought for him. It was the alien's first experience with sugar. Ridley wondered if the strange foods would have any long-term effects on the alien's metabolic functions.

"Were you successful?" said Azrnoth-zin.

"Yeah. I got hold of Jake. At first I thought he was becoming forgetful - mixing up locations and events. I went along with him, trying to humor him. Then I realized he was warning me. They must have the phones bugged. That means they're on to us now."

"What did he say to you?"

"He made a remark about almost landing in a den of rattlers - they're a species of poisonous snake - in Sendario Wash. We never encountered the snakes there. We had that experience up at the summer roundup near Williams. Damn! Snakes, of course. I can't believe I almost missed it."

"What is that?"

"Ever since I can remember, Jake has referred to people of questionable reputation as "snakes." He usually calls them "two-legged snakes." What he was telling me there was more than one agent hanging around. I hope they don't get wise to the tip-off he gave me."

"Ridley, I do not wish harm to come to your people because of me. Perhaps it would better for all if you were to leave me. I have survived on other alien worlds quite well before with much less at my disposal."

Ridley narrowed his gaze at the alien. "But this is earth. A guy could get killed here." He looked around the parking lot as if he expected agents to start popping up. "I don't think Jenks is going to do Jake and Marjorie in. Especially, if we're still at large. I know Jake doesn't want me to come in. I'm more than a little worried that his heart isn't up to all of the stress."

"You should go to them and make sure they will not be harmed," said Azrnoth-zin. "I will make it back to the rendezvous point."

"Right now, you're the only trump card I've got, and I plan on keeping you up my sleeve until it's time for you to go home. I'm betting that Jenks will be on hand to make the trade at Sendario wash. He likes to grab the limelight at any chance."

Azrnoth-zin eyed Ridley suspiciously. "What are you thinking of doing?"

"Oh, I don't know. Maybe just pay a little visit to the ranch. I'm kinda homesick."

"You cannot be thinking of going back there and trying to free your friends. That would be a foolish undertaking."

"If I know Jenks, he'll pull out all the stops to have a big reception waiting for you and me. That's if Jenks bought into the story."

"You are willing to risk your life based on a great deal of conjecture."

"Hell, no one knows the lay of that ranch better than I do. I can get in and out before they even know it. They will be concentrating all of their agents out in Sendario wash."

"You cannot accomplish this task alone, Ridley. I will assist you."

"Forget it, Arnie. If they have you, then they have no reason to keep anyone of us around for posterity. Me, Jake, Marjorie, even the ranch hands. Sorry, *amigo*, but you are to be stashed someplace for a while and you're not to move until I get back or a certain amount of time has elapsed."

Azrnoth-zin bristled, the first time Ridley saw anything resembling anger coming from the visitor. "I come from a proud, warrior race of people. We have never backed down from a battle in 900 years of fighting. At present, I am an outcast, branded as a coward and a deserter. You have repeatedly risked your life to protect me and aid me in getting back to my people. Now, because of me, those close to you are in grave danger. I cannot allow you to do this alone. I will go with you and those are my final words." Azrnoth-zin stared at Ridley with a mixture of defiance and resolve.

"Or what? You gonna mix it up with me?" Ridley said.

"If necessary," said the alien. "But I do not think we have time for activities now other than the immediate one. Besides, I may have some things that will reduce the odds in our favor." He patted the nylon backpack.

Ridley stared at the alien. Then, a slow, crooked smile spread across his lips. "Okay, Arn, you're in. I guess it's back into the snake pit for us."

The agent stood with his back to them, about fifty yards off and semi-concealed against an old mesquite tree. From another angle he would be almost invisible. Ridley sensed movement ahead of the one agent and saw another shift his position near the horse corral. He and Azrnoth-zin were lying against the near bank of a shallow wash that would pass close to the ranch house. They had taken a back road into the property that was not on any of the local maps; he and Jake had cut that road themselves ten years back. The wash was overgrown with palo verde trees, mesquite, and catclaw acacia. Reddish welts were forming on Ridley's and Azrnoth-zin's arms and faces from crawling through the desert undergrowth.

The agent turned toward them, causing Ridley to hunker down even lower. It was then Ridley saw the semi-automatic rifle cradled in the agent's arms.

"Looks like I was right so far," Ridley whispered. "They took most of them to Sendario wash."

"What is your plan, Ridley?"

"Well, I figure to sneak up behind that guy and hit him over the head with a large and heavy object."

Azrnoth-zin looked at Ridley, almost imitating perfectly the squint that Ridley had used so often when he addressed the alien. "You call that a plan?"

"Do you have a better one?"

"Yes. I believe I do. We can neutralize him from here. With this." Azrnoth-zin produced the horseshoe-shaped object from his pack.

"Will it make much noise?" said Ridley.

"A small amount," admitted the alien. "But it reduces our risk considerably. I can adjust the frequency to neutralize both of them."

"Save it, it may come in handy later. Right now we need to be as quiet as possible. Can you take the close one?"

Azrnoth-zin nodded.

"Okay. Meet back up at the corral where the second agent is. Move when I move." Ridley slid down onto the floor of the wash and crawled into the underbrush. The alien waited until he saw Ridley emerge from the wash and squat behind a fallen cottonwood log. Azrnoth-zin pushed over the top of the wash and walked slowly and purposefully toward the agent using whatever cover he could find. He was able to cover the fifty yards quickly.

Meanwhile, Ridley had made it to the far side of the corral and was down on the ground, the horses nearby snorting nervously. Several of them kicked up their hooves, throwing a small cloud of dust into the air. Ridley could see the agent's legs through the slats in the fence. He tightened his grip on the cottonwood branch he held in his right hand.

Looking up, Ridley saw Azrnoth-zin close the final distance between himself and the first agent. Ridley took advantage of the dust cover and moved around the corral, coming out behind the agent.

"Hey," said Ridley softly as he raised the club. The agent wheeled around and Ridley splintered the branch against the side of the agent's head. The agent crumpled like a marionette whose strings had been cut. Ridley looked up to see the alien running toward him, carrying the semi-automatic. The other agent was no longer visible.

"Good plan," Azrnoth-zin said, catching his breath when he reached the corral. "Is this something we can use?" he said, holding up the rifle.

"I don't want to use deadly force if we don't have to," Ridley said. He peered through the slats in the corral toward the house. Two more agents were stationed just outside the door.

"Why can't this be easy?" said Ridley. "If there's two outside, there's at least two inside with Jake and Marjorie."

"How do you know this?" said Azrnoth-zin.

"I know how Jenks thinks. I used to serve under him." Ridley looked at Azrnoth-zin. "I think it may be time to bring out the high tech stuff. Give me seven minutes to get in position on the inside. Then do what you need to do to stop those two on the porch. Can you stop them without killing them?"

"I can adjust the beam on the phase weapon to emit a strong pulse, not deadly, but enough to stun the two on the porch," said Azrnoth-zin.

"I'll follow your lead this time," said Ridley. "After you make your move, I should be in position to get a drop on the two in the house." Ridley drew a deep breath. "God, I hope there's no more than two in there. Be careful, Arn. Nothing fancy, okay?" Ridley patted Azrnoth-zin on the shoulder and disappeared around the corner of the corral.

Ridley was able to cover the distance between the corral and the back of the two-story ranch house without being detected. The rear of the house faced west and was shaded by an old cottonwood tree, whose leaves were just beginning to turn. Ridley had climbed up and down this tree innumerable times as a boy, and found it handy for youthful stealth missions, usually to meet young girls or to sneak out to the barn to smoke some of the "devil weed."

He climbed up the tree and stepped gingerly inside the bedroom window, removing his shoes before he placed his feet on the floor. Ridley stood and listened. The house was quiet, except for the tick-tock of the grandfather clock in the hallway downstairs. Ridley made his way to the doorway and opened it cautiously. The upstairs appeared to be clear. He slid along the wall and moved to a place at the top of the stairs. Peering around the corner, he could see the back of one of the agents, who sat in a chair opposite Jake and Marjorie. Ridley could not see the second agent from this vantage point. He either must be in the kitchen or in the spare room off the living room. Ridley began to inch down the stairway.

Outside, Azrnoth-zin counted off the final seconds and then moved quietly toward the house. In his hand, he held the device, now quietly resonating. The alien removed his sunglasses and stepped into the open. The two agents drew their weapons and almost simultaneously, their mouths dropped open.

"I do not wish to harm you," said Azrnoth-zin, approaching. "Place your weapons on the ground and move away from them."

The sight of the alien and then the brusque command caused the agents to hesitate slightly. Azrnoth-zin activated the phase weapon. A parabolic shock wave emanated from the weapon, hurling the agents backward. One crashed through the picture window. The other was slammed against one of the supports on the porch. The front of the house wavered, then buckled inward, sagging on its framework.

The agent inside was thrown to the floor, momentarily stunned. The shock wave flung Jake and Marjorie back against the sofa as shards of broken glass rained down on them. Suddenly, the other agent came running out of the back room toward the window, gun drawn. Ridley vaulted after him and landed on the agent's back driving him forward. They both hit the front door hard and crashed through it landing on the porch and rolling down the steps into the dirt.

The wind knocked out of him, Ridley lay on the ground gasping for air. He pulled his face out of the dirt long enough to see the agent scrambling for his gun several feet away. Ridley pulled himself up and screamed hoarsely at Azrnoth-zin, "Now!"

"I cannot. You are too close," the alien said.

Ridley summoned all of his remaining strength and lurched after the agent, tackling him around the waist. They both rolled in the dust, legs and arms flailing. Ridley was able to reach the pistol and fling it out of the way. The agent assumed a catlike stance and maneuvered toward Ridley. Suddenly, a silvery flash appeared at the tip of the agent's right shoe. The agent began to circle closer, trying to get within range for the stiletto.

"Shit," said Ridley, moving backward. "Arn!"

"You are still too close!"

The agent lunged at Ridley, his right leg kicking out with great force. Ridley spun and the blade passed within inches of his face. The agent landed, then was on the attack again. He made a thrusting kick with his leg that raked Ridley across his left side, tearing his shirt and grazing his skin.

The agent circled him again, grinning from a dust and blood-flecked face. Ridley's legs and arms felt leaden. The agent crouched to make another deadly parry. Ridley stepped on something. Looking down, he saw that it was part of the front door panel. He reached for it as the agent leaped toward him. The agent's foot came crashing toward Ridley's neck. In one desperate move Ridley brought the panel up. The stiletto and the foot came through the panel just missing Ridley's face.

Now off balance, the agent staggered backward, still attached to the door panel. Ridley was up on his feet, fists hammering at the agent's face. The agent went down on the third punch.

Ridley stood over the downed agent, gasping for breath. Looking askance at the alien, he said, "Thanks for the help."

"You appeared to be doing well," Azrnoth-zin replied. "At this distance, I may have severely damaged you both."

"You just about destroyed the house and everything in it. That was supposed to be the stun mode?"

"It may require some recalibration. The moisture from the cave may have affected its internal matrix."

"So much for high - ".

"Look out!" Jake yelled from inside. The agent stepped outside, his gun pointed at Ridley's head. Ridley looked down the muzzle of the pistol and in that microsecond, knew the agent was going to pull the trigger.

A flash occurred. Ridley thought the gun had misfired. The agent disappeared in a hot glowing light, leaving behind the smell of ozone. Ridley looked over at a grim-faced Azrnoth-zin who was still holding the device pointed toward where the agent stood seconds ago. Ridley looked back toward the porch. A faint outline against the wall traced the figure of the crouching agent.

"What the hell was that?" Ridley said, stunned by the quickness of the death. He looked back and forth between the alien and where the agent used to be.

Azrnoth-zin stared at the weapon in his hand. "Now, I am truly dead to my people."

"Holy Mary, sweet mother of Jesus," came Jake's voice from the porch. He and Marjorie had stumbled out from the ruined front room and were staring wide-eyed at Azrnoth-zin.

"He…he…just vanished," Marjorie stammered.

"Who in the hell…What are you?" said Jake, still dazed from the events of the last minutes.

"Uncle Jake and Aunt Marjorie, permit me to present Azrnoth-zin from Delfinus," Ridley said dusting the dirt off his shirt and wincing when he encountered the cut on his side.

"I apologize about your house," was all the alien could say.

"He's the reason those men were here. He's the reason they'll kill whoever stands in their way until they can bring him in," Ridley said.

"That's one hell of a weapon," Jake said, his face still registering shock.

"That's why I need to get him back home, Jake. We're not ready for this level of technology yet. We can't even control the weapons we have now."

"Where will you go?" said Marjorie, coming out of her initial stupor.

"It's where we will go," said Ridley. "It's not safe here any longer. When Jenks returns and sees what happened here, there's going to be hell to pay. You both need to grab a few things and you're going on a spontaneous holiday, to Aunt Lil's in Redwood City."

"We can't leave the ranch," protested Jake.

"Uncle Jake, you don't understand and I don't have time to explain it to you. Please, get your things now. I'll explain everything on the way to the airport."

"What about the horses? We can't just leave them."

"I'll take care of that. Right now, we need to be gone." As Jake and Marjorie hurried off to pack some belongings, Azrnoth-zin checked on the unconscious agents.

"How're our friends?" said Ridley.

"They will survive," said the alien. "Several of them sustained some damage from the pulse. I will attend to their injuries while you prepare for departure."

"Make them as comfortable as you can until I get back. I'm going to run over to the bunkhouse and grab a few things for the road."

When Jake and Marjorie returned with their luggage, Ridley turned to his uncle. "Jake, I need to switch out plates on the Toyota. Can I use the plate from the Chevy?"

"Be my guest. Lately that truck has been relegated to brush and manure hauling."

"Thanks. We need to hurry folks. By now Jenks has probably figured we're not coming to his reception."

Azrnoth-zin led Jake and Marjorie through the underbrush toward the truck parked a mile away, tucked in a mesquite bosque. Ridley ran over to the corral and opened the rolling gate. Inside, the herd began whinnying and bunching together at the back of the corral. Ridley ran at them, arms flailing, trying to urge them toward the opening. At first, one, then two horses ran toward freedom. Soon, the rest of the herd flowed out of the corral and galloped toward the open chaparral. Ridley picked up the suitcase and followed the wash back to the truck.

"So, that's it in a nutshell," Ridley said as they turned off Benson Highway and made for the airport. "Give it five days, then book a flight back. Carlos and his family will keep things together until you return. I spoke to his mother and aunt at the line shack."

"Dear God," said Marjorie. "I hope Carlos is all right."

"Carlos is a pretty savvy kid," said Jake. "He can disappear pretty quickly when he has a mind to."

Jake, Marjorie, and Ridley were crowded into the cab of the Toyota. Azrnoth-zin was lying in the back, positioned between the suitcases and sleeping bags. The rear window was left open so the alien could listen to the conversation.

"Where will you be going now?" Marjorie asked.

"Azrnoth-zin has a rendezvous with his people in less than five days, as soon as he is able to extrapolate the coordinates from our maps. He thinks the pick-up point is somewhere to the south of here, possibly back in Mexico. This area has gotten a little too crowded for my tastes recently, so I think it's time for a little road trip to see an old friend up in the White Mountains."

"You're going to stay with that lunatic, the Dutchman?" said Jake. "I wouldn't trust him as far as I could throw him."

"The Dutchman is okay, Jake. You're not still pissed at him, are you? That was more than six years ago he liberated that bottle of bourbon from your liquor cabinet."

"That wasn't bourbon, "Jake said. "That was Paddy, the finest sipping whiskey distilled in Ireland."

"Remember, he didn't drink it alone."

"Oh, I haven't forgotten your role in that debacle."

"Well, he replaced it, didn't he?"

"With an inferior brand, I might add," Jake said. The old rancher looked at Ridley and a smile softened the lines on his face. "Just keep your ass out of harm's way so we can cork that bottle when you get home."

"I'm looking forward to it, Uncle Jake."

The Toyota pulled into the airport and Ridley made for the terminal check-in lane. He pulled over and kept the motor running, went back and opened the camper shell. Azrnoth-zin, once again in full human attire, handed the suitcases out to Ridley.

Jake turned around in the seat to face the alien. He stuck his hand through the rear window. "It was nice to meet you, Mr. Azrnoth-zin. I'm sorry I didn't get a chance to chat with you more. There are a lot of things I've wondered about - about things out there. Thank you for all your help."

"I regret I did not have more time or that the circumstances were different," said Azrnoth-zin, shaking the old rancher's hand. "I can understand where Ridley derives his character. Like him, I can see you are not afraid to face extreme difficulty."

"Mostly too dumb or stubborn to know any better," Jake said with a smile. "Coop always had a penchant for the lost and castoff. I'm not surprised he found you. Good luck."

Marjorie grabbed Azrnoth-zin's hand next and said, "Thank you. Take good care of yourself and safe journey home."

"At least she didn't tell you to "drive safely" like she does me every time I leave the ranch," Ridley said.

Ridley stood before Jake and Marjorie. Marjorie had tears in her eyes when she hugged him. "I don't care if you think it's corny," she said. "But I mean it. You drive safely, you hear? And come home in one piece, too."

Ridley kissed her on the cheek. "Five days from now, things will be back to normal, I promise."

Ridley turned to Jake. His uncle passed something into Ridley's palm. Ridley looked down at the seven one hundred- dollar bills wrapped around a Visa card. "I wouldn't use that card unless you absolutely have to," said Jake. "Chances are, they'll be on the lookout for it."

"Thanks, Jake. Take care of yourselves. I'll be in touch soon."

They hugged and then Jake turned to Marjorie. "Come on, mama. I believe there's a plane with our name on it in there."

Ridley watched them pass through the door, and disappear into the evening rush of passengers. He felt an odd sense of melancholy as his aunt and uncle walked away. Perhaps it was the realization that they were becoming more frail and vulnerable.

He got back into the truck and merged with the rest of the outbound traffic. Once on the surface streets again, Ridley pointed the truck northward. Azrnoth-zin stuck his head through the rear window opening, looking forward.

"As soon as I can find a place to pull off, you can climb up front again," said Ridley.

"Where are we going, Ridley?"

"Sometimes, when things get a little hot in the desert, it's a good time to impose on old friends who live at a higher elevation. We're heading for the White Mountains."

CHAPTER TWENTY-SIX

Richard Jenks bent over the blackened shadow that was now part of the front wall of the house. He traced his finger along the border, then examined the carbonized particles on his fingertips.

"I believe this was agent Miller," Jenks said. Standing, he then turned to the five remaining agents who were being treated for their injuries on the grass in front of the house. "Did any of you see what happened here?"

"Sorry, sir. We were out of commission," volunteered one of the wounded agents. "All I remember was a man - or what looked like a man - pointed something at us and there was this strange sound, and that was it."

"What do you remember about this man? Anything at all would be favorable for all of you."

The agent said, "It was his eyes, sir. I've never seen anything with eyes like that. It was as if they burned a hole right through you. They were…like…like a blue fire."

"That's great," said Roberson. "We are now looking for a human-like alien with burning blue eyes."

"Shut up, Roberson," said Jenks. "We just got skunked again by Ridley, if you haven't realized it already. What else, Burosky?"

The agent stared ahead, trying to recall the events of the last few hours. He shook his head. "I don't know, sir. It seems as if I can't remember much of the events. Wait! There was something odd about the alien's hands. He was dressed like a regular human, but his hands had extra skin on them, like they were - webbed, or something like that."

"Can you describe the weapon he used on you?"

"All I remember was that it fit into his hand and had a rapidly moving series of strange lights to it before it discharged."

Jenks walked over and stared at the caved-in house. "Whatever it was, it had the power to almost knock down the front of this house. It seems our visitor has decided to use deadly force. Get the word to the rest of the teams that the rules of the hunt have changed and to use all necessary precautions. The visitor is armed and dangerous."

Jenks turned back to Roberson. "What about the Mexican? Have you located him yet?"

"Not yet, sir. He couldn't have gone far. I'm positive I hit him when he tried to make a run for it."

"Keep four agents out there until he's neutralized or captured. I want a report when he's located."

Roberson knew the next question to his superior could meet with any number of reactions. "About Ridley, sir -."

"Ridley and the visitor are moving out of the area. I want our efforts focused on his contacts for the surrounding areas. That includes all states bordering Arizona. Twice now Ridley has outsmarted us. Number One was right. I have grossly underestimated Ridley's resourcefulness. It also appears the alien is actively cooperating with Ridley at this point. The two of them could be much more formidable than I had anticipated."

"What about this place? What do you want to do about it?"

Jenks pulled a cigarette from his breast pocket, lit it and exhaled the fumes skyward. "Torch everything," he said, and walked away from the group of men.

The pain in Carlos' shoulder had decreased from excruciating to barely tolerable. He limped between the creosote bushes, slowly heading to the north. He had lost a considerable amount of blood and was in a state of shock. By the deep throbbing, he was fairly certain the bullet had shattered his shoulder blade.

Carlos thought back to several hours ago when Jake had beckoned him to the ranch house. When he saw the agents, he knew they would use him as bait to entrap Ridley. Jake's deliberate glance told him all he needed to know: Ridley would not be meeting him. It was then that Carlos began plotting his break. He was sure these *hombres* would not let him leave the desert alive.

As the agents marched Carlos past a thicket of cat-claw acacia, Carlos dove into the thorny bushes and scrambled for his life. He dodged and rolled, crawled on all fours, and came up running. The two closest agents became ensnared in the vicious undergrowth. Carlos and his family had navigated brambles like these many times coming up from Mexico crossing into Arizona.

The agents began firing into the thicket. Carlos was almost out of the thicket when the slug hit him high and outside the right shoulder, sending him sprawling into the dirt. He was up on his feet and running, not realizing for several seconds that he had been shot.

That was several hours ago. He suspected that he was back on the Holtzman property now, but through the painful fog was not sure of his bearings. Only sheer will kept driving him forward to reach his wife, mother, and children, still in hiding at the line shack. He hoped Jake's old Chevy truck was still there.

Carlos topped a low-lying hill and stopped in his tracks, his heart sinking at the sight before him. In the distance, plumes of black smoke billowed skyward. Carlos knew then they had burned down the ranch in their anger. He wondered what Ridley had done to incur such wrath from the government agents.

Carlos ran down the hill, more resolved than ever to make it to the line shack and his family. He could no longer feel his fingers on his right hand, but at least the bleeding had stopped. His running soon gave way to a jog-walk, then to lurching, and finally to stumbling over the rocks. Through his delirium, Carlos thought he saw the outline of the line shack in the fading afternoon light. Two figures were running toward him. At first he thought to run away, thinking they must be the *hombres muy malos* coming to make the kill. But his legs would no longer cooperate. He sank to his knees and awaited his fate. In the next moment, he was being cradled in his wife's arms and family members were yelling and crying all around him. The last thing he remembered before he passed out was his five-year old daughter kissing him on the cheek.

CHAPTER TWENTY-SEVEN

Azrnoth-zin stared at the grayish-brown cloud that hung suspended over the Tucson valley. He and Ridley were driving northward on Oracle road, the traffic stalling and moving with a consistency of lukewarm tree sap. The windows in the truck were rolled down allowing the unmistakable smell of burnt car emissions to permeate the cab. Looking behind him, Azrnoth-zin could not see an end to the vehicles at a near standstill.

"It is remarkable," he said, "that you humans foul your own planet with inefficient and toxic hydrocarbons. Your vehicles do not even attain speeds sufficient for transport."

"Pretty disgusting, I agree," said Ridley.

Ridley pointed to a large, black Hummer inching along in the right lane next to them. "The oil companies and the automobile manufacturers convinced the American consumer that we need to drive these gas guzzling behemoths, even though ninety percent of them have never even seen a dirt road."

Azrnoth-zin turned to Ridley. "This technology is not difficult to achieve. Earth has all the necessary resources to develop alternative means of transport that are less destructive. Solar energy is much more efficient to use."

"Oh, that's a given. But, as I said, the oil corporations dictate policy to the car manufacturers, buying up or squeezing out any alternative designs that come down the pike. They'll make the change to other fuel sources when it will serve their interests for more profit."

"This profit and monetary system you use is a strange phenomenon to me," said Azrnoth-zin. "I find it hard to believe that earth societies base their existence on the rise and fall of financial markets. It is as if you are a civilization of merchants." The alien said this as if he had bitten down on something distasteful.

"I'm probably not the one to explain supply and demand economics to you," said Ridley. "I have a pretty skewed view of the whole mess. Suffice it to say, even though it has its problems, it's still better than some of the other doctrines that sprouted up in the last century."

"Do not the people have a voice in determining policy of the government?"

Ridley laughed. "Well, we do have elections. It is unfortunate that, once a lot of these politicians get into office, the desires of the people often take a back seat to their own personal agendas. Many of them support and are, in turn funded by big business."

"Why do the people not revolt against those who make policy?"

Ridley let out a great sigh. "Because it's easier to drive your car, live in your beautifully furnished house, and collect your retirement check than it is to make waves."

Azrnoth-zin was silent for several moments as the traffic picked up pace and they started pulling away from the mass of vehicles. "Ridley?"

"Yeah?"

"You are a - cynical? Is that the correct form of the word?"

"Cynic. That's right. Cynicism and irreverence, my constant companions."

Ridley continued up Oracle road, passing north of the Santa Catalina Mountains until he picked up state route 77. From there, they drove a worn two-lane blacktop that would pass through several small and dying mining towns. After that, it would be a gradual ascent into the rim country, the gateway being the passage through the Salt River Canyon.

Ridley was afraid to stop for any long break other than to refill the gas tank in Globe. He hoped to make the White Mountains by sunset, but soon realized they were going to spend another night out in the open. After a time, it became evident that the alien was getting hungry again. He began reading the billboard signs out loud, announcing the fares of various restaurants along the way. Ridley was amused at this, but also was able to reflect on what a strange world this would appear if you were seeing these things for the first time.

They pulled into Show Low after seven that evening. Ridley was tired, sore, filthy, and hungry. Locating a small roadside cafe on the outskirts of town, Ridley pulled into the nearly empty parking lot.

"I don't think I can find the Dutchman's house in the dark," Ridley said, climbing stiffly out of the truck. "Last time I saw him, he still didn't believe in phones, which is probably good for us. After we grab some chow in here, we'll find a place farther up the road to set up camp for the night. We'll make Dutch's place by mid-morning."

"Who is Dutch?" asked Azrnoth-zin.

"His name is Steve van derWahl," said Ridley, smiling. "He's called the Flying Dutchman because of his reputation on the ski slopes. He does things on a pair of skis that defies the laws of gravity. He's also a helluva rock climber."

"He will help us?"

"Dutch and I have known each other since junior high school. We've shared many sordid adventures over the years."

"This skiing and climbing. I am not familiar with such activities."

"They're recreational activities that we humans engage in when we have leisure time. Some humans feel the need to go very fast down an icy mountain or climb a difficult peak."

"It is a very strange concept, Ridley, this recreation and leisure. Why do you do this?"

"For the rush, the adrenaline, I guess. And just for the fun of it."

"Fun?"

"Arn, I'm tired and I'm hungry. We'll talk more after we sit down and eat something."

"Is what we are doing now considered fun?"

Ridley rolled his eyes.

After introducing Azrnoth-zin to the great American Cheeseburger and a dessert of apple pie a la mode, Ridley felt gorged and sleepy. His side was still throbbing from the slash of the agent's blade, but he didn't think it warranted asking the alien if he could borrow that flashing- healing thingy for something that, he was sure, Azrnoth-zin would consider merely a scratch. What kind of government agent carries a stiletto tucked inside his shoe anyway? Ridley thought there must be some very interesting recruiting programs going on in Washington these days.

They found a forest service road outside of Pinetop and pulled the truck far enough back off the main highway and into the trees to avoid detection. Ridley got out and opened the camper shell, laying out the sleeping bags. He crawled into one bag and, shortly thereafter, felt Azrnoth-zin settling into the one beside him.

For several minutes, they were silent. Ridley thought the alien was already asleep when he spoke.

"Ridley, what is that odor? It is most pungent."

Ridley did not answer. He was too tired. Before he drifted off, he realized the smell was coming from him. He vowed to find a shower as soon as they reached the Dutchman's.

Ridley awoke to light pouring in the window of the camper. He was having a difficult time adjusting his eyes to the sunlight; they felt puffy and swollen. He realized that Azrnoth-zin was not next to him. Sitting up in his sleeping bag, Ridley rubbed the sleep out of his eyes, and clumsily climbed out of the back of the truck.

The morning air was crisp and cold, the smell of conifers filling his nostrils. Ridley stretched and noticed the aspen grove they had camped in was awash in burning golds. Change was coming. The smell of fall was in the air.

Azrnoth-zin was nowhere to be seen. Ridley wasn't going to start worrying about him until after he had a cup of coffee.

After relieving himself against the nearest tree, Ridley returned to the truck and splashed water on his face. He pulled the small butane stove from one of the side compartments. Soon water was boiling in the stainless steel cook pot.

Ridley was on his second cup of coffee when the alien appeared from around a bend in the road.

"I was just getting ready to come looking for you," said Ridley. "You care for some coffee?"

"I would like that Ridley," said the alien. "This is a wondrous place. It is unlike anything I have seen before."

"There are some mighty pretty places on this planet," said Ridley. "Too bad it's all going to go to hell in a hand basket."

"I saw creatures. Magnificent creatures. There must have been twenty or more of them. Some of them had sharp projections on their heads. They watched me closely and then ran into the forest."

"Sounds like you stumbled onto a herd of elk, Arn," Ridley said, handing Azrnoth-zin a tin cup of steaming black coffee.

"The air is different here," said Azrnoth-zin. "There is reduced oxygen content. I did not notice the change in elevation until I began walking."

"We're close to 9000 feet elevation from sea level. You've basically climbed that since you crash landed."

"How much further to our next destination?"

"About an hour. If I can remember the right turnoff. You have any more luck figuring out where your rendezvous is?"

Azrnoth-zin sipped the hot coffee, savoring the aroma and taste. "It is not on any of the coordinates from the charts in your possession. I have performed some extrapolations and am now quite sure the location is south and west of the large city we passed through."

"As soon as we get settled in over at the Dutchman's, I'll head into the nearest town and scoop up all the area maps I can find," said Ridley. "I just hope your friends aren't planning to pick you up back in Mexico. I'm not sure I want to run that gauntlet again."

An hour and a half later, Ridley eased the truck up the dirt incline that led to Steve van derWahl's place. He knew he had found the Dutchman's place when he came to a narrow track that climbed gradually. All along the narrow road, the white trunks of the aspens appeared like a giant picket fence. A carpet of yellow and red leaves disturbed by the airstream of the truck fluttered behind the white Toyota like the tail of a kite.

Ridley pulled the truck in front of the mountain cabin and turned off the motor. Dutch's jeep was visible under the covered carport to the left of the main house. Ridley pushed the door handle to let himself out when suddenly a great force slammed against the door, knocking him back into the truck. Ridley looked up to see big white canines in a large black face. A low growl came from the dog's throat.

"Jesus, J.B.! You scared the shit out of me!" Ridley sat back waiting for the huge mastiff to recognize him. After the dog heard his voice, it cocked his head and its tail began a rhythmical thump-thump against the door of the truck. Ridley leaned forward and slowly rolled down the window. He tentatively let the dog smell his hand. The dog responded with a whine and increased tail wagging. Ridley leaned in closer and was instantly slathered in dog slobber.

"It's okay. We can get out of the truck now."

Azrnoth-zin regarded the whole encounter with a mixture of amusement and revulsion. His hand lay on the metallic device in readiness. "What is this creature?"

"It's called a dog. We keep them as companions and pets." Ridley opened the truck door slowly and stepped out. The large dog was on him immediately, knocking him to the ground. The bull mastiff licked Ridley's face, while Ridley, laughing, tried to wrench free from the weight of the animal.

"Ow! J.B., get off me, you big dufus!"

Azrnoth-zin came around the cab and stood several feet away, weapon held at ready in his palm. "Should I neutralize this creature?"

"I'm okay, Arn. He's just glad to see me."

A voice boomed from the porch. "What the hell you doing with my mutt?"

Ridley rolled over to see Steve van derWahl standing on the edge of the porch, grinning at the spectacle on the ground.

"Dammit, Dutch! Call your dog off me. I'm about half drowned here."

"J.B.! Come!" The mastiff looked up at its master, took two steps toward Dutch and froze in front of Azrnoth-zin. A low, throaty growl emerged from deep within the dog's chest, his ears flattening back and his hackles rising.

Azrnoth-zin stood his ground and slowly lowered himself down to the dog's level maintaining eye contact the entire time. J.B. cocked his head first to one side, then to the other. The dog let forth a soft whimper and moved toward the alien. Azrnoth-zin held out his hand and J.B. leaned into it allowing the stranger to rub his chin.

"We have reached an understanding," Azrnoth-zin said, gently caressing the dog's ears.

"I've been around that dog for a long time," said Dutch. "I've never seen him take to someone that quick."

"I have a way with dogs," Azrnoth-zin said.

"I guess you do. Ridley, you look like shit."

"Good to see you, too, Dutch," Ridley said, picking himself off the ground and dusting the dirt from his pants. "I'm getting real tired of ending up in the dirt all the time."

The big man strode over to where Ridley stood and gave him a great bear hug, lifting him off the ground. He had no difficulty lifting his friend off the ground. Dutch stood at least a foot taller than Ridley. His long blonde hair, streaked with some gray, was tied behind his head in a ponytail. Under his blonde beard and mustache, the Dutchman's face had the angularity of an elite athlete.

"It's been a while, *amigo*," said Dutch grinning. "What's it been? Two, no, three years. Last time I heard, you were running blockades on Japanese whaling ships."

"I guess it's been that long," Ridley said, somewhat sheepishly. "Sorry, pal. A lot of water has gone under the bridge since we last climbed together."

Dutch made it a point of sniffing the air around Ridley. "Ooo-ee boy, are you ever ripe. How long have you been carrying that dead gerbil around in your pocket?"

"Give me a break. This is an easy fix if I can use your shower." Ridley turned toward Azrnoth-zin. "Dutch, this is Arnie Zinn, a friend of mine. Arnie, meet Steve van derWahl, aka, the Flying Dutchman."

Azrnoth-zin tentatively shook hands with the big man, awed by his stature. "It is good to meet you." Azrnoth-zin's social skills were improving, Ridley thought.

"Any friend of Ridley's -," Dutch said, and then a slightly quizzical look crossed his face after he let go of the alien's hand. "I still can't get over how quickly J.B. took to you. He's usually pretty skittish around strangers. His former owners kicked him around a lot."

"I know," said Azrnoth-zin. "He told me."

"Excuse me?" said Dutch.

"Uh, hey Dutch. You okay with having a couple of gypsies in the palace for a few days?" said Ridley, attempting to distract the big man.

"Yeah, no problem. You know, *mi casa…*"

They moved inside the split log cabin and Ridley and Azrnoth-zin stood in the living room. It was rustically furnished, with no rhyme or reason to the decor, obviously the abode of a bachelor.

"Care for a beer, boys?" said Dutch making his way toward the kitchen.

"Thought you'd never ask," said Ridley. "Hey Arn, why don't you use the shower first. I need to bring Dutch up to speed on our situation."

Azrnoth-zin nodded and Ridley directed him to the bathroom. Dutch reappeared with three bottles of beer in one hand and a bag of pretzels and chips in the other.

"I told Arnie to go ahead and use the shower if it's okay with you."

"Yeah, no problem." Dutch and Ridley sat opposite one another at the rough-hewn dining table. After a pull from the beer, Dutch said, "sorry to hear about you and Liz, man. I heard about it from Jake when I called to check on your whereabouts."

"I guess I owe you an apology, Dutch. After the split, I wasn't much good to myself or anybody else for that matter. I figured the best thing to do was to fade into the sunset for a while."

"No, dumbshit. That's when you lean on your friends. Ridley, honest to God, I don't understand you sometimes. When I was down, you were right there for me. Why shouldn't it go both ways?"

"Because it was my fault. It was a pill I had to digest on my own. Sometimes a little self-flagellation goes a long way."

The sound of running water from the bathroom down the hall ceased. It was replaced by a splashing sound and a monotone that sounded like someone chanting underwater, followed by more thrashing of water.

Dutch looked toward the bathroom, then back at Ridley, a big grin outlining his bearded face. "So what planet did you pick this guy up on?"

Ridley almost spit out his beer. "What?"

"I swear, Ridley. You really take the cake. It doesn't matter if it's stray animals or humans, you have a knack for bringing home the weirdest of the weird."

"Oh. Well, you see, Arnie's not from around here."

"Yeah, I figured that out already, Einstein."

Ridley felt the cold beer foaming on the way down his throat. He set the bottle on the table and leaned back in the chair. "It feels good to sit for a while. The last few days have been pretty hectic."

"I've been waiting to hear the reason you ended up here, instead of down in the smaller latitudes that you prefer."

"Hey, can't a guy visit his old climbing partner?"

"Ridley, I know you pretty well after all these years. It's not like you to just show up. That's more my m.o.. So, what's up?"

Ridley held the half-full beer bottle in his hand, as if he were studying the label. "Dutch, I need a favor from you. Arnie and I need to keep a low profile for a few days. I figured your place was off the beaten track."

Dutch stared at Ridley. "Are you boys in some kind of stew with the law?"

"Not like you'd think. Let's just say there's some fairly unscrupulous people that want to ask Arnie some questions that would be potentially embarrassing to him."

Dutch eyed Ridley with a narrow gaze. "He's not some Euro-trash terrorist, is he?"

"No. Nothing like that," said Ridley. "Let's just say he's an illegal alien - of sorts."

The bathroom door opened and Azrnoth-zin walked over to the table, dressed like he was before. Ridley noticed the paleness of his skin against the dark sunglasses and hat. The bandanna still covered his head and ears.

Dutch pushed a beer toward Azrnoth-zin. "I hope you like beer."

Azrnoth-zin flexed his hand, revealing the webbing between the delicate fingers and wrapped them around the bottle. When Ridley saw Dutch's eyes widen, he said, "Go ahead, Arn, you can show him." Turning to his friend, Ridley said, "You were always good at keeping secrets. Can you keep another one?"

"You know me, Ridley."

Dutch looked at Ridley in confusion and then back to the alien as Azrnoth-zin removed the cap and bandanna, revealing slicked-back black hair, or something that resembled hair, a prominent forehead with ridges angling back from the brow and small rounded ears, set back in the head. The alien then slowly removed the sunglasses with his head down, and placed them on the table. He looked up at Dutch, the burning cerulean eyes boring a hole to the back of his optic nerve. Startled, Dutch knocked his beer bottle over, spilling the contents all over the table.

"Jesus H. Christ," murmured the big man. For a moment, all that could be heard in the room was the drip-drip of beer through the slats in the table.

"Steve van derWahl, I'd like you to meet Azrnoth-zin of the planet Delfinus. He crash-landed in the Sea of Cortez a few days ago. It's a long story, but I was led to him by a group of dolphins and ended up smuggling him out of Mexico. He has a rendezvous with his people in four days and I mean to see that he keeps his appointment."

Dutch tried to say something, his mouth working, but no intelligible sounds came forth.

Azrnoth-zin took a sip from the amber bottle and nodded toward the Dutchman. "You spilled your beer."

CHAPTER TWENTY-EIGHT

Ridley wondered if the noises he made in the shower were as weird as Azrnoth-zin's. He scrubbed himself until it almost hurt, shaved, and put on a fresh change of clothes. Passing the refrigerator, he grabbed another cold one. Azrnoth-zin and Dutch were sitting on the porch, fresh beers in their hands. The dog, J.B., sat at the alien's feet.

"Ridley, I still can't believe my own eyes," said Dutch. "Arnie has been telling me about his people and how you found him. He was just getting to the part about you going back to Jake's place. And your ol' buddy Jenks, too. Who'd of thunk it?"

"Jenks is being funded by some branch of the government I'd bet the average taxpayer knows nothing about," said Ridley. "He has men, weapons, boats and planes at his beck and call. Kind of makes you feel all warm and fuzzy inside, knowing Jenks and his merry band of assholes are out there protecting us from the evil invaders."

"I'm still in a state of shock. There are so many questions I want to ask you," said Dutch to Azrnoth-zin. "I don't even know where to start."

"Feed him Mexican food and he'll probably tell you more than you'd ever care to learn," said Ridley with a laugh.

Azrnoth-zin was thoughtful. "I am limited in what I can divulge to you. There are events that are unfolding now that would defy any experience you have had."

"Did he tell you about the Trochinids?" said Ridley.

"The who?"

"I think this should be dinner conversation, especially after a few more of these." Ridley held up the beer bottle. "What do we need for dinner anyway?"

"Not a thing. I've got some rainbow trout that I caught last week and fresh froze. Trout, baked potatoes, salad, and cerveza. That should be the ticket."

They spent the afternoon sitting on the porch, sipping cold beer and attempting to get Azrnoth-zin to open up. It took some prodding and an unending supply of cold beer, but gradually the alien began to talk of his homeworld, the 900-Year War, and space exploration.

"Care for another beer, Arnie?" Dutch said, rising from the chair.

"No. No, thank you," said the alien. "I have achieved a very interesting state of being at present."

Ridley leaned over and looked closely into the alien's large elliptical eyes. "I think you're cut off for a while, pal. At least until we can get some food into your system. That would be a hell of a first impression, wouldn't it? Send you back to your people half in the bag."

Together, Ridley and Dutch prepared the evening meal. In short order, they sat down at the table to trout almondine, baked potatoes, and ceasar salad, topped off with a bottle of chardonnay. Ridley and Dutch watched the alien savor his food and wine.

"Boy, you sure do seem to enjoy eating and drinking," said Dutch. "What's the food like where you come from?"

"Our food is designed to provide the maximum amount of energy to sustain you in periods of extended combat." Azrnoth-zin helped himself to more salad. "Unfortunately, taste is a luxury we do not enjoy."

Ridley pushed his empty plate away and leaned back in the chair. "Dutch, I need to find an outdoor store or sporting goods store, someplace that would carry topo maps of the southwest region. Azrnoth-zin has the coordinates for his pick-up point, but it's south and west of anything I've got in my possession. Possibly back in Mexico. His rendezvous with his people is in less than four days."

"There's two or three stores like that in Springerville, maybe one in Eager," said Dutch. "Want me to go and see if I can find them?"

"No, I'd better go. I have a pretty good idea of what to look for. You keep Arnie entertained tomorrow while I head into town. Are there a lot of law enforcement types hanging around?"

"No more than the usual. Small town police department. Highway patrol cruises through a couple times a week, usually more toward the weekend when the flatlanders come up from the valley." Dutch looked at the alien. "Well, Arnie, what do you want to do tomorrow? I think I can take a day off to entertain a visiting dignitary."

"I would like to see the forest and examine the plants and animals found there."

"Done. One of my favorite pastimes anyway."

"How's the contracting work these days?" said Ridley.

"Pretty good. I've been doing a lot of remodels lately for the folks at White Mountain Country Club. They're a pain in the ass to work for, but the pay more than makes up for their surliness."

"Here's another one," Ridley said. "Four years of college and he'd rather do construction."

"Yeah, I see that you've been lighting 'em up with your credentials, too," Dutch said.

As Ridley had predicted, the alien's tongue loosened as the evening wore on. He spoke of the Trochinids at length. Every once in a while, Ridley would look over at Dutch who either sat slack jawed or rubbed his bearded chin contemplatively.

Azrnoth-zin began asking questions of Ridley and Dutch as well, requesting explanations on phenomena or behaviors he had witnessed. He was particularly interested in aboriginal cultures of earth, especially after his encounter with the Seri myths. Ridley and Dutch tried to answer the alien's queries about the native peoples, but Ridley felt ill equipped to supply Azrnoth-zin with the information he sought.

Later, Dutch produced a bottle of tequila and the three shared a round of shots. Shortly thereafter, Dutch brought out two old guitars, giving one to Ridley and settling onto the couch with the other.

"I guess if we're facing imminent invasion we'd better get a few songs in before the Trochinids come to call," said Dutch. "I always thought you and I were the last of a dying breed, Ridley, but I never figured we'd all go the way of the dinosaurs."

"Only difference here is that when they get through, if what Arnie is saying is fact, there'll be nothing left behind to show we were even here," said Ridley. Strumming the strings, he said, "I haven't played one of these in a long time. What should we do?"

Dutch smiled. "I was thinking of "Hey, Mr. Spaceman." "

"Or how about "Space Cowboy," that old one by Steve Miller?" Ridley and Dutch both laughed while Azrnoth-zin looked on, amused at the earthlings' word games.

"I've got one," said Ridley. "Let's do that one by Jimmy Buffett. "Wonder Why We Ever Go Home." "

Ridley awoke to the smell of fresh coffee and bacon frying. He unrolled himself from the couch and sat up, trying to focus his eyes. The Dutchman was moving furiously through the small kitchen, sliding bread into the toaster and breaking eggs into a large skillet, then removing bacon from another pan and placing the strips onto a large grease-soaked paper towel.

Ridley walked stiffly over to the coffeepot and poured a cup. "Hey," he mumbled.

"Hey, yourself. Sorry if all my banging around woke you up, but by the way you were sleeping, I figured we wouldn't eat until tonight."

"That's okay," Ridley said, yawning. "I haven't been getting much sleep lately. Man, does this coffee taste good." Ridley took another swallow of the black beverage and looked around the room. "Where's Arnie?"

"Bathroom, making those real weird noises again. What the hell do you think he's doing in there?"

"Ask him. But remember, he may ask you a very embarrassing personal question later on."

"I think you'd better ask him. You've been around him longer. Why don't you make yourself useful and set the table while you're regaining consciousness," said Dutch. "This'll be ready in about two minutes."

"What time did Arnie finally turn in?" Ridley mumbled.

"He didn't. Wanted to stay up and watch videos. I lasted through half of "Butch Cassidy and the Sundance Kid," then had to crawl off to bed."

Ridley walked over to the makeshift entertainment center and picked up several of the DVD's. He scowled. "Jesus, Dutch. "Teenage Vampire Lust?" He's already got a skewed version of earth society. Don't add more fuel to the fire."

Ridley found the dishes and silverware and also was able to locate a jar of hot sauce in the cupboard. As he finished placing the last of the mismatched silverware onto the table, Azrnoth-zin walked into the room.

"Morning, Arn. Dutch wants to know what you were doing in the bathroom a little while ago."

Dutch shot Ridley an angry stare.

"I was performing the water ritual," the alien said matter-of-factly, pouring himself a cup of coffee. "On Delfinus, this is a ceremony of daily purification. In space, we cannot partake of the ritual. Because Delfinus is considered one of the few worlds with more water to land mass, water is the basic fabric of Delfinians existence. Most of our cities are under the surface of our oceans."

"See?" said Ridley. "I told you there was reason he was running up your water bill."

"Eggs are ready. Shut up, sit down, and eat."

The breakfast plates were cleared and another pot of coffee was put on. Ridley lingered over the last of his coffee, savoring the taste and the smells that go along with a mountain cabin.

"Here," said Dutch, sliding a piece of paper across the table toward Ridley. "I've got a small list of things for you to pick up in Springerville."

Ridley picked up the list and studied it. "I didn't know I was doing your grocery shopping for the next month."

"I figured Arnie may not get to eat tasty food for a while where he's going. May as well introduce him to as many dishes as possible in the next couple of days."

Ridley smiled. "Dutch, the idea is to get him to go home. He may decide to take up permanent residence."

"I have given this matter a great deal of thought," said Azrnoth-zin, "and I have decided to stay on earth."

Ridley and Dutch looked at each other, then at the alien. Azrnoth-zin twisted his mouth into a smile and took another sip of his coffee. "I made humor," he said.

Later that morning, Ridley waved to Dutch and Azrnoth-zin as they climbed into the big man's jeep. At the last minute, J.B. jumped into the back and the jeep roared down the incline. Ridley finished cleaning up the kitchen, showered, and was soon winding his way along the stand of aspens in the old white Toyota.

The morning sunlight filtered down through the trees, illuminating the colors of red, gold, and green. The sky was a brilliant blue, the air was crisp, and there was a gentle breeze pushing through the aspen leaves, causing them to quake slightly. Ridley felt renewed.

It was a half-hour drive to the interstate, and another hour to Springerville. Being a weekday, the town was quietly going about its daily routines. This was the slow season; the time between the influx of prostrate tourists from Phoenix and Tucson seeking escape from the heat of summer, and the next wave of skiers and snowmobilers who plied these mountains for the fresh, dry powder.

After a few inquiries in town, Ridley located the first of the stores on his list. Unfortunately, the first two stores had topo maps that were limited to the immediate area. An hour later, Ridley located the map in a skiing, climbing, and kayaking store. He checked the coordinates Azrnoth-zin had given him and located the corresponding maps. Ridley's heart sank when he saw the general coordinates would take them south of the border.

He rolled up the four maps that were the most likely choices and wandered around the store, searching for nothing in particular, but still seeking that one thing he could not live without. Funny, he thought. He had recently jettisoned almost all of his material possessions and hadn't given it more than a passing thought. Perhaps he was beginning to achieve that Zen state the Tibetan monks go through when they no longer require the trappings of the material world.

A Swiss Army knife caught Ridley's attention and all thoughts of Zen dissipated. It was the deluxe model, the one with pliers, screwdrivers, file, and a bottle opener. It would make a dandy going away gift for the alien. Hell, everyone, even extra-terrestrials, should have at least one Swiss Army knife.

Paying for the items with some of the cash Jake had given him, Ridley tucked the rolled-up maps under his arm, pocketed the knife, and returned to the truck. He found a gas station and filled the tank, again paying with cash. He was nervous about using the credit card.

Ridley located a Safeway and filled the list - and then some - that Dutch had provided. While standing in the checkout line, Ridley perused the magazine rack that housed all of the scandal sheets and tabloid newspapers. One in particular, the *Weekly World Report,* caught his attention. On the front page, the headlines read, *Alien Ship Crashes in Mexico!* There was a very poor rendition of a spaceship crashing into the ocean. Below it, in smaller print, were the words, *Visitor from Outer Space Held in Mexican Jail.* A picture next to this text showed some artist's rendition of a three-eyed, hairy creature, slobbering out of a fang-filled mouth, peering out from behind bars. Ridley laughed out loud and snatched the newspaper from the rack and added it to the contents of the grocery cart.

Leaving the store, Ridley glanced at his watch. It was already 12:30. He suddenly felt the overwhelming urge to locate the great American cheeseburger before he began the trip back to the Dutchman's. He stopped at another gas station and asked the attendant where he would go to get the best cheeseburger in Springerville. The attendant gave him directions and minutes later Ridley pulled into the nearly full parking lot of a place called Kate's Corner Cafe.

The attendant did not steer Ridley wrong. The burger, fries, and chocolate shake were the epitome of what you would expect from a roadside diner. As Ridley munched down his meal he failed to notice the highway patrol car that passed slowly through the parking lot. The officer almost missed the white Toyota completely, but then stopped and backed the patrol car up to see the license plate once more. He checked the clipboard on the seat next to him. The plates did not match but the description of the vehicle did. Strange, he thought. The instructions were to report it, but not to detain or apprehend. The patrolman was about to call in the Toyota when the radio crackled informing him of a semi-tractor trailer rollover outside of Nutrioso. The white Toyota would have to wait.

CHAPTER TWENTY-NINE

Jenks' face was still crimson following the dressing down he received from Number One. A half-full plate of what was once Mexican food now adorned the opposite wall of his temporary office, located in an abandoned warehouse in south Tucson. Twice now, Ridley and the alien had slipped through his hands. He doubted Number One would tolerate another screw up. Many of Jenk's colleagues had paid dearly for lesser infractions.

He stood up and walked over to the map of Arizona and Mexico located on another wall. Ridley's and the visitor's trail had gone cold. There'd been no reports of any sightings since they had backtracked and made the daring rescue of the aunt and uncle.

Richard Jenks seethed with anger. For all he knew, the two fugitives could be in any one of the four corner states by now. Concentrated, the task force could cover one state quite well; spreading out to three or four states including northern Sonora would make for one thin blanket.

There was a knock on the door. Jenks said irritably, "What is it?"

Roberson stuck his head in the office. "Sir, I think we may have something."

Jenks spun around to face Roberson. "Talk to me, Roberson."

Roberson entered the room and strode over to the map on the wall. "A few minutes ago, we received a report from a highway patrol officer in a place called Springerville. It's right… here." Roberson pointed to the location on the map. "A vehicle matching the description of Ridley's was called in."

"Did the plates match?"

"No. But he ran them through DMV, anyway. The name that came up with the plate was Jacob Holtzman."

"That son of a bitch switched out license plates," said Jenks acidly. "Did he follow the truck?"

"Apparently not."

"I don't believe it," said Jenks. "Is everyone we're dealing with not functioning on all cylinders?"

"From what we understand, the information he received from his station commander was vague."

"I'm dealing with a village idiot's convention. Where's this guy now?"

"He went off duty around thirty minutes ago. We've got some people trying to raise him by phone right now."

"When you get him on the phone, I want to talk to him."

Roberson disappeared out the door and Jenks turned to look at the map once more. Why had Ridley chosen the White Mountains of eastern Arizona? It was not even that far from Tucson. Jenks figured Ridley to put as much distance as quickly as possible between him and the pursuit, perhaps head into New Mexico, Colorado, even California. There must be a reason he was still hanging around.

Jenks looked at his watch. It was almost 3:30. They could be mobilized in less than an hour, then another hour to cover the distance by chopper. Mentally he ticked off the details of the assignments to the subordinate agents: location of the nearest airport, pre-arranged vehicles, and cooperation from local authorities.

Roberson stuck his head inside the office again. "He's on line three."

Jenks went over to the phone, punched line three, and picked it up. "This is special agent Richard Jenks, Phoenix Project field director speaking." Jenks loved to hear his name with a substantial moniker on the end of it.

"Yes, sir, this is Officer Tom Wadkins, Highway patrol, Sitgreaves substation."

"Officer Wadkins, it has come to my attention that you think you were able to positively identify a white Toyota pickup truck in a cafe in Springerville earlier today. Is that correct?"

"That is correct, sir. I spotted the vehicle at approximately 12:50 and made a note in my logbook. Unfortunately, I was unable to investigate further as I was called away to a semi-tractor trailer rollover carrying flammable liquids near Nutrioso. Later, I called in the plates and the department informed me that it was not a match."

"Did you see anyone in the truck, Officer Wadkins?"

"No, sir. I didn't. I can only assume the owner of the truck was in the cafe."

"Has anyone seen the truck since then?" said Jenks, growing more irritable with each passing minute.

"We're short of units in that sector. There's one other unit that patrols there regularly."

"Mr. Wadkins, I am going to need the name of your superior officer and his location. You may have lost a suspect that we have been searching for. This person has been eluding federal agents from Mexico to Arizona. Are all of you people this inept?"

"I am sorry, Agent Jenks. It was not listed as high priority on my APB sheet. We had no way of knowing this fugitive was wanted for questioning by your agency based on the information we received. Besides, your bulletin was not listed by my department as urgent."

"The name of your superior," repeated Jenks.

"That would be Captain Hawley, sir. He can be reached at the Show Low headquarters. I'll be happy to give you the number."

"Thank you, Officer Wadkins. I'll have you give it to my second in command. Hold the line for a minute."

"Uh, sir?"

"Yes?" said Jenks. "What is it?"

"Can I ask what these suspects are wanted for?"

"I cannot divulge that information at this time," said Jenks. "Let's just go off the record and say they're enemies of the state, they're armed, and very dangerous. Good bye, Mr. Wadkins." Jenks punched the hold button and motioned for Roberson to get the phone number of Captain Hawley and to debrief officer Wadkins.

Jenks went back to the large wall map and with a red felt tip marker, circled the area where Ridley's truck was last seen. He then began to write down all of the roads leading in and out of Springerville and all the possible routes of escape.

Moments later, Roberson got off the phone and looked at his boss. "Here's the number for Show Low. What's our next move?"

"Mobilize all of our sections and have them converge on these coordinates," said Jenks. I want every available agent pulled into a circle encompassing this area." He circled an area on the map that included Show Low, Pinetop, and all the way to Greer and Springerville. "Focus our efforts here, but keep a few agents for this area in New Mexico. We need to reach out and touch the forest service and find out about all of the useable roads, paved or unpaved, that they may access."

Roberson nodded. "I'll get on the ground transport, sir. We can have the choppers ready in thirty minutes."

"Make it fifteen," said Jenks. "Make sure all of the agents have standard issues checked out. I don't want to lose another agent if I don't have to."

Roberson left the office once more. Jenks went back to the map and tapped the circled area.

"The net is closing in on you, Ridley. You're about out of time and luck."

CHAPTER THIRTY

Ridley arrived back at the mountain cabin to find it deserted. There was no sign of the Dutchman's jeep. Although it was approaching late afternoon, there was still plenty of time before he had to start worrying.

He parked the truck close to the house, and carried the bags of groceries, maps, and supplies inside. Tossing the maps on the table, Ridley put the groceries away. He spread the maps out on the table and arranged them in a connected fashion, from north to south, for the alien to peruse when he returned. Finally, pouring himself a tall glass of cold well water from the tap, Ridley went outside to the front porch and flopped on the tattered old sofa.

It was the kind of fall day tailor-made for a long walk in the woods. The afternoon air was cool. The shadows of the sun lengthening through the aspens cast a radiant golden glow. Ridley thought about getting up off the old couch and snooping around a bit, but gravity was winning. Nothing wrong with parking his butt here for a while.

He hoped the maps would give Azrnoth-zin the information to complete the final calculations for his rendezvous point. Ridley thought the signal had contained some sort of homing beacon, but the alien had never explained its function. For the first time in many days, Ridley was able to reflect on the mind-numbing events that he was now a part of. If he had not seen it with his own eyes, he would have chalked it up to a case of severe sun stroke or a bout of delusions born of some intestinal illness picked up in Mexico.

Ridley opened his eyes to the sound of a vehicle rambling up the dirt road. He must have fallen asleep. He rubbed his eyes and checked his watch. 5:30. The jeep pulled up to the cabin and around to the side. Azrnoth-zin, Dutch, and J.B. appeared from around the corner. J.B., upon seeing Ridley spread out on the sofa, sprinted up the steps and in one muscular bound landed on Ridley's stomach, knocking the wind from him. The great dog straddled Ridley and began barking loudly, inches from his face.

"Get off me, you chowderhead," said Ridley, half-laughing, half-gasping for air. "Jeez, what did you roll in today? You stink."

"He anointed himself with "Ode de Dead Skunk" just for you," said Dutch.

"Call him off me Dutch. I'm serious. Between his breath and his b.o., I'm about ready to puke."

"You're lying in his bed," said Azrnoth-zin. "He does not like anyone lying in his bed."

"Is that what he told you?" said Ridley. "Okay, Okay, J.B., I get the message loud and clear. Now just get off me!" Ridley pushed the big canine off to the side and sat up. "Dutch, don't you ever bathe that dog?"

Dutch shrugged. "When he needs it."

"How was the field trip?" inquired Ridley.

"Most interesting," said Azrnoth-zin. "I have recorded over 75 species of plants and animals today. Dutch summoned several of those large animals called elk by performing a ritual called bugling."

"Yeah. The Dutchman knows these mountains well," said Ridley. "If you were ever faced with a survival situation in these woods, he'd be the guy to have hanging around. What else did you see?"

"I observed a creature that resembles another life form that I have encountered on my voyages. You call it a bear."

"You saw a black bear?"

"Yes. It was an intriguing animal, but all similarities to the Mawhrbahts ceased after the morphological comparison."

"The elk and later the bear just walked right up to him," said Dutch. "Damnedest thing I've ever seen."

"I got to see him do that with the dolphins in Mexico," said Ridley. "He says he can read their thoughts."

Dutch looked down at J.B., then back to Azrnoth-zin. "Don't believe a word that dog tells you. He lies all the time."

Ridley got up from the sofa and followed Dutch and Azrnoth-zin into the house. J.B. padded after them choosing to remain close to the alien. Azrnoth-zin's attention was immediately drawn to the topo maps laid out on the table. He began plotting points on the maps and performed the mental arithmetic to extrapolate the coordinates he was searching for. Ridley pulled the *Weekly World Report* from one of the empty shopping bags and walked over to where the alien was poring over the maps. He held the paper up in front of him so Dutch could see the front-page headlines.

"Hey, Dutch. What do you think?" said Ridley grinning.

The Dutchman had just opened a fresh bottle of beer that he retrieved from the icebox. Turning to face Ridley, he read the first few lines and almost spit out his beer, laughing. Azrnoth-zin looked up, a quizzical expression on his face.

"I think it captures his essence, don't you?" said Ridley. He could no longer contain himself and began shaking with laughter.

"I - I - believe you're right," said Dutch, between bouts of laughter. "I can see the artist captured the total malevolence of his character. I just think the eyes are a bit too close together, though."

"Whose eyes? The pictures or Arnie's?"

Azrnoth-zin snatched the paper from Ridley's hands and read the lines, a disgusted look on his face. After several moments, he looked up and said, "What is a *"chupacabra"?"*

Ridley laughed again. "Is that what they're calling you in that rag?"

Azrnoth-zin read, "Mexican farmers have reported a rash of cattle mutilations since the alien craft landed. Many believe the alien to be an extra-terrestrial *chupacabra*."

Ridley had just finished wiping the tears from his eyes and broke into another fit of laughter after hearing this. "It's a slang term,

Arnie. Probably not in your translator's data banks. Loosely translated, it means goatsucker, a form of vampire."

Azrnoth-zin threw his head back and emitted the strangest of sounds, unlike anything Ridley had ever heard before. He and Dutch ceased their merriment. They looked at one another, then back at the alien.

"What's he doing?" said Dutch, backing away slightly.

"I'm not sure, but I think he's laughing," said Ridley. "Either that or we pissed him off enough to vaporize us."

Just as quickly as he had started, the sound coming from Azrnoth-zin's throat stopped. The alien's face had a surprised look on it and he placed his fingers at the base of his throat.

"Arn, are you okay?" said Ridley.

"Quite well," replied the alien. "But I think I have been in the company of humans for too long. I found myself - laughing at this." He pointed to the article. "That is a sound I have not heard among my people. I do not know how I made that sound, either."

"How did it feel?"

"It felt - cleansing."

Ridley looked at Dutch. "It's okay. He's not going to nuke us."

Azrnoth-zin again scanned the paper, reading the bylines aloud. "Moth Baby Devours Own Mattress. Dog-Faced Boy Goes to Pound for Chasing Cars." He made the same sound once more, this time a little longer. "Your people read this?"

"A lot of people swear by it," said Ridley. "Scary, huh?"

"I wonder how humanoids rose to the level of biological supremacy on this planet," Azrnoth-zin said.

"It's a mystery," said Ridley.

Ridley grabbed two beers out of the refrigerator, opened them and handed one to Azrnoth-zin. He watched as the alien went back to calculating where he was to be picked up.

"Will these maps work for you?" said Ridley.

"I am not sure. It appears the lines of your longitude and latitude are converging near where the coordinates are located." A moment later, Azrnoth-zin pointed a slender finger to the lower right hand corner of the bottom map. "The ship will come to meet me here."

Ridley leaned across the table and whistled through his teeth. "Looks like we're heading back to Mexico, boys. The *Pinacates*. Hell of a place for a rendezvous."

"What is this place?" said Azrnoth-zin.

It's a series of extinct volcanoes and cinder cones, creating one of the most pristine and formidable wilderness areas in this part of the world. During the summer months, it's damn near inhospitable. The roads going in are marginal at best. Do you know where the pick-up point is once we get to the Pinacates?"

"I have an estimation of an area the size of this." Azrnoth-zin circled an area around one of the larger volcanoes.

"That's not good," said Ridley. "There are no roads into that area. We're on foot from this point on." He indicated the last of a primitive road petering out near the base of the mountain.

"Ridley, it is not necessary to accompany me past this point. You have done too much already."

"Sorry, Azrnoth-zin. You have some amazing survival skills, but you don't know those mountains. I've spent some time in the *Pinacates*. I can help you get there quicker. Besides, I want to see firsthand, what an honest-to-God spaceship looks like."

"Looks like you boys can't do this alone," said Dutch. "I'd better tag along just to make sure you don't get lost."

Azrnoth-zin raised his hand. "I will risk no more lives than I have already. Your offer is appreciated, Dutch, but I cannot allow you to accompany us."

Dutch was about to protest when Ridley interjected. "There's not enough room in old Blanco for the three of us anyway. I started this, Dutch. Now I need to see it to its end. And you know well that's something I've not done very often in the past."

The Dutchman scowled. "That's a lame-ass excuse, Ridley. But since Arnie thinks it would be better if I didn't go along, well, I respect that. It's just that I'd love to see what kind of chariot is picking him up, that's all."

"How long will it take us to get there?" said the alien.

"It's seven to eight hours drive from here to the border. Another hour to the *Pinacates* turnoff, another hour to the end of the road. After that, it's all on foot," said Ridley.

"Do you think Jenks and his men are still hanging around?" said Dutch.

"Undoubtedly," said Ridley. "Jenks has been skunked twice now. He not only would kill to get what Arnie's got, but he has another reason to continue the hunt. He doesn't like to look bad to the people he has to answer to. We kind of rubbed his nose in it."

"What's to say he won't keep dogging you even after Arnie here is long gone?" said Dutch. "You said yourself that he carries a grudge."

"There's no percentages in him coming after me once Azrnoth-zin is safely off the planet. Besides, I plan on putting a lot of water between me and Jenks once this is over." Ridley turned to Azrnoth-zin. "Any idea when your people will pick you up, what time of day?"

"Three days from now," replied the alien. "By my calculations, the time corresponds to three and one-half hours past the midday point."

"Well, that means we need to be on the road sometime tomorrow if we're going to get you to the rendezvous point on time. I'm thinking we'd be better off traveling at night again. So, if it's okay with you, Dutch, we'll crash here another night and then hit the road after dark tomorrow."

"Fine by me," said Dutch. "As it turns out anyway, I'm supposed to have a dinner date tomorrow night. I was thinking of canceling if you two were to invite me on your little soiree, but I guess I'll keep my appointment."

"Don't start pouting on me, you old faker," said Ridley. "I've never seen you spurn the opposite sex to spend time with the guys. Why start now?"

The Dutchman smiled wryly. "I've waited for a long time to get a chance to go out with this lady."

"Do I know her?" Ridley asked.

"I don't think so. She runs the ski lodge and resort at Sunrise. I met her while on ski patrol last year. This is the first time when neither of us have had other commitments."

"That's the Dutchman I remember."

They feasted mightily that evening on shrimp in garlic and butter sauce, steamed vegetables, hot bread, and a Caesar salad accompanied by a bottle of merlot. After the meal, Dutch set a blazing fire in the hearth and the three lounged in the living room enjoying an after dinner brandy. With urging from Ridley and Dutch, Azrnoth-zin continued with his tales of intergalactic battles, unknown civilizations, and bizarre life forms. The universe began to unfold before the two humans, who sat in rapt attention as the traveler wove a strange and wonderful tapestry of life beyond their solar system.

That night, Ridley dreamed he was being pursued down a long corridor by hideous looking creatures. He came to the end of the corridor and found only steel walls and a floor. He could almost feel their fetid breath upon his shoulder. Turning, he saw ominous apparitions lurching through the shadows toward him. He tried to open his mouth to scream, but no sound came.

CHAPTER THIRTY-ONE

In spite of the disturbing dream, Ridley slept deeply and awakened feeling rested. The first rays of light from the sun were arcing through the living room window. Ridley sat up in the rollaway and surveyed the room. Dutch and Azrnoth-zin must still be asleep, he thought. Ridley unwrapped himself from the warm blankets and relit the fire in the fireplace. He then stumbled into the kitchen and set the coffee to brewing. Soon, a fire warmed the chilly room and Ridley sat at the table enjoying the first cup of coffee for the day.

After breakfast, Ridley took a walk out behind the cabin, enjoying the forest in the cool autumn morning. Upon his return to the cabin, he found Azrnoth-zin waiting for him on the front porch.

"Ridley, I request the initiators to your vehicle."

"You mean my keys? What for?"

"I desire to make some modifications on your fuel intake system. I believe I can improve the efficiency of your truck."

"I don't know, Arnie. I'm not sure I want anyone messing with that truck."

"Trust me," said the alien. Ridley was beginning to recognize some of his own idioms now peppering Azrnoth-zin's dialogue.

Ridley tossed the keys to Azrnoth-zin. "I've been driving that truck for eleven years. I really don't think it needs to be modified."

The alien half smiled and turned toward the open garage on the side of the cabin. Ridley was tempted to follow him and observe, but decided to wait and see the end result. Walking into the kitchen, Ridley found Dutch cleaning up the last of the morning dishes.

"What's Arnie up to this morning?" said Dutch.

"I don't know," Ridley said. "It seems he wants to monkey around with the old Blanco. Said something about improving the fuel efficiency."

"Maybe that explains why he wanted me to show him how to use the arc welder while you were out communing with Mother Nature. He picked it up real fast. Within ten minutes, he was laying down a fine bead - looked like he'd been welding all his life."

"Still," said Ridley. "It's the white truck. There's nothing wrong with the way it's running now."

"Oh, quit your whining. You can't do anything to hurt that P.O.S. Maybe he's converting it into one of those cool air cars, like in Star Wars."

"Give me a break, Dutch."

Dutch threw the wet dishrag over the faucet. "Well, gotta go back to work today. There's a cabinet job to finish in Pinetop. You and Arnie up for a farewell beer before you hit the road tonight?"

"I don't see why not. Azrnoth-zin wants Mexican food again, so we'll meet you after he gets his last hurrah. We'll look for a place in or near Show Low."

"How about the Hanging Oak around 7:30?"

"The Hanging Oak? I haven't been in there for years. Still a rough and tumble place?"

"Not like the old days. Oh, there's still the occasional brawl, especially after payday, but these days you see a smattering of all kinds frequenting the place."

"The Hanging Oak works for me. Do we get to meet the mystery woman?"

Dutch hesitated. "Maybe it's not such a good idea, with trying to keep a low profile with Azrnoth-zin, and all. If you know what I mean."

"No worries there," said Ridley. "Arnie's got the human disguise down pretty well by now. I'll bet you twenty bucks she doesn't figure him out."

"What the hell," said Dutch. "Later I can tell her she had a beer with an honest to God extraterrestrial."

"Oh, to be a fly on the wall when you do that," said Ridley.

After Dutch left for work, Ridley busied himself by reviewing the roadmaps of Arizona, determining the least traveled but most direct route into Mexico. He packed enough food and water to last them for three days. Following his shower, Ridley stuffed his meager wardrobe of clothes into the backpack. Finding he was running out of things to keep occupied, Ridley's curiosity got the best of him and he ambled around the side of the house to the garage where Azrnoth-zin was still working.

The big dog bounded out from behind the Toyota to greet Ridley as he approached, panting happily. The hood was up, and the alien was tightening down some God-awful contraption that was perched on the manifold.

Ridley leaned over the hood, then looked at Azrnoth-zin disdainfully. "What the hell did you do to my truck?"

"These internal combustion engines are rudimentary and inefficient. I have made the necessary adjustments to provide the maximum performance from this vehicle."

"My God. Look at all that…stuff…sitting on top of the engine. It looks like someone cooked spaghetti on the manifold. This will never pass emissions," Ridley said sourly.

Azrnoth-zin closed the hood and tossed the keys back to Ridley. "It's better now. I suggest we conduct a trial run."

Ridley went around to the driver's side, grumbling the entire time. Azrnoth-zin slipped into the passenger seat and immediately harnessed himself in.

"I suggest you fasten your seat belt. It's the law, you know."

Ridley cast a sharp look at the alien, then buckled in. He turned the key in the ignition and the truck belched out black smoke and shook furiously, then died with a violent convulsion.

"Some improvement, ace," Ridley said.

Azrnoth-zin nodded toward the keys in the ignition. "Try again."

Ridley cranked the engine again. This time the engine exploded into life, rumbling and popping like a Saturday night dragster.

"This sounds worse than before," Ridley shouted above the din.

Azrnoth-zin motioned for Ridley to drive down the road. Ridley engaged the clutch and the truck lurched down the leaf- covered road, blowing leaves out to the side in a psychedelic wake. Ridley was worried the truck was going to shake itself apart before they even reached pavement.

When they reached the highway, Ridley turned the truck back toward Show Low. There was a long stretch of open, little used road ahead. The engine continued its complaining as Ridley shifted into third gear. Ridley gave another displeased look at Azrnoth-zin. In fourth gear Ridley kept checking the rear view mirror, anticipating seeing a transmission lying in the road behind them.

Ridley depressed the clutch and began to shift into fifth gear as Azrnoth-zin said in a monotone, "If I were you I would prepare for accel -."

"What?" Ridley yelled as the gears engaged. His head was slammed back into the headrest; his body felt like it was being sucked through the back of the seat as he experienced the force of sudden and severe acceleration. In the first few seconds, Ridley almost threw the truck into the ditch along the road. He had to fight the wheel with all of his strength just to keep the vehicle on a straight line. The truck sounded like the engine was going to drop out of the chassis any moment, the whine of the pistons increasing in pitch.

Azrnoth-zin tapped on the instrument panel. "Good! Good!" he shouted to Ridley. "The temperature is within functional limits."

Ridley wasn't sure if he wanted to glance away from the road for fear of leaving it abruptly. His eyes quickly scanned the panel; the speedometer and tachometer were pegged to the right. The temperature read just above the normal range. Ridley found his hands sweating and his breathing labored.

"Begin deceleration," said Azrnoth-zin. "The road is beginning to curve. It may not be stable on curves."

Ridley eased off the accelerator and then shifted into fourth. He and Azrnoth-zin were thrown forward in their seats. The motor returned to a loud clanging sound.

"I think we need to work on your deceleration techniques," said the alien.

Ridley pulled the truck onto the shoulder of the road. Turning to Azrnoth-zin, the alien could see the whites of Ridley's eyes. "What kind of go juice did you put in here?"

Azrnoth-zin looked amused. "It appears, Ridley, that you are not accustomed to sudden acceleration."

"Not in this truck. How fast do you think we were going?"

The alien shrugged. "It is difficult to determine. I am not familiar with earth measures for velocity. The test was a success, would you not agree?"

"Are you going to tell me what you did?" said Ridley. "It still sounds like hell. We won't get past the first highway patrol we come across with all the racket Blanco makes now."

"That is a minor modification," said Azrnoth-zin. "I have in essence, made a fuel converter. The fuel is broken down and the molecules are rearranged to form a more unstable bond. A high-pressure injection system forces the re-mixed fuel into the cylinders when you reach the fifth stage of acceleration. It functions as a crude booster, very similar to a booster rocket. The problem that exists is that it can only be used for brief periods of time."

Arriving back at Dutch's cabin, Ridley parked the white Toyota in the garage again. He watched as Azrnoth-zin made the adjustments to the engine. Soon, the truck was idling only slightly higher than normal.

"You must promise me that you will dismantle the fuel re-mixer when I have left," said Azrnoth-zin, wiping the grease from his hands.

"No problem there," said Ridley. "I can't imagine ever finding a mechanic that could tune up this truck in its present condition anyway."

The rest of the day was spent in packing up food and belongings and loading them into the back of the pickup. Azrnoth-zin spent considerable time with the big dog. They sat on the porch, J.B. looking up at the alien adoringly. Every now and then, the dog's tail would beat furiously, even though no spoken words came from Azrnoth-zin's mouth.

Late in the afternoon, Azrnoth-zin emerged from the back bedroom in full human costume. He was dressed in a pair of faded jeans, a dark blue denim shirt, red Converse tennis shoes, hat, sunglasses and bandanna. Ridley laughed, shaking his head at the same time.

"Arn, you're definitely looking like one of the locals. I swear you're becoming more and more human each day."

Azrnoth-zin stopped in front of the mirror near the entryway. "A few days ago, that observation would have led to a combat challenge," he said.

Ridley picked his backpack off the couch. Azrnoth-zin shouldered his own pack and they walked through the door. The dog was lying near the front steps appearing to Ridley like he was in the throes of despair.

"I think that old hound is going to miss you," said Ridley.

"I can understand why you humans bond with these creatures so strongly," said the alien. "I will miss his companionship as well." Azrnoth-zin knelt beside the dog scratching J.B.'s ears. The dog responded by whimpering and licking his hand.

Ridley patted the dog on the head and then headed down the steps. "Better get going, Arn, before you decide to pack that dog in the back of the truck and take him with you."

Azrnoth-zin stood and walked down the stairs. The big dog attempted to follow behind, but stopped when Azrnoth-zin turned and faced him one last time. J.B. lay down on the porch, his muzzle in his paws.

"That's the look that got them into the cave fifty thousand years ago," said Ridley, as he slid into the front seat.

Ridley and Azrnoth-zin pulled into the Hanging Oak tavern. There were a dozen vehicles, mostly four-by-four trucks, parked in the lot to the side of the bar. Ridley always held his breath before they entered a public place. The alien's disguise had passed on many occasions by now, but Ridley still wondered what would happen if someone decided to take a really close look.

After entering the bar, Ridley and Azrnoth-zin walked to the far corner, to the other side of the pool tables. They sat at the bar opposite an elevated television, which was tuned to ESPN. Ridley ordered two beers and two shots of tequila. Azrnoth-zin stared at the television screen.

Ridley gave a quick look around the room. There were three men wearing dirty coveralls standing at other end of the bar, laughing and talking loudly. There was a wide variety of humanity represented here tonight. They ranged from people who looked like they just walked off the eighteenth green to those who looked like they came off the back forty. Cigarette smoke hung in the air and an old Patsy Cline song warbled from the jukebox.

Among the tables were half a dozen couples, some sitting very close, lost in each other's eyes, or twosomes that seemed to be looking every where except at their date. Ridley noted one couple that was almost sitting in each other's laps. Must be a new romance, he thought. No suspicious types in here tonight.

"That's called television," said Ridley, turning his attention back to Azrnoth-zin. "Just about every home in the United States has one of those things in it."

"Does it recieve messages as well as send them?" inquired Azrnoth-zin.

"One way only. We have many channels to chose from on various subjects. Unfortunately, you have to wade through a lot of junk to find something that doesn't insult your intelligence."

"What subjects?"

"Well, for instance, the channel that's on now is dedicated to sporting events." Ridley looked around. No one was in the immediate vicinity, so Ridley asked the bartender if he could borrow the remote. The bartender grumbled something and handed the remote to Ridley.

"You see," said Ridley, surfing through the channels, "there's movies, music, sports, news -," he stopped at CNN. "This is a news and information channel. It gives you current events that are occurring all over the world." Ridley turned up the volume for the alien.

An attractive black woman in a business suit was addressing Congress.

Ridley nodded toward the screen, keeping his voice low. "That's the president of the United States, Claire Chatsworth, the first woman to hold the nation's highest office. For two years, she's had an uphill run against all of those good ol' redneck boys in Washington."

The announcer was commenting on the recent environmental legislation that the president was trying to get pushed through. Her bill had met with severe opposition from the Senate, spearheaded by the speaker of the house, Norman Hunsaker.

"You have a single ruler of your country?" said Azrnoth-zin.

Ridley sighed. "I apologize, Arnie. I should have been trying to get you as much information as possible on things like governments, economics, politics, technology. There's a lot to show you and it seems like all we've been doing is running."

"I have learned a great deal since coming here," said the alien. "Enough to change my opinion of your people and the world in which you live."

Ridley took a sip from the long neck beer. "The people elected her to office. But we have three branches of government; the executive, the legislative and the judicial, which all function as a system of checks and balances to prevent one from becoming too powerful."

"So can the president be overruled by the other two bodies?"

"Yes. She is a very popular president among the people. She strongly supports issues that the status quo doesn't champion. She's been fighting the development of the last of the wilderness areas for oil exploration. Those are issues that a lot of us care about a lot. That's why I voted for her." Ridley raised his beer bottle toward the screen. "Give 'em hell, President Chatsworth."

The bartender came back over and stood in front of Ridley and Azrnoth-zin. "If you want to watch the flippin' news, retire to your living rooms. Here, it's ESPN or the country music channel," he said sourly.

Ridley shrugged and handed the remote back to the surly bartender. "I guess some things never change."

A Jimmy Buffett song came on the jukebox. Azrnoth-zin perked up when he heard the words from "Fins." Ridley laughed.

"What do you find amusing, Ridley?"

"Oh, I don't know. It struck me as funny what impressions you're going to go home with - Mexican food, beer, Jimmy Buffett music and a 30-second lesson on American politics."

"More can be learned from a culture or a civilization if you have a ground level view," said Azrnoth-zin.

Ridley leaned his beer bottle toward Azrnoth-zin's. "Here's to a safe journey home and a warm reception when you get there."

The alien clinked his bottle to Ridley's. "That is a favorable wish, but I am sure my return will not be met with great warmth. However, I will state the case for your people to the best of my ability."

"Thanks. And don't forget about the delfids either."

Azrnoth-zin smiled. Ridley could see he was still getting used to using those muscles in his face. "Anything else you would like me to pass on to the Water Council?"

"No, I think that's about it." Ridley reached into the pocket of his coat and set the box with the Swiss Army knife in front of Azrnoth-zin. "A little going away present. A memento from the late, great planet earth."

"What is it?"

"It's a Swiss Army knife. What? You don't have these in outer space? I can't believe you made it this far without one."

Azrnoth-zin examined the box and then slid the shiny red knife into his hand. He began to methodically unfold each of the blades and tools until the knife was fully opened.

"Don't forget this one," said Ridley, pointing to one of the smaller curved blades.

"What function does this one perform?"

"The most important one," said Ridley. "It opens your beer bottles,"

The alien, even through the disguise, was beaming, admiring his new acquisition. "It is a worthy gift, Ridley. I thank you."

As the song finished, Ridley sang the last line in sync and slightly out of tune with Jimmy. "...and you're the only bait in town."

Azrnoth-zin grew fidgety. "I have never known a friend like you, Ridley. Out there, friendships are fleeting. It is best not to get too close to someone. The war will most likely claim you or those close to you. I am - envious of your ability to maintain lasting friendships with your fellow humans."

"Now don't be going soft on me, Azrnoth-zin. I was just getting used to the haughty and pompous traveler that I picked up in Mexico," Ridley said, smiling.

"Pompous! I am not pompous!" protested the alien.

Ridley laughed. He clinked his near empty beer bottle to Azrnoth-zin's once more. "Here's to friendships that span star systems."

"To friends," said Azrnoth-zin, and he drained the remainder from his bottle.

"I hope I didn't turn you into an alcoholic," said Ridley. "Frankly, I'm glad you're going back home. Another week of this and I'd have to check myself into the Betty Ford clinic."

A voice from directly behind Ridley and Azrnoth-zin spoke. "Well, if it isn't Butch Casualty and the Moondance Kid."

Jenks had finally caught up to them.

CHAPTER THIRTY-TWO

Jenks leaned between the two of them, a sinister smile plastered to his face. "I've been waiting for this moment for a long time," he said. "I finally get a chance to meet our distinguished visitor. We have a great many things to discuss, and I'm sure you'll enjoy the hospitality that the Phoenix Project will provide."

"Yeah, like a laboratory rat, complete with scans, dissecting tools, and a team of hired thugs to try to figure out what makes him tick, right?"

Jenks put his face close to Ridley's, who was still staring straight ahead. "I'm going to personally enjoy dealing with you, Ridley. You are about to embark on a long and very painful journey. Once I get through with you, you're going to wish your mother had aborted."

By now, several of the bar patrons were looking on at the group of men that confronted the two at the bar. The bartender attempted to come down to see what the problem was, but Jenks waved him away with some sort of identification.

"This is government business," Jenks said sharply. "Remain in your seats or where you stand." Jenks turned to one of the men standing behind him. "Call in the chopper for pick up. We have our passengers."

Out of the corner of his eye, Ridley could see the other agent talking quietly on a cell phone. Jenks leaned in and looked closely at Azrnoth-zin. "Not bad for a disguise. I can see how you slipped by them. I must say that it is a personal thrill to finally get to meet a traveler from space."

Ridley noticed that Jenks' hand rested on the curved portion of the bar as he addressed Azrnoth-zin. He knew he had one chance to create a diversion so Azrnoth-zin could get to his weapon.

"Hey, Jenks. So you outsmarted us. The least you could do is let me finish my beer before you take us away."

"You're a bigger fool than I first suspected, Ridley. Did you truly believe that a loser like you could outrun the men and resources from the Project?"

"Silly me," said Ridley. He winked at Azrnoth-zin, brought the beer bottle to his lips and drained the rest of the beer, tilting his head back while increasing the arc of his arm. In one move, Ridley brought the butt of the beer bottle crashing down on the back of Jenks' hand. Ridley heard crunching in the small bones as the bottle shattered. Jenks howled in pain and lurched backward, but not before Ridley's left elbow caught Jenks squarely in the mouth. Although Jenks was half a head taller and thirty pounds heavier, Ridley was quicker. Ridley was off the barstool and landed a foot to Jenks's stomach before two agents grabbed him and threw him against the bar.

By now, agents were drawing guns and people were diving for the floor. Two other agents leveled their weapons at Azrnoth-zin, who was standing a short distance from Ridley.

While Jenks lay gasping on the floor, a third agent advanced on Ridley and began working him over. The agent landed a punch to Ridley's face, then another to his midsection, doubling him over in pain. Azrnoth-zin made a move to intervene, but was shoved back by two other agents.

Jenks gathered himself and stood. Blood was trickling out of the corner of his mouth.

"Hold the son of a bitch!"

Ridley looked up in defiance as Jenks drew back and crashed his right fist into Ridley's cheek. He proceeded to throw a barrage of hammering punches to Ridley's face and shoulders. Blood poured from Ridley's nose and split lip. He could no longer see out of his left eye. His consciousness ebbed.

With most of the attention focused on Jenks' brutal beating of Ridley, the two agents guarding Azrnoth-zin did not notice when the alien touched the outside of his Levi's jacket pocket near his chest. A low humming sound began to build and the agents turned back to see the alien smiling slightly.

Suddenly, a shock wave of intense energy emanated from Azrnoth-zin, enveloping everyone in the bar.

Agents and customers collapsed onto the floor or sprawled across tables. Jenks went down like a sack of flour, a warm stain spreading across the crotch of his pants. Azrnoth-zin noticed many of the others had lost control of their bladders as a result of the stun pulse.

Ridley lay on the floor, leaning against the bar, barely conscious. On some level, he willed himself to get up and move, but his body would not obey. He knew Azrnoth-zin had used some sort of weapon, but he was not sure if his inability to move stemmed from the stun pulse, the beating, or both.

Azrnoth-zin surveyed the room. The only sound he could hear was the blare from the jukebox. Then his ears picked up another sound, growing louder. Helicopters. That meant more of the agents would be here soon. The alien quickly checked the collapsed forms lying around the barroom, then went to assist Ridley. It was no good; the only way Ridley was leaving this place was to be carried out.

Azrnoth-zin leaned over Ridley. "I really must remember to get that device recalibrated. I think it would be wise for us to be going now."

He struggled to lift the heavier Ridley and finally had to settle with half-carrying, half-dragging him toward the front door. Before he left the building, Azrnoth-zin activated the personal force field. A shimmering curtain enveloped the alien and Ridley as they emerged into the chilly September night air.

A large helicopter was setting down on the fringe of the parking lot, its halogen searchlight illuminating the night. Azrnoth-zin saw figures pouring out of the flying machine and running toward him. Something sparked and pinged off the force field. Then came another shot with a high pitch whine that faded off into the night. Azrnoth-zin realized the agents were firing guns at him. He stopped long enough to activate the stun pulse once more. The agents dropped in their tracks.

He was almost to Ridley's truck when he heard the approach of another vehicle. Azrnoth-zin turned to face his would be assailant, raising the weapon toward the oncoming headlights. Only at the last minute did he recognize a familiar yellow jeep skidding through the parking lot dust.

Dutch flew out of the jeep when the headlights focused on Azrnoth-zin and the bleeding form of Ridley. "What the hell happened?" he shouted. "Jesus, what happened to Ridley?"

Azrnoth-zin looked out into the parking area for any agents that might be lurking in the shadows. Satisfied they were all neutralized he deactivated the force field and propped Ridley against the fender of the truck.

"It seems our friend here has no concept of diversionary tactics. He attempted to neutralize Jenks and all of his men by himself. I believe the agents would have killed him. As it is, he has sustained minor damage."

An attractive, auburn-haired woman got out of the jeep slowly, staring at Azrnoth-zin and Ridley, the color drained from her face. Azrnoth-zin knew she had seen the deactivation of the force field. It would be up to Dutch to provide the necessary explanations.

"We need to leave now," said Azrnoth-zin. "I am not certain how long the effects of the stun pulse last. Jenks and his men are undamaged." Together, Azrnoth-zin and Dutch were able to carry Ridley around to the passenger side of the truck. Azrnoth-zin fished the keys out of Ridley's pocket, and, not very gently, lowered him into the front seat. Ridley grunted in pain.

Dutch turned to the woman. "Stay put, Jackie. I'll be right back." He sprinted off in the direction of the helicopter and the parked government vehicles. He stopped and checked on one of the fallen agents, then continued on. Several minutes passed and soon Dutch reappeared in the bright lights of the helicopter, running back toward them. In his hands were a tangle of wires and connectors.

"This should buy you a little more time, "said Dutch. He handed the car's distributor wires and helicopter battery leads to Azrnoth-zin.

"Toss those out of the truck when you get down the road a few miles," said the Dutchman. "How'd you do that?" He pointed to the fallen agents. "They're breathing, hearts are working, even their eyes are open. It's like you hit them with a mega animal tranq."

"It is a lengthy explanation and we're out of time," said Azrnoth-zin taking the wires from the Dutchman.

Azrnoth-zin walked around to the driver's side. Before he got in, he looked at Dutch and said, "I will not forget your friendship and assistance, Dutch. Ridley has made a wise choice in comrades. He is to be envied."

"Take care of yourself, Arnie," said Dutch. "And make it home."

The alien and Dutch exchanged handshakes. Azrnoth-zin slipped behind the wheel and started the truck. He pulled the truck around and, spinning the tires in the gravel, disappeared into the darkness.

Dutch watched the red taillights fade into the night, then turned back toward Jackie. She was staring at him, some of the color returning to her face.

"Tell me I didn't see what I just thought I saw," she said.

"Come on," said Dutch. "Let's get out of here and find some place where we can split a bottle of champagne and have a long talk. I think you're going to need that champagne."

CHAPTER THIRTY-THREE

Azrnoth-zin pulled the truck off the main highway and onto a seldom-used forest service road. He bumped the truck over innumerable ruts and potholes until they were well concealed among the Douglas firs. Reaching into the glove box, he found a flashlight and shined it on his semi-conscious passenger.

Ridley was a mess. A cut above his left eye was still oozing blood, as was the split on his lip. Dried, encrusted blood ran down his right cheek and there were bloodstains on his shirt. Both of Ridley's eyes would be black by morning.

The alien directed the scanner over Ridley's head and torso. Ridley experienced an odd tingling sensation all over his head and face. His skin grew progressively warmer.

Satisfied there were no life-threatening injuries or permanent brain damage, Azrnoth-zin began to treat the cuts and bruises with the device. Slowly, the wounds began to cauterize, the bleeding slowed and finally stopped. If the treatment was painful, Ridley did not let on.

"I had no other choice," Azrnoth-zin said as he put the scanner back into his backpack. "I had to make sure all of those men were sufficiently neutralized. There should be no long lasting side effects from the stun pulse. Within a few hours, all of the effects should be gone. Scans of your body and head reveal no permanent damage. I do not believe I could make that statement if we were in there a moment or two longer."

Azrnoth-zin started up the truck and found a place to turn around. He drove back out to the highway. Turning to Ridley, he said, "Which direction?"

Ridley tried to speak but only a few garbled sounds emerged from his throat. Ridley rolled his good eye in frustration.

"Do not try to talk now," said the alien. "It will come back in time. I want you to focus your mental energy. Project in your mind the route you want me to take."

Ridley focused through the lingering pain. *Right. Right. Go right.*

Azrnoth-zin turned right onto the main highway. "Now, where?"

Again Ridley focused. *Superstition Wilderness. We can hide there.*

"How far away is this wilderness?"

Two hours, Ridley mentally projected.

Azrnoth-zin engaged the truck's gears and they sped southward along the deserted highway. He knew they had to put as much distance as possible between themselves and the agents before the phase stun wore off.

"Superstition Wilderness it is," said the alien.

By the time they reached the top of the Salt River Canyon, some of the feeling was returning to Ridley's fingers. He thought he could move his feet a little, too. Finally, with great effort, Ridley was able to turn his head toward Azrnoth-zin.

"- eed - y - ants-," Ridley forced the words out.

Azrnoth-zin turned his head to face Ridley. "What?"

Ridley took a deep breath. "Th-that goddamn thing made me pee my pants!"

"I apologize for the embarrassment," said the alien. "If it is any consolation, everyone else in the bar suffered the same fate. Some were in a much more compromised position than you."

"That's s'posed to make me feel better?

"How do you feel, Ridley?"

"How do you think I feel? Like I've been drug through a knothole backwards. How long before I can start moving again?"

"All of your systems, musculoskeletal and neuromuscular, should be fully functional within several hours."

"How did you do that, that mind connection thing?"

"Delphinian children have the water link instilled in them at a very young age. On our homeworld, much time is spent in the water developing this portion of our brains."

"How was it," said Ridley, "that you were able to hear my thoughts and I have had no formal training?"

"It is a simple matter to pick up your thoughts, Ridley. You are only a transmitter. From the information provided from the scans, I do not believe that part of the human brain is developed to receive the unspoken words."

Ridley thought about this for a moment. "How far away can you communicate with others?"

"It depends," said Azrnoth-zin, "on the level of..." Azrnoth-zin furrowed his brow, searching for the right words. "...on the level of connectedness you have with that individual. I was able to communicate with my mate Resar-dan from a great distance in space. In the water, I can also link over great distances."

"That explains why you were able to pick up on the dolphins so well," said Ridley.

"I believe most of the other species on your planet have at least rudimentary capabilities. I am surprised that you humans lack this attribute."

"Oh, I don't know. I have heard that aboriginal cultures were able to employ telepathy. I think there's just too much unfiltered garbage coming at the majority of humanity. Daily we're bombarded with images from the television, increased traffic, corporate stress, you name it. It's a wonder most of us can even think anymore."

"You said it, not me," said Azrnoth-zin.

"You never cease to amaze me, Arnie."

"And you never cease to amaze me either," said the alien. "I wonder if you have a secret termination wish. Creating a diversion by challenging a roomful of hostile government agents is not the action of a rational being."

"Hell, I was real close to having the situation well under control," retorted Ridley. He tried to laugh, but winced from the residual pain.

"Good. I hope the pain acts as a reminder to you." Azrnoth-zin shook his head, suddenly becoming more serious. "I am concerned for your safety, Ridley. I think the man called Jenks would not have stopped beating you until he killed you."

"I'm telling you, Arnie. Once we get you off this rock, Ol' Dickey Boy will be up to his ass in alligators explaining to his superiors how he let the find of two millenniums slip away. He's going to have a lot more to think about than exacting revenge on me. Besides, it's a great big world. There's a lot of oceans I haven't paddled yet."

Ridley drew one leg up at a time and then extended them back out. "My legs feel like they've been encased in concrete," he said. He flexed and unflexed his hands in front of him.

"Hey?"

Azrnoth-zin again shifted his gaze to Ridley. "Now what?"

"Why don't you find a place to pull over. I'd like to change my pants."

They made it to the southern boundary of the Superstition Wilderness by early morning. Concealing the truck in an arroyo that was overgrown with palo verde and mesquite trees, they opted to lay low during the daylight hours and continue their run under the cover of darkness.

In the afternoon, Ridley and Azrnoth-zin reviewed the topo maps one more time, choosing the least likely routes back to the border. The alien had been right. Most of the effects of the stun pulse had dissipated after several hours. Considering he almost had been beaten to death the night before, Ridley felt pretty good. Some residual soreness around his right eye socket and a slight headache were the only reminders of his encounter with the agents.

Ridley was frowning as he studied the map of the Pinacates. "I don't like this part," he said, indicating a road-less track. "I don't think we can get Old Blanco in there. It's going to be a long hike and we'll be out in the open. And that's if we can get through the border, which will be akin to a major miracle."

"This is the area where the signal designated that I should be for the rendezvous," said Azrnoth-zin, pointing to a large crater.

"That's *El Elegante*," said Ridley. "It's a good five to six clicks by foot to the base and then the fun really begins. There's not a lot of used trails on that cinder pile."

"Do you think there will be agents at the border?" said Azrnoth-zin.

"Hard to say. I don't think so. Jenks and his lackeys shouldn't have a clue as to which direction we're heading. That and traveling at night should give us the edge we've been looking for."

"It seems close but at the same time it seems like it is a very distant goal," said Azrnoth-zin.

"I know exactly what you mean," said Ridley.

Dark clouds formed out of the southwest and by late that afternoon it appeared Ridley and Azrnoth-zin were going to get wet. Storm warnings with flash flood advisories had been issued for the southwestern portion of the state. The air smelled of approaching rain. The wind picked up and a few large droplets spattered the dust on the windshield of the white Toyota.

"This could be a good thing," Ridley said as he strapped himself in. "Darkness and a nice little storm to hide us."

Azrnoth-zin climbed into the passenger seat and adjusted the seat belt. "Are you quite certain you are fit to pilot this vehicle?"

"I'm fine, Arnie. I'll drive until I need a break, then you can take over."

By the time they were back on the solid pavement of State Route 77, the sky had released a deluge. There was no sundown this evening. The sky went from gray to black. Visibility was reduced to less than fifty feet. Ridley had to slow the truck, fearing the lack of visibility could cause him to plunge into a swollen wash crossing the road. Just outside of Tucson, the Toyota was pelted with thumbnail-sized hailstones that rattled off the roof and rendered conversation impossible. Given the time of day and severity of the weather, the truck passed unnoticed through Tucson.

Ridley found the turnoff onto State Route 86 which would lead them back to Mexico. He aimed the truck west through the continuing downpour. At Three Points, Ridley chanced a stop for gas at a Gas n' Go. While Azrnoth-zin filled the tank and the extra gas can, Ridley went inside to pay. They were in and out of the convenience mart in less than five minutes.

The traffic gradually thinned as they headed west toward the Tohono O'odham reservation. Through the rain-streaked windshield, Ridley noticed the turnoff to Kitt Peak observatory. He imagined the looks on the faces of the astronomers if he walked in out of the storm with Azrnoth-zin.

Just before Sells, Ridley was suffering the effects of severe eye swelling and fatigue. He was hunkered over the steering wheel peering into the driving rain, the windshield wipers acting like a metronome, orchestrating the first of the winter storms.

"I think it is my turn to drive for a while," said Azrnoth-zin. "You look like you are about to fall asleep."

"Yeah, I think I'm ready. Next place you see that looks good to pull over, call out."

A wide spot in the shoulder presented itself soon and Ridley changed positions with Azrnoth-zin. When he got back into the truck, Ridley was soaking wet, his hair plastered to his head.

"Be careful up ahead, Arn. For the next 90 miles or so, there are a lot of washes that crisscross the highway. A storm like this could fill up one of those arroyos in a hurry. I don't want to get any wetter than I already am."

Azrnoth-zin nodded and geared up the truck once more. Ridley cranked up the heater; he was already starting to shiver from the cold.

"Wake me up before we get to Why or if something significant happens," Ridley said, pulling his leather jacket over his shoulders.

"Why?" said the alien.

"Because, you need to wake me up, that's all."

"No. What's why?"

"Oh. Why's a small town. A bump in the road. It's where we turn toward Mexico."

"Why Why?" said Azrnoth-zin, enjoying the word game.

"Just wake me up before we get there, okay, smart ass?" Ridley closed his eyes and was asleep instantly, lulled by the drone of the engine and the drumming of the rain.

Ridley awoke to being shaken vigorously by one shoulder. "Wha-What is it? Where are we?"

"Approximately 36 miles from the place called Why," said Azrnoth-zin. Ridley could barely make out his features from the sparse dashboard lights. "You told me to wake you if something significant occurs."

"This better be good," said Ridley.

Azrnoth-zin indicated behind them. "We are being pursued."

Ridley whipped around to see the flashing red lights of a highway patrol car coming up fast on their rear.

"Dammit! How long has he been riding our butt?"

"The lights came on only a minute or two ago. The vehicle has been behind us for twenty minutes."

"I think he's ID'ed us. I'd bet he's holding back until the big guns arrive," said Ridley.

"What is the road ahead like?" said Azrnoth-zin.

"Fairly straight, but, no, wait. There's a series of banked curves coming up and then it's pretty much a straightaway to Why. Got any brilliant ideas? Because if you do, now is the time when we could use a brilliant idea."

"Do you know of any alternative routes from here?"

"There's a few. But in this rain, we'd be bogged down in five minutes."

"Then I believe we will have to outrun them," said the alien.

"Good plan," Ridley said. "I like the simple solution."

Azrnoth-zin accelerated the truck without engaging the overdrive. The trucks speedometer hovered close to eighty miles per hour, then pegged over to the right. The engine strained, the truck hydroplaning through some of the larger puddles. Visibility was almost nil as the rain pelted the windshield in continuous sheets. The lights behind them grew larger.

"My guess is he'll try to overtake us, either forcing us onto the shoulder or he'll pass us and block the road," said Ridley. "I'd get ready for a reception at Why. It's a crossroads of sorts. He'll have support coming from two other directions." Ridley kept turning around to mark the progress of the approaching patrol car. "Oh, yeah, one more thing."

"I hope so," said the alien.

It's a hard left at the Why junction. You're going to have to decelerate there."

"Anything else?"

"No. I think that about covers it."

The patrol car was almost upon them, the air splitting from the screech of the siren.

"Here he comes," said Ridley. "Watch for his move."

The patrol car swung into the passing lane and continued to accelerate. Ridley guessed they were traveling at over 90 miles per hour in conditions where they should be doing 35. The highway patrol vehicle pulled even with the Toyota. Through the din, a bullhorn sounded.

"SLOW DOWN AND PULL OVER TO THE RIGHT SHOULDER IMMEDIATELY!" boomed the authoritarian voice. It was impossible to see into the interior of the patrol car due to the slashing rain.

"He's going to make his move now," said Ridley.

The patrol car moved ahead of the truck. Every rut was like a chasm, every puddle formed a lake. The only way to stop was to careen off the road into the rocks. At this speed, the highway patrol vehicle was having the same trouble staying on the road. The black and white was two car lengths ahead of them. More lights appeared from the rear. A second car was approaching, its flashing lights now evident through the rear window.

Ridley held up two fingers in front of Azrnoth-zin. "Now it's a party." He peered ahead into the rain, which was now coming at the windshield horizontally.

He almost didn't see it. Ridley blinked once. Twice. The rain and the condensation on the inside of the cab made it almost impossible to see ahead. There it was again. Ahead in the road. Ridley detected movement, a brown flowing mass.

Ridley barely had time to react. "Punch it, Arn!"

Azrnoth-zin reacted quickly and thrust the gears into overdrive. The Toyota rocketed forward throwing Ridley and Azrnoth-zin back in their seats.

The truck squirted by the patrol car as if it were standing still. The truck became airborne. Below them, Ridley glimpsed rushing water, with massive pieces of debris being pulled in its current. He felt the rising and falling of his stomach. The hood of the truck was angled slightly downward. They hit and a huge curtain of muddy water enveloped them. The impact threw Ridley and Azrnoth-zin forward, seatbelts straining to their limits. The truck's wheels spun through the water looking for solid purchase. Lurching forward, the truck's tires connected with solid ground.

The truck blasted out of the brownish torrent like some slime creature from a grade B horror movie. Azrnoth-zin lost control as the truck reached the incline on the other side of the arroyo and became airborne again. The truck spun on the gravel on the shoulder and turned 180 degrees before coming to rest. The headlights faced the rain-swollen wash. The white Toyota stalled.

Ridley was aware the patrol car was still trying to match Azrnoth-zin's former speed. The slower, heavier patrol car came off the incline and was airborne.

"It's not going to make it," said Ridley.

The highway patrol vehicle landed in the middle of the wash with a spectacular splash. The rushing water began pushing the car downstream. Within seconds, the patrolman was climbing out the window and crawling onto the roof of the car.

Ridley was out of the truck and into the back of the camper before Azrnoth-zin could ask him what he was doing. Ridley retrieved an old perlon rope, long since retired from his last climbing adventure. He ran through the rain and reached the edge of the rushing water, unwinding enough coils of rope to reach the other side.

"Grab the rope and tie it around your waist!" Ridley yelled into the wind and rain.

He threw the rope toward the stranded patrolman in an underhanded movement. The rope fell short by several feet.

Ridley reeled in the rope and coiled it again. He moved along the bank in the direction of the flow. He would have only one more chance to reach the patrolman before the car disappeared from view and he was out of range.

Ridley brought his arm back and let the rope sail. The patrolman lunged for it and tied the rope around his waist. Ridley began hauling in the cop as the car disappeared from sight.

Azrnoth-zin got behind Ridley and pulled on the rope. The current tried to suck them both in. The two of them finally landed the soggy officer on the shore. The second highway patrol car pulled to the edge of the wash, its headlights playing down on the dramatic rescue unfolding. The patrolman lay in the shallows, gasping like some prostrate fish.

Together Ridley and Azrnoth-zin dragged the patrolman the rest of the way up the bank. Through the downpour, the other cop was yelling something through his megaphone but Ridley couldn't understand the words.

Bending over the patrolman, Ridley said, "Are you all right?"

The patrolman nodded weakly and coughed. Ridley noticed that the patrolman's sidearm was missing from the holster. Here was one cop who wasn't going to make a collar this evening. Ridley ran back to the truck and found the emergency blanket. He returned and draped the silvery blanket over the patrolman's shoulders.

"This should help keep out the chill until help arrives," said Ridley.

The cop looked up at Ridley and Azrnoth-zin. "You're both under arrest," and then coughed up some more water.

"Maybe later," Ridley said.

Azrnoth-zin and Ridley sprinted back to the stalled truck and got in, this time Ridley at the wheel. He turned the key in the ignition. The truck's engine turned several revolutions and promptly stalled again.

"Come on, Blanco," pleaded Ridley. "Just one last time. You can do it."

Ridley drew a deep breath. He floored the accelerator and let his foot off quickly. Then turning over the ignition, he pumped the gas pedal again. The truck chug-chugged and then stalled again.

Ridley felt panic enveloping him. They had come too far to give up here on this lonely stretch of road on this rainy night. He tried once more. The truck sputtered, popped and belched, then caught.

"Yee-hah!" yelled Ridley.

The truck spun its wheels, mud and gravel cartwheeling out behind it. Ridley swung the truck around and sped off into the torrential night.

CHAPTER THIRTY-FOUR

The white Toyota careened through the parking lot of the Why gas station, throwing up plumes of mud. Ridley cranked the steering wheel furiously to the right, trying to avoid the two patrol cars that attempted to block their way. Ridley looked down at the gas gauge; it was going to be close making it to their destination. There would be no fill-up here.

Ridley out-maneuvered the highway patrol cars converging on the crossroads and fishtailed onto highway 85, heading south. The two patrol cars followed in close pursuit.

"Don't ever let it be said that I don't know how to show an out-of-towner a good time!" Ridley yelled over the noise of the sirens.

The alien cast Ridley a blank stare and then continued to look over his shoulder at their pursuers. "Do you think they have contacted the others?"

"Bet on it," said Ridley. "I think there's going to be a large and not very friendly reception waiting for us at the border. Any new developments on your elaborate plan?"

"I am still considering our options," replied the alien.

"We don't have a lot of options," Ridley snapped. "These guys are pushing us down a long funnel with the bottleneck being the border crossing."

Azrnoth-zin reached into the backpack and produced the orb Ridley had first seen in the cave.

"I am unsure how effective the force field generator is from the inside of this vehicle. It will take me some time to adjust the new parameters," said Azrnoth-zin.

"Will that make us bulletproof?"

"That depends."

"Depends on what?"

"On how much charge is left in the cells and the caliber of weapons used against us."

Ridley let out a long breath. "I sure hope that thing's equipped with a Die-Hard battery."

Azrnoth-zin performed some deft manipulations with his hands at various locations on the sphere and the orb opened like a split melon. He found the beam direction and attempted to make the necessary adjustments. He looked over at Ridley.

"There is an additional fine adjustment that is necessary, but I do not have the implement that will complete the calibration. Without it, I can adjust for one frequency only."

"What about your knife?"

Azrnoth-zin was doubtful. "This is a very sophisticated piece of technology. I do not think there is a device in this knife to adjust the particle force field."

"Just try it." Ridley said, his voice edgy.

Azrnoth-zin began pulling the different blades out and seeing if any of them could be used for fine mechanical manipulation. He finally settled on the punch tool. After several minutes, the orb suddenly closed, lifted from his hands and began spinning, bathing the cab of the truck in an eerie blue-green light."

"Did you get it?" said Ridley.

"I believe the force field is functional to contain the truck now."

"Nice going, Arn."

The alien held up the Swiss Army knife admiringly. "A worthy gift, indeed."

"So are we bulletproof now?"

"That remains to be seen."

They continued traveling south in the darkness. Two patrol cars maintained a safe distance behind them. Ridley glanced at the sign for the turnoff to Organ Pipe National Monument as they sped by.

"Too bad you can't see this place in the daylight," said Ridley. "It's one of the prettiest pieces of desert around."

He continued to monitor their pursuers in the rear view mirror.

"Get ready for a reception at the border, Arn. Those two cops are just making sure we don't decide to slip out the back door."

The force field was pulsating and filling the truck cab with a not unpleasant vibrating sensation, which Ridley felt deep within his core. The wind and the rain slackened slightly, the rain now coming in intermittent squalls.

Just before the border near Lukeville, Ridley noticed two more highway patrol vehicles had joined the other two. The cars were spread across both lanes of the two-lane highway.

"They must have both lanes closed up ahead," Ridley said grimly, "waiting on us." He slowed the truck to assess the situation ahead of them. Approaching the border crossing at Lukeville, they rounded a curve in the road.

Ridley's heart sank.

A solid mass of cars and SUVs blocked the road ahead. A Cobra helicopter hovered ominously above the array of highway patrol and *federale* vehicles. To the sides were a couple of half-tracks, each one with a manned .50 caliber machine gun atop. Ridley guessed there were several hundred armed agents and law enforcement personnel stationed around the border crossing.

Ridley slowed the truck to a crawl, then stopped. The vehicles behind closed the distance and stopped a safe distance behind them. Ridley and Azrnoth-zin were bathed in a flood of halogen light. The place was lit up like Fenway Park.

"Hell." Ridley looked over at Azrnoth-zin and shrugged. "It's your call, Arn."

Azrnoth-zin pulled the small horseshoe from his pack and adjusted the settings. The device hummed into readiness. He moved the device slowly in an arcing fashion from left to right.

"There." he declared, on the second pass. Pointing between a highway patrol car and a *federale* SUV, he said, "That is the area of least molecular concentration. If there is a weak point in the barricade, it is there."

"So-o-o, am I to assume that I'm to drive at that spot, balls out?"

Azrnoth-zin looked over at Ridley, an attempt at a slight grin etched to his angular face. "Balls out," he said.

"Seats and lap tables in the upright position ladies and gentlemen," Ridley said, gunning the engine. "Hang onto your ass."

The truck leapt forward, tires spinning on the wet pavement. Ridley ran through the preliminary gears quickly. He needed to have enough acceleration to make the jump to fifth to use the truck as a battering ram.

Ahead of them, soldiers and personnel were scrambling to their positions. Small sparks pinged off the front of the force field as the blockade opened fire. Ridley saw a large flash; the conflagration rocked the front of the truck, but the force field held. Ridley reached 50 miles per hour and pushed into fifth gear. The truck bolted forward, the front line of vehicles looming ahead.

A growl emanated from Ridley's throat, one long, drawn out sound that escalated into an open-mouthed yell. He steered the truck toward the nether space, as directed by Azrnoth-zin. Azrnoth-zin looked at Ridley, looked ahead at the small army of agents, looked back at Ridley, looked ahead and opened his mouth, emitting a similar noise. Another explosion off to Ridley's left created a huge starburst effect.

Ridley and Azrnoth-zin braced for impact. They saw men frantically diving out of the way. In the next instant, Ridley felt a great jolt, the force field acting as a battering ram, parting the two vehicles. As the Toyota tore through, rending metal caused sparks to fly. The force field flickered and resumed its revolutions.

"I don't believe it! We made it!" said Ridley.

The truck barreled down the straightaway from the border that led to the town of Sonoyta on the Mexican side. Ridley knew there were dangerous curves up ahead and the road was wet. He began deceleration.

"Arn, you're a fucking genius. That was - amazing."

"Do not sing my praises prematurely," declared the alien. "We are still being pursued." Azrnoth-zin indicated the roof of the truck. Over the roar of the engine, Ridley could hear the pumping rotors of the helicopter above them.

A series of high-pitched pings resounded over the noise. In front of the hood, small explosions formed, then ricocheted into the darkness as the fifty caliber slugs were deflected by the force field. Ridley saw the helicopter pull slightly ahead. Two white tanks attached to the skids released a whitish vapor, which drifted down to them.

"I don't believe it!" Ridley yelled. "They're trying to gas us!" He looked quickly over to Azrnoth-zin who was adjusting the orb. "Can it get through the force field?"

"I believe it is adjusted to control finite particles. Unfortunately, this creates an even greater drain on the energy cells. At present levels of function, we will lose the finite barrier in less than fifteen minutes."

"Bastards!" Ridley called out. "People live here!"

The sounds of bullets and tracers diminished as they reached the series of turns winding down a long hill to the main part of town. Not surprisingly, the main drag, usually full of people after dark, was nearly deserted during the recent deluge. The helicopter still dogged them, but for the present, had ceased firing on them. The other vehicles lagged several miles behind now.

The rain intensity began to pick up once more. The sounds of the helicopter's rotors were drowned out by the rain. Suddenly, the orb's light faltered, the revolutions and humming slowing.

"We're losing power in the field," said Azrnoth-zin. "The finite array drained more energy from the cells than I thought."

"We need to lose that helicopter fast, before he douses us again," said Ridley. "How much time do we have left?"

"Five, perhaps ten minutes," said the alien. "The cells have received no more than portable charges, which are weak and not designed for a large workload."

Ridley steered the truck through the last of the Sonoyta streets and headed into the darkness once more. He looked over at Azrnoth-zin. "I have an idea."

"I'm listening."

"Just how good are you with that stun gun?"

"I hit what I aim at."

"Moving at a 160 miles an hour?"

"That should not present a problem."

"Okay, hot shot. Once the orb goes, I'm going to give us a quick blast of juice and move ahead of the chopper. That's when you roll down the window and disable it."

Azrnoth-zin nodded and took the horseshoe object in his hands adjusting the beam. He looked over at Ridley and said, "Ready."

The orb began to flicker. The light faded altogether for a moment. The force field shimmered, then lifted like a sheer curtain. The orb's light reappeared after a few seconds, much dimmer this time.

"If those boys up there can see that, they may open up on us again," said Ridley. "Next time that thing goes out, I'm going to fifth. You'd better get ready."

Azrnoth-zin rolled down the window. Instantly, he was assaulted by the driving raindrops. The helicopter, sensing something was wrong began to make its pass overhead. The orb's revolutions slowed, the hum barely audible. The blue-green light sputtered, then went completely dark.

"Now!" said Ridley, engaging fifth gear.

The truck roared ahead. Following the initial acceleration, Azrnoth-zin spun around in the seat and leaned out the window facing backward. The pelting rain felt like a thousand stinging needles on his back and arms. He brought the device up and fired. A flash of light arced under the belly of the helicopter. The pilot swerved erratically. The helicopter corrected and Azrnoth-zin saw the flash from its mounted guns. The truck pulled away. The helicopter was almost at level attitude again. A splay of bullets created plumes of mud and water off to the right and behind, stitching their way toward the truck.

Azrnoth-zin steadied himself over the vibrating truck, took a breath and fired. The streak of photonic energy connected with the tail rotors, creating an explosion amid a shower of sparks. The helicopter veered wildly and began to corkscrew toward the earth. It crashed into a copse of palo verde trees off the side of the road.

Azrnoth-zin pulled himself back into the cab, dripping wet. Even in the dim light from the dashboard, Ridley could see that the alien was grinning. "Piece of pie," he said.

"That's piece of cake," said Ridley. "That, my extra-terrestrial *compadre*, was one hell of a shot."

Azrnoth-zin was beaming. "Yes, it was, wasn't it?"

Ridley kept the truck in fifth gear for a few more minutes, until noticing the temperature gauge beginning to creep toward the red line. The gas gauge read one quarter. It was going to be close. Ridley downshifted to fourth, gripping the steering wheel hard to avoid skidding off the road. Regaining control, he looked in the rear view mirror. The lights from the pursuing vehicles were distant pinpoints.

They reached the turnoff for the *Pinacates* going better than 60 miles per hour. Ridley almost lost control as the road went from pavement to soft sand. Bouncing along the sodden washboard road, Ridley began to think they were going to make it. One thing was evident; the Toyota truck was not going to be driving out of here. The gas gauge needle was hovering around the 'E' and Ridley figured there to be three to five miles left in Old Blanco before it quit.

Suddenly, the truck was bathed in harsh halogen lights. From above, another Cobra helicopter swooped down and closed in on the truck from behind. An explosion off to the left showered the truck in mud and rocks. Ridley pulled the wheel wildly to the right and continued bouncing over the ruts.

"Where in hell did he come from?" Ridley yelled.

"They must have been following at a safe distance after they witnessed what happened to the other helicopter."

Automatic fire peppered the side of the truck. Ridley could hear the sickly penetration of each slug as they tore through the side panel.

"Shit!"

"What?" said Azrnoth-zin. "Are you hit?"

"No, dammit. There goes my trade-in."

The helicopter fired in front of them. Ridley overcompensated with the steering wheel, pulling hard to the right. The front wheel caught in a pothole and the truck rolled over onto its side and slid through the mud. It crashed into a pile of lava boulders, shattering the windshield. Ridley found himself lying on top of Azrnoth-zin, covered in broken glass, rain spattering his face. He struggled with the seat belt, finally releasing it. Pushing the door upward, Ridley crawled out and jumped to the ground. He rolled to avoid fire from the helicopter. Azrnoth-zin was behind Ridley and fell to the ground.

Ridley rushed over and helped the shaky alien to his feet. The helicopter was coming back for another pass, its lights bearing down on Ridley and Azrnoth-zin. In the lights, Ridley could see the alien had a gash on his forehead, blood running down his face mixed with rain and mud.

The helicopter's lights found the two standing together and Ridley was momentarily blinded, like a deer on the highway. The alien's face was that of dark determination. In his hand, he held the weapon, aimed at the approaching assailant. A brilliant ray shot from the weapon and blew away the tail rotor.

The helicopter veered away from them and began losing altitude quickly. The pilot tried to steer it away from the lava fields and toward the sandy expanse north of them. The iron bird landed with a crash, the sound of metal tearing, audible even above the storm's fury.

Ridley and Azrnoth-zin lurched toward the lava fields. When they were several meters from the twisted volcanic formations, Ridley took the weapon from Azrnoth-zin and aimed it at the crippled truck. The truck exploded in a burst of flame, the concussion almost sending them sprawling. The old white Toyota, a veteran of over 400,000 miles, had come to its final resting- place in a desert of extinct volcanoes.

"Sorry, Blanco," said Ridley. "It's been a nice ride." Ridley handed the weapon back to Azrnoth-zin. They turned and stumbled through the darkness, in the direction of *El Elegante* crater.

CHAPTER THIRTY-FIVE

The rain had finally stopped. Ridley looked out from under the sheltering crevice. In the east, the first rays of sunlight were highlighting the rolling cloud formations.

Ridley could not remember a time when he felt more miserable. Every muscle and joint felt like it was on fire. He was damp and the chill permeated to all parts of his body. Unable to turn his head to the right, he kept Azrnoth-zin on his left side as much as possible.

Azrnoth-zin was in no better condition. His head bore a nasty laceration, which was only partially healed by the device. The last of the energy reserves were giving out. Ridley had finally brought the bleeding under control.

"Sun's coming up soon," Ridley said, hunkering back into the cleft in the rock. Azrnoth-zin was leaning against the black volcanic wall. He opened his eyes when Ridley spoke, the glowing blue a contrast against the dark basalt.

"We'd better get a move on," Ridley said. "I have a feeling it's going to take us the better part of the day to make it to the rendezvous point, especially the shape we're in."

Azrnoth-zin stood up stiffly. "Did you see anything out there?"

"Just the smoldering remains of my former truck. I didn't see any other movement from this vantage point. You can bet they're out there slinking around."

Ridley and Azrnoth-zin emerged from the crevice and began the arduous climb up the steep volcanic cone. Between the two of them, they had a one-liter water bottle and some freeze-dried snacks. The rain had left standing pools in depressions in the rocks; water acquisition would not present a problem.

They rounded a small crest, which gave them a clearer view of the desert floor below them. They saw the concentration of vehicles parked at the base of the lava fields. From the flurry of activity, Ridley assumed the agents had set up a base camp not far from where they had left the truck.

"Well, at least for now they're on foot, too," said Ridley. "But there'll be air support once the light gets a little better."

Ridley and Azrnoth-zin continued their ascent of the large crater, stopping only to catch their breath or take a quick drink of water. By late morning, they were better than two-thirds the way to the summit. At one point, Azrnoth-zin stumbled and slid backward on the loose black lava rock, abrading his hands. Ridley followed back down after him and assisted him back to a flattened area near a series of basalt columns. The columns were latticed with crevices and chimneys, some of which appeared to snake toward the top of the crater.

"The way I see it," said Ridley trying to catch his breath. "Is that we can either go up from here - maybe buy ourselves some more time - or else follow the wall around until it plays out. What do you think?"

"We can climb that?" said the alien.

"Piece of pie," said Ridley, half-smiling.

The air filled with the sound of machinery moving rapidly toward their position. Ridley and Azrnoth-zin ducked under the basalt ledge just as the helicopter buzzed over them and dropped down below their position.

"As soon as they see us, it's only a matter of time before they drop people all over the ridge and cut off our way to the top," Ridley said.

Azrnoth-zin gave Ridley a resigned look. "I guess we're going up here, then."

"Just follow my lead, Arn. All you do is alternate placing pressure between your hands and your feet. You just kind of shimmy up the inside of the chimney."

"Delfinians do not "shimmy"," said Azrnoth-zin indignantly.

"Right."

Ridley turned and crawled inside the space between the two basalt columns. Placing his feet on opposing walls, he to inched his way upward until he was out of sight. Several minutes passed. The only sound was Ridley's labored breathing and the clattering of dislodged rocks.

Finally, Ridley called down. "It's okay, Arn. You can come up now."

Azrnoth-zin struggled with the technique at first, but soon was able to develop a reasonable rhythm of movement. He reached Ridley and hoisted himself onto the ledge, then fell flat onto his face.

"You do this for entertainment?" said the alien, his voice muffled.

Ridley shrugged. "I've been told I have low serotonin levels." He looked up, eyeballing the configuration of the next pitch. "I can't tell for sure, but I think we should be clear once we top out on the next section. The only problem is that there's an exposed part up there, where you have to come out onto the face. It gets real thin there, but I think it's do-able."

The helicopter rotors echoed through the basalt cliffs all around them. It appeared to be above and to the right of them. The noise faded as the helicopter dropped into the giant cinder cone.

A low humming sound, different from the drone of the helicopter, filled the rocky space. It took Ridley a moment to register where the sound was coming from. Azrnoth-zin reached into the backpack and pulled out the horseshoe device. The air around them felt electrically charged.

"I think that's your ride," said Ridley.

Azrnoth-zin made the calculations quickly and looked up at Ridley. "We are close to the rendezvous point. It is - over the top of the crater and down at the bottom - in the depression. They will use the cloud cover for their descent."

Ridley stood up in the cramped space, sizing up his moves for the climb. "We're close, Arn. One last push and you're home."

Azrnoth-zin watched as Ridley stemmed up the chimney. Soon, Ridley was on the exposed face, calculating the moves to reach the final chute to the top. Azrnoth-zin observed the number of handholds thinned out considerably. He watched Ridley deftly execute the balance moves and continue the climb.

"Come on, Azrnoth-zin. Get your extra-terrestrial ass up here," Ridley's voice echoed down.

With grim determination, the alien followed Ridley's lead, his pace quickening after the first pitch. He moved up easily to the exposed section, then stopped. The rock face, daunting from below, appeared impassable from this perspective. Azrnoth-zin tried to retrace Ridley's movements. How had Ridley negotiated this part? He made the mistake of looking down. Below, the lava flows spread out like a giant black apron. In and among the jagged features, Azrnoth-zin detected movement. Agents were moving up the slope, dispersed in a broken line.

"Let's go, Arn! This is no time for admiring the scenery!"

The alien looked up and muttered an epithet in Delfinian. He stepped out onto the rock face and groped for anything to hold onto. His right hand closed around a small but pronounced projection. He moved up. With his other hand, he located another hold, this one not nearly as substantial. His breathing coming in labored gasps, Azrnoth-zin focused all of his concentration on the rock face in front of him. He willed the rising panic back down into that dark place within him.

He was almost to the last chute, when the irritable sound of the helicopters rotors were upon him. The helicopter swung in from the west and hovered over the basalt cliffs. Azrnoth-zin expected to feel the bullet in his back any second, but the flying machine held its position. With a lunging movement, the alien leapt for the safety of the last chimney. The helicopter moved up and over the black cliffs.

Above him, Ridley was able to see the approach of the helicopter in time to blend back into the overhang. He, too, saw the line of U.S. agents, Mexican *federales,* and police moving steadily up the slope. When the helicopter flew out of sight, Ridley figured it was reporting their position and keeping an eye on them until the ground forces caught up.

Azrnoth-zin reached the summit and crawled to where Ridley crouched under the escarpment.

"Took you long enough."

Azrnoth-zin spoke between gasps, "Delfinians…are… swimmers. Not…climbers."

Ridley looked at his watch. "If your people are on time, we have less than one hour to make it to the rendezvous point."

"I think I can proceed now," said Azrnoth-zin.

"At least the last part is downhill," said Ridley. "Those guys just don't quit, do they?"

The alien snorted. They turned and scrambled up the talus slope. When they rounded the top of the crater, the helicopter was waiting for them. The pilot pulled it away from the mountainside, well aware of the firepower that had crippled its sister ships.

Ridley knew that from here it was going to be a foot race. The agents below would be topping out soon. Ridley sent out a silent prayer to the cosmos that the Delfinians knew about Mountain Standard Time.

They hit the steep down-slope running for all they were worth, creating a wave of black dust and scree rolling toward the bottom. Ridley ran straight down until the momentum threatened to pitch him head over heels. He changed his descent tactic to a serpentine motion, zig-zagging his way toward the bottom. Azrnoth-zin followed Ridley's example. The alien, not used to running on a leg that several days before had been fractured, stumbled several times. Then, Azrnoth-zin turned his ankle and began rolling down the steep grade. Ridley heard the alien's cry of pain and turned around to see Azrnoth-zin tumbling out of control toward him. Ridley caught the alien by the shirt and they both tumbled into a heap.

"I have twisted my leg," the alien announced. He was covered in a grayish dust, a small trickle of blood running down his forehead.

"Can you walk? We're almost there."

Azrnoth-zin stood up and attempted a step. He wobbled and almost went down. Ridley slipped the alien's arm over his shoulder and supported him as they continued downward. Their pace was slowed considerably. Still, the helicopter hung back far enough to view the proceedings.

Ridley cast a glance back to the summit. Tiny figures began appearing all around the rim. Ridley and Azrnoth-zin continued on, performing a very bad rendition of the three- legged race. The slope flattened out and Ridley half-walked, half-carried, and half-dragged

Azrnoth-zin to a cleared area. Upon reaching it, the two collapsed onto the ground.

Ridley lay in the dirt, face down, trying to catch his breath. His legs felt leaden, his lungs were on fire. He willed himself to move, but his body refused to respond.

Ridley noticed a strange sensation overtake him. A deep resonance permeated deep into his chest. Then he realized the deep vibration was present all around him. The rocks were moving slightly, the sand shifting under his body. Rolling over onto his back, his heart skipped a beat. He was awed by the sight of the object that was descending through the cloud cover.

A great shadow passed over Ridley and Azrnoth-zin. Above them a ship descended toward them. Its shape reminded Ridley of a huge overfed manta ray. Ridley looked over at Azrnoth-zin who was standing favoring his injured leg. The alien looked up at the ship and then back to Ridley. Ridley got to his feet, smiling his crooked smile. Azrnoth-zin was also smiling.

The ship settled above them, the vibration from it rising and falling rhythmically. A portal opened on the belly of the ship and a brilliant blue-green beam formed between the ground and the ship a short distance from where they stood.

Ridley stuck out his hand. "Tell them about us," he said. "Let them know that planet earth ain't such a bad place."

"I will tell them. Ridley, I will never forget your friendship. Thank you."

Ridley hugged the alien fiercely, then pushed him away. "Get out of here. You don't want to miss your taxi."

"Take care of yourself my terran friend." Azrnoth-zin hobbled over and stood in the center of the intense light. The light waves began to flicker and the alien began to disappear, as if he was being pulled away, layer by layer, from a sketch- pad. Ridley watched the ghost image fade until only the blue-green beam remained. The beam drew up quickly into the ship.

The resonance increased around him again. The ship appeared to shimmer, then rose slowly upward. Ridley watched until it disappeared into the low-lying clouds.

Ridley had forgotten all about their pursuers. Looking up, he could see a ring of armed men closing on his position. Many of them were still looking skyward, transfixed by the sights of the past few moments. As they drew closer, Ridley saw many of them had guns trained on him.

He looked down at his shredded clothes, his bruised and raw hands. His skin was covered in volcanic dust and cinders. Every square inch of his body screamed at him, either from exhaustion or soreness. Part of him wanted to lay down right here and sleep. But there was the other part, the part of him that felt the jubilation. Cooper Ridley had finally seen something through from start to finish.

A voice from a bullhorn broke the silence. "YOU ARE SURROUNDED. LAY YOUR WEAPONS ON THE GROUND. MAKE NO ATTEMPT TO ESCAPE."

Ridley recognized Jenks's voice. He shook his head and laughed.

"No shit, Jenks. Now, where the hell would I be going?"

The armed men were drawing into a closer half circle, with Ridley at the center. Ridley stopped to retrieve the handkerchief from his back pocket to wipe some of the dust from his eyes.

A voice yelled out. "He's going for a gun!"

"No!"

Ridley felt the slug tear into his chest before he heard the report of the rifle. He was thrown backward several feet, landing on his right side. The world around him suddenly shifted into slow motion. He could not get his breath back. He reached down and touched his chest, his hand coming away warm and sticky.

Ridley attempted to stand but was caught by a fiery pain ripping through his right shoulder. Another bullet shattered his left knee knocking him back to the ground.

His breath came in shallow, rapid pants. He no longer felt any pain, only the irresistible urge to close his eyes and sleep. He lay on his back, his eyes fixed on the scudding storm clouds above him. *It's going to storm again*, he thought dreamily. *I'm cold and it's growing darker.*

The last thing Ridley saw was a deep blue light.

EPILOGUE

Maria Morales walked down the gently sloping beach toward the water. Behind her, the lights from the houses of *Punta Chueca* cast her figure in a long shadow on the sand. The evening was cool, a freshening breeze coming out of the west. The air smelled of salt and the slightly decaying aroma of sea grasses washed up on the beach.

In the pumice colored moonlight, she spotted a lone figure crouched at the end of the sand spit, near the water's edge. A small red flare from a pipe briefly illuminated the face of her husband Enrique.

"I thought I would find you here," Maria said as she sidled up next to him.

"It is a good night for a walk by the shore," Enrique said, emerging from his reverie. "Are the children asleep?"

"Yes, finally. Jorgé was full of questions. It was difficult to get him to lie down tonight."

Enrique did not respond immediately. Maria felt her husband heave a great sigh. "In the morning, I will talk with him."

Maria's attention was drawn to the darkened water just beyond their feet. Loud, explosive exhalations broke the stillness of the calm night. Sharp percussive whacks like a palm slapping the water's surface, were interspersed with the respirations of the dolphins several yards offshore. Maria was able to discern triangular shapes of dorsal fins arcing out of the water, momentarily catching reflections from the moonlight before they slid beneath the surface.

"I see the dolphins are taking advantage of the moon to find food," said Maria off-handedly.

"Hmm," said Enrique. "Yes. Perhaps they came here fishing for mullet tonight."

Enrique and Maria stood quietly for several minutes listening to the rhythmic breathing of the dolphins. Maria broke the silence.

"Did you hear anything at the meeting of the elders?"

"Joaquim returned from *Disemboque* around two hours ago. He reported that several from the village saw the *gringos federales* and *Mexicanos* come down from the top of the mountain. They claim they saw the great ship leave. But I do not know how. The clouds were very low that day. The top of the *El Elegante* must have been hidden from view."

"And what of Ridley? There are rumors going throughout the village that he has been killed," said Maria.

"Joaquim told me there were no bodies taken off the mountain," said Enrique.

"How can you be sure? There were reports of gunfire coming from inside the crater."

"Joaquim also spoke to one of the young *federales* who was at the mountain. The *gringos federales* were not happy when they came down from *El Elegante*. They would have acted differently had they killed Ridley and captured the visitor."

Enrique nodded toward the dolphins. In the moonlight, Maria could see a faint smile etched into the face of her husband. "Besides, if Ridley or Azrnoth-zin were dead, the dolphins would have told me."

"What else did the dolphins tell you?" said Maria.

Enrique placed his arm around Maria's shoulder. "They told me not to let my beautiful wife stray too close to the water's edge, or they may take her away."

Maria half-smiled and leaned in closer to her husband.

"I can't help but feel that Ridley is in danger or lying injured someplace," said Maria, her voice catching.

"The visions show me that he lives, even though he suffers and his course is treacherous. But think, Maria! Think what he has accomplished. Now, his future lies in the hands of the Sky People."

The air suddenly became more saturated as an offshore fogbank moved over the western end of Tiburon Island. The waning moon slid behind the fast moving clouds, deepening the darkness. Maria shivered from the moisture-laden night air. Leaning in closer, Enrique wrapped both arms around her.

"Sometimes, I wish I had your faith," said Maria. "Perhaps I have lost touch with much of our people's traditions and ways."

"You have the teachings within you," Enrique said, looking into Maria's eyes. "They have always been there. You can no more forget who you are and where you come from than you could forget to breathe the air."

"I will pray that Ridley is still alive," said Maria with conviction. "That he will return home, alive and well."

"Of this I am sure: Ridley's journey is only just beginning."

Maria and Enrique continued to listen to the dolphins until the last of their exhalations faded into the night.

Printed in the United States
76006LV00003B/1-99